A

"Then we hav

"Pax," she agreed, holding her hand out to seal the bargain. Instead of shaking it, as she expected, he brought her gloved fingers to his lips. "And . . . and thank you for sending over Monsieur Vincente to do my hair this morning. I shall repay you, of course, but it was very thoughtful."

"No, I won't hear of it. I owed you for my boorishness. Besides, it was worth every penny, for the curls are delightful."

Maylene colored at the compliment, then recalled that he was still holding her hand. "My lord, we really ought not be stopping here like this, apart from everyone else."

He sighed, but released her hand after pressing a light kiss to the palm. "That's right. I am not a rake."

"And I am not a light-skirt."

They both sighed. The earl gave the horses the office to start, then cursed. "Dash it, I am no monk, either." And he reached over, pulled Maylene closer, and kissed her. . . .

Miss Treadwell's Talent

Barbara Metzger

A SIGNET BOOK

SIGNET
Published by New American Library, a division of
Penguin Putnam Inc., 375 Hudson Street,
New York, New York 10014, U.S.A.
Penguin Books Ltd, 27 Wrights Lane,
London W8 5TZ, England
Penguin Books Australia Ltd,
Ringwood, Victoria, Australia
Penguin Books Canada Ltd, 10 Alcorn Avenue,
Toronto, Ontario, Canada M4V 3B2
Penguin Books (N.Z.) Ltd, 182–190 Wairau Road,
Auckland 10, New Zealand

Penguin Books Ltd, Registered Offices:
Harmondsworth, Middlesex, England

First published by Signet, an imprint of New American Library,
a division of Penguin Putnam Inc.

First Printing, August 1999
10 9 8 7 6 5 4 3 2 1

To all my new Internet friends,
especially Rosemary

Chapter One

Her mother was a mystic. To Miss Maylene Treadwell's discomfort, her mama spoke to spirits. Thisbe, Lady Tremont, relict of the late, unlamented Baron Tremont, held discourse with the dearly departed. Or the not so dearly departed. So long as they were dead.

She did not hold dialogues with her deceased husband, since she'd barely spoken to him in life and saw no reason to disturb an otherwise pleasant widowhood with Tremont's ill temper. He'd been a curmudgeon for his two score and six years; one could only imagine his mood in eternity. Instead, Lady Tremont examined the afterlife with an entity known as Max.

This was not, perhaps, the best recommendation a young woman might have upon entering London's Marriage Mart. In fact, Mama and Max together were some remarkably heavy baggage for a debutante to carry on her journey through a come-out and subsequent Seasons. Maylene had had too many Seasons, thanks to her father's gambling away her dowry and her mother's gamboling through the hereafter. Maylene was of average looks, if one discounted her unmanageable, flyaway blond hair, and perhaps above average intelligence. Her mother rejoiced in Maylene's loyal, caring nature. Her mother despaired that Maylene was one-and-twenty, and unwed.

Since her mother's patrons provided the wherewithal for their continued existence on the fringes of Polite Society—nay, for their continued existence, period—Maylene had learned to silence her reservations about Lady Tremont's pastime. Lud knew Maylene couldn't silence her mama—or Max.

Maylene was not sure about Max, but she dearly loved her mother. So did the *ton*, thank goodness. Eccentrics were the

spice in a bland diet of balls and dinners and card parties with
the same faces, the same interests, the same conversations.
Thisbe, Lady Tremont, was an original. She was also of good
birth, bore a respectable title, and was without the least hint of
scandal. She was also without two shillings to rub together. If
she enlivened—endeadened?—the beau monde's evenings,
they were willing to make generous contributions to the Fund
for Psychical Research in return.

The Fund for Psychical Research was otherwise known as
the household account. On account of an empty coalbin, therefore, the little house on Curzon Street was holding another of
Lady Tremont's ghoulish gatherings.

Maylene shuddered, and not from any spectral force sending
shivers down her spine, nor from the chill in the parlor due to
the recently lighted meager fire, nor yet the odd trancelike state
her mother entered. Maylene trembled because she was forced
to hold the flaccid, damp, toadstool-white left hand of Lord
Shimpton, without benefit of gloves. Mama had insisted the
fabric kept their thoughts from uniting, making the flow less
powerful, too thin to reach the otherworld and Max. Maylene
wondered if the peer's perspiration would dilute the aura. It certainly disgusted her. She'd rather hold a dead carp in her hand.
Now that she thought of it, that was precisely what Shimpton's
hand felt like.

Lady Tremont's eyes snapped open. "Someone," she hissed,
"is not concentrating."

Maylene closed her similar blue eyes and tried her best to
think of those who had passed beyond, instead of those who
merely smelled that way.

There was a small circle this evening, unfortunately. Two pe-
titioners sat on either side of Lady Tremont, with Campbell, the
butler, and Maylene's great-aunt, Regina Howard, making up
the numbers at the round table. Sometimes enough aspirants
came to seek their dear defunct that Maylene did not have to
take part, but could sit in the corner and take notes for future
reference, or research, as Mama preferred to term it. She could
also figure how many wax candles Lady Crowley's donation
would purchase, if Mama and Max were able to reassure the recent widow that the late Lord Crowley had indeed reached the

Light after being lost at sea. Judging from his past behavior, the loutish lordship was more likely dinner for the devilfish in hell.

Her mother might have one foot in the ether, but she knew as well as Maylene which side their bread was buttered on, and whence came the butter. Max was probably going to tell them that Lord Crowley could not come hear his young wife's final farewell because he was too busy learning the harp. Yes, there came the faint sound of strings, so soft no one would have heard it, except for the held-breath hush in the small parlor, which just happened to abut the smaller music room, where Lady Tremont's faithful maid Nora just happened to be dusting the instrument.

"Max says he needs practice," Mama whispered now, her eyes still closed as she swayed in her chair.

Lady Tremont believed in spiritualism, not starvation.

Last week she'd convinced Lord Applegate that of course his dead father would forgive him for running off with that actress. Certainly the man's erstwhile fiancée hadn't forgiven him, nor had her brothers, who were rumored to be out for Applegate's blood. Fearing his own imminent mortality, Applegate had sought an ally in the afterlife. Maylene had been able to pay the grocer from his gratitude.

Maylene would have liked to think that her mother's patrons wished to commune with their friends and relations out of a great love for the deceased; perhaps they'd forgotten to express that love before it was too late, or hadn't time for proper farewells, like Lady Crowley. Instead, she'd come to believe that it was fear and uncertainty and loneliness that sent a great many of them to Lady Tremont's spirit circles. Miss Treadwell found the séances sad, even if they provided her sustenance. But her mama was providing a service, Maylene almost convinced herself: if the soul-seekers left somewhat poorer in the purse, they were rewarded with peace of mind. That way she did not have to feel guilty about accepting the money. Besides, no matter what Maylene thought, her mother believed in what she was doing. No actress could have attained that sublime smile, the look of beatitude that came over the older woman whenever Max was talking to her, like now. She sat straighter in her chair, as if her mind were that much closer to Paradise.

"Ah," she said, her eyes still shut as if she could conjure an image behind her lids, "there you are, my dear. Look who else is visiting us this evening. It is Lord Shimpton, come to speak with his beloved mother. Remember, he was here a few days ago, and we asked if you could make contact with the dear woman for us."

Max usually needed a sennight or so to find the right spirit. The beyond was a large place, Mama told her clients, explaining why reaching their loved ones often took two or three visits—and two or three donations to the Fund for Psychical Research, which was unobtrusively but unmistakably housed in a Chinese urn on the table in the entry hall. If one of the callers should happen to overlook the urn's label, perhaps in an excess of emotion, the Treadwell House butler could perform a creditable imitation of a tollgate. Campbell would block the door, clear his throat, stare pointedly at the jar, and neglect to hand over the guest's wraps. If neither donation nor *doucour* was forthcoming, neither was Max on the next visit. Lord Shimpton had been desperately eager to ask his mother if he could properly put off mourning after two years. The urn was overflowing.

"Have you found her, Max?" Lady Tremont asked. "The poor boy misses her so much, surely she will come talk to him."

The poor boy had to be perilously close to thirty years of age, Maylene thought. Viscount Shimpton sought his mother's forgiveness, her blessing, and her guidance. In Miss Treadwell's opinion, he should have been seeking for his brain, since the dowager viscountess seemed to have taken it with her to the next life. She'd taken his manhood in this one. The viscount's chin seemed to have decamped at birth, obviously choosing not to spend a lifetime with such a weak willy. Perhaps Max could suggest Shimpton grow a beard—and longer hair to cover ears that stuck out sideways. Maylene would mention it to Mama, if the viscount returned.

"Is she there?" he whispered hoarsely. "Mumsy, where are you?"

He'd return.

"I always knew Mumsy would go to heaven." Lord Shimpton sighed ecstatically until Aunt Regina shushed him.

"That's not how it works," she told him in an aside while Lady Tremont waited for Max to nudge the old virago of a viscountess out of her eternal slumber. "Only the saints and innocent infants go straight to the blessed beyond. True sinners go to the baser beyond. Everyone else has to wait around for Judgment Day. That's why the in-between is so crowded. Otherwise Max could find your mother in jig time—if the unincorporated can dance a jig."

Maylene's mother cleared her throat and frowned at Aunt Regina. "That's incorporeal, not unincorporated, Auntie." She needed a few moments to redirect her thoughts skyward. Then, when all was quiet again, Lady Tremont shook herself, took a deep breath, and raised her chin, like a bulldog. "Frederick? Is that you?"

Maylene marveled at the change in her mother's voice. Suddenly, Lady Tremont sounded as if her mouth were full of lemons and her heart was full of limestone. "Sit up, boy. And straighten your neckcloth. How many times have I told you not to slouch?"

"Mums! It is you!"

Maylene prayed Mama didn't overdo the shrew, but Viscount Shimpton was nodding happily. His eyes screwed shut, he was squeezing Maylene's hand so hard she'd have watermarks, like stationery. "Ask her about colors," he whispered. "Can I have that new puce waistcoat?"

"You'll look like a filleted salmon," his fond parent replied, through Lady Tremont's lips. "But pearl gray might be nice, with a tracing of embroidery. And none of those yellow Cossack trousers, Frederick. Do you hear me?"

"Yes, Mumsy. No, Mumsy, I wouldn't."

Maylene was hoping her mother didn't intend to oversee the nodcock's new wardrobe or they'd be here all night. Besides, Maylene's army of information gatherers had discovered details about the viscount's household that he ought to be told, in fair trade for his largesse to the research fund. Aunt Regina knew her Debrett's inside and out, while Campbell knew the inside of every pub and tavern that catered to those who catered to the nobs. Treadwell House's two young footmen, Campbell's nephews, had contacts among fences and flash houses about which Maylene never inquired too closely, and the abigail, Nora, was privy to every scrap of gossip passed in a ladies' retiring chamber, dressmaker's fitting room, or companion's corner. If the War Office had such an efficient squadron of spies, the Corsican upstart would have been long vanquished.

"You have more important things to think about than your clothes, sonny," Mama rasped, remembering her lines, or Lady Shimpton's. "That housekeeper you hired is cheating you blind, Frederick. She makes the merchants pay her for your business, and then she doubles the accountings. She feeds you inferior foodstuffs, while you pay for the finest. Her staff is underpaid, despite the enormous payroll she presents to you. You're being fleeced, you gudgeon."

"I am?" Shimpton was still regretting the yellow Cossack trousers. His lip was quivering. "What should I do, Mums?"

He should grow a backbone, Maylene thought to herself. Then she shrugged. They'd given him the facts; it was up to the viscount to act on them. But through her lashes, she could see that tears were coursing down the clunch's cheeks. Added to his sweaty palms, the humidity would make Maylene's hair curl even worse than usual. Still, how could she not feel pity for the poor fool, who'd never had a thought in his brain box that his mother hadn't put there? She and Campbell would go have a talk with that housekeeper in the morning.

Her mother must have noticed the viscount's distress, too, and her tender heart led her to reassure him: "But you're not alone anymore, sonny. These nice, honest people will help you."

Maylene groaned. Mama was forgetting Lady Shimpton's character and letting her own sweetness come through. She coughed to get her mother's attention. Her ploy worked, for Lady Tremont's voice returned to a harsh screech. "You'll never amount to anything, Frederick, the way you moon around. Why, you'd have been swindled out of your inheritance if I hadn't made all the arrangements with the solicitors. What you need, boy, is a wife."

Maylene's eyes snapped fully open. Oh, dear, her mother was improvising. She shook her head, but Mama was warming to her theme.

"That's right, Frederick, you need a wife who will look after your household and go with you to the tailor's, the way I used to. Why, the right wife can help you find your way about in Society, without offending all the hostesses by arriving late or without an invitation, or not showing up at all, the way you did at Lady Bricechurch's dinner, leaving her numbers uneven."

"I did? I do? A wife? But . . . but I ain't in the petticoat line."

"A man has to settle sometime," Aunt Regina informed him. Campbell, the equally ancient bachelor, nodded vigorously.

"A wife? Where would I find the right wife?" Shimpton asked with a whimper.

"Right under your nose," Lady Tremont snapped at him.

The only thing under the cabbage-head's nose was the perspiration on his limp upper lip. Maylene glared at her mother, who pretended to go back into her trance, consulting with Max. "Yes, Max agrees," she said in her own normal tones. "The perfect wife for you is quite near to hand."

Maylene dropped that damp hand so fast Lord Shimpton's wrist hit the table with an audible crack. He rubbed the injured member against his cheek, and whined, "I could never find the right woman without Mumsy's help."

"Nonsense," Lady Tremont told him, realizing that subtlety was wasted on a gentleman with spun sugar for brains. "My daughter will help you find a wife."

"Mama!" Maylene yelped, but her mother merely patted the viscount's much-padded shoulder. "Max reminds me that dearest Maylene is excellent at finding things. That's her talent, don't you know."

If Max wasn't already dead, Maylene thought, she'd strangle him.

Chapter Two

A wail pierced the silence in the Treadwell House parlor after Campbell had gone to show the guests out, past the Chinese urn. Aunt Reggie had sought her bed, and Lady Tremont sat slumped in her chair, exhausted after the evening's efforts. This was no spectral keening, a shade moaning from the netherworld, nor a spirit protesting its disturbed slumber at the baroness's meddling.

This was a strident: "Mama, how could you!"

Lady Tremont feigned a yawn. "How could I do what, dearest?"

Maylene sputtered. "What? What? Why, you practically threw me at that poor man's head."

"Oh, no, dearest. He is not a poor man at all. Quite well to pass, I understand from your own notes. And I am sure his trustees will loosen the purse strings even further should he take a calm, capable wife such as you."

Maylene Treadwell was anything but calm at this moment. Her blue eyes were flashing, her hands were at her narrow waist, and what order she'd managed to bring to her unruly curls disappeared with the flying hairpins as she shook her head. "Mama, the man has less intelligence than a turnip!"

"Yes, he was quite dense about the matter, wasn't he? You'll just have to work a bit harder to show him how suitable such a match can be, won't you, dear?" Lady Tremont touched her own blond hair, which was as neat under its frilly cap as it was that morning when her maid had pinned it. "I daresay you'll manage. You always do."

"But, Mama, I do not want to manage such a catastrophe! Lord Shimpton and I wed?" She wailed again.

"Well, dearest, you must admit you are not getting any younger."

Maylene was growing older by the minute. Juggling nonexistent finances, worrying that Polite Society was laughing at them, feeling like a charlatan, was taking its toll. Why her hair hadn't already turned gray from all the worrying she did was a miracle itself. Likely it would tonight, from such an outrageous suggestion. Perhaps she'd put on caps, too.

Mama was going on: "And eligible gentlemen are not crowding our drawing room, are they?"

No, only dead gentlemen were, Maylene thought. "But Lord Shimpton?"

"The viscount has endearingly boyish qualities."

"A boy who has been playing in the muck, I swear."

"I am certain you could easily convince him of the benefits of more frequent washes, May."

"That harridan who raised him was likely afraid he'd drown himself in a hip bath. He is a mooncalf, Mama," Maylene insisted.

"Who can be taught to follow your lead."

"If I wanted a pet, Mama, I would get a dog, not a husband."

"Faugh, you are being too particular, dear. You know Lord Shimpton will neither stray nor gamble away his patrimony."

"The way my father did."

A frown creased Lady Tremont's pretty face when she recalled her late husband. "You would not wish to wed a domineering sort, like Lord Crowley, I am sure."

And like her father, Maylene thought. Then she said, "No, I am much too managing a female to be a complacent, compliant wife. That does not mean I wish to become a nursemaid to my husband. Lord Shimpton needs a keeper, Mama, not a spouse."

Her mother stroked Maylene's cheek. "Very well, dearest. You don't have to have the viscount. But you will help him find a suitable bride, won't you? I'm afraid the poor dear will make a mull of it on his own." She waited for Campbell to wheel in the tea cart before adding, "You do have the talent for such endeavors."

Maylene gave an unladylike snort. "There is no such thing as a finder's talent, Mama, and if there were, I wouldn't possess it. You are the one who believes in magic, not I."

Lady Tremont frowned over her teacup. "Powers of the mind, dear, not magic. We all have strengths beyond our puny understanding, if only we are willing to reach for them, accept them, let them flow through us like the purest light from on high."

Now Maylene yawned. She had heard the lecture before. Her mother should save the fustian for the paying customers—or for Max. She added another lump of sugar to her tea, to rid herself of the sour taste the reminder of the family business left in her mouth.

"Deny it all you want," Lady Tremont was going on, as if she could see into Maylene's mind, as well as into the beyond. "But you do have a knack for finding things, dearest. An intuition, if you will. Why, I'll never forget the way you found Lady Ponsonby's brooch that time, within seconds of her mentioning it, and you no taller than an end table."

The story of the long-ago afternoon call to Ponsonby Place had grown apocryphal in time. Maylene knew her efforts were futile, but she tried. "Mama, as soon as Lady Ponsonby said her jewel had gone missing, that maid dropped a teaspoon. She looked as guilty as a fox in a feather boa. Anyone could have made the deduction."

"But you were the one who suggested the maid be sent on an errand so we could search her room. And there it was!"

Maylene sighed. "And if the maid had been wearing the brooch pinned to her petticoats, or had already sold it, Lady Ponsonby would still be missing her heirloom."

"No, you would have found it. A mother knows. You're always finding my reticule for me, and Aunt Regina's spectacles."

"Those items are merely misplaced, not lost or stolen. I simply go looking until I find them, nothing more. It's logic, Mama, not witchery."

"And finding Lord Castleberry's watch? Mrs. Jarrett's little nephew? The key to your father's lockbox?"

"Logic, Mama," Maylene insisted. "And careful research. Campbell and his nephews scoured the backstreet jewelers for the watch, and the child was hiding in the stables, where anyone with an iota of knowledge about little boys would have thought to look. Castleberry and Mrs. Jarrett were more comfortable endowing scientific research than paying a gentlewoman a reward; that's how you were able to convince them of my so-called talent. I did not call forth any special forces to guide my search, Mama. I am not a sorceress."

Lady Tremont patted her daughter's hand. "We cannot all be mediums, dearest. Be proud of your own gift."

Maylene ground her teeth in frustration. She'd make one last attempt for the night. "If logic and reason are gifts, then I will accept them, especially when they help put food on our table. As for my father's lockbox, you were the one who begged me to keep looking for the key, rather than blowing the thing up with his dueling pistol. It was empty except for yet another gambling debt. We'd have done better to have left it unopened."

"I never claimed to be fortune-teller, May. I was afraid the contents would be destroyed if we exploded the box. And I was hoping Tremont had left something of value there, a bank book or a deed or a piece of jewelry, anything we might have lived on so I could have provided you with a dowry."

Lady Tremont dabbed at the moisture in her eyes with a delicate lace-edged handkerchief. Maylene was lost, and she knew it. "Very well, Mama, I will help Lord Shimpton find a wife." She raised her chin. "But I will not marry him myself. I cannot think of another gentleman I would less like to be bound to for the rest of my earthly days. And eternity, if you and Max are correct."

"What about Cousin Grover?" her mother asked.

"I said gentleman."

Her mother clucked her tongue. "Grover Treadwell is as wellborn as any sprig of the nobility."

The current Baron Tremont, Maylene's father's scurvy cousin Clarence's son, Grover, was of an age with Maylene. That was about all they had in common. "Very well, Mama, you are correct. Cousin Grover makes Lord Shimpton look like young Lochinvar. I would still rather wed the coal man than either one of them."

Unfortunately, she might not have the choice. Not content to inherit a mortgaged country estate and empty coffers—and

Maylene could not really blame him for his ire—Grover was
determined to get his hands on the Curzon Street house. Not
part of the entailment, Treadwell House had been a wedding
gift from Lady Tremont's parents. Grover would get it, as part
of his cousin's estate, but not until his cousin's widow died,
remarried, or went to live with one of her children. Thisbe's
marriage contract guaranteed that. Grover's pecuniary shortcomings guaranteed that he coveted the well-appointed, presti-
giously located property. His social ambitions guaranteed that
he found his cousin's relicts an embarrassment. He blamed
them, in fact, for his failure to attract an heiress, any heiress.
How many birds could he kill with one stone? If he married his
spinster cousin, Maylene, he could ship the lot of them off to
the country, where, with any luck, the widow would be burned
at the stake for her outré notions. He could sell Treadwell
House and set himself up as a man of the town, or he could con-
vert it into a polite gaming hell.

Grover thought he'd like living rent-free in Curzon Street—
and like having his pretty cousin in his bed. With Cousin
Thisbe's encouragement, Maylene's lack of the same did not
faze him one whit. In fact, he was so determined to have her
and her house, that Maylene's refusals fell on deaf ears—deaf
ears that had hair sticking out of them, besides.

Short of a dagger through his heart, Maylene couldn't discover a way to make her point, that she would never wed the
clunch. And he was growing more possessive daily, as if his fa-
miliarity would compromise her into accepting his hand in marriage. More than once she'd been forced to tolerate his touch,
rather than create a scene. She would *not* be forced into wedding Grover the Groper.

"Grover has more hair than wit, Mama, and he'll be bald before he's thirty. Furthermore, he always has that revolting drip
at the end of his nose."

"He was sickly as a child, too. Still, he is eager."

"He is eager to escape his rented rooms, that's all. Grover
should find himself a bride from the merchant class, since no
right-thinking aristocrats will let him near their daughters. One
always hears how mill owners and bankers will take on an im-
provident son-in-law for the sake of his title."

"But I do not think Grover wishes a wife with connections to trade. You know how he deplores our simple efforts to make ends meet." Her mother replaced the tea things on the tray and stood, ready to retire. "Well, you'll figure it out, dear. You really are good at finding whatever needs finding."

"I've been lucky in locating things that have gone missing. Females missing a few cogs are another matter. Only a wantwit would want either Shimpton or Grover."

Lady Tremont bent to kiss Maylene's cheek. "You can do it, dearest. You have the talent."

Chapter Three

Being a finder was better than being a future Baroness Tremont or, heaven forfend, a Lady Shimpton. Maylene stayed on in the parlor, sipping her cold tea, thinking about her mother's words.

She liked playing at detective, liked organizing her spies and informants, and liked earning the reward monies. She did not feel so helpless, so at the mercy of Society's fickle whims. Despite her mother's concerns, she did not *have* to marry, to be dependent on a feckless male, if she could support herself. As a female without great beauty or fortune or social standing, Miss Treadwell was pleased to get by on her wits, a commodity sadly lacking among the Quality. Why, when Mama told her callers that whatever they were missing—key or coin or important paper—was in the last place they'd look, they hung on her words as if she were the Delphic Oracle. And when they begged her to delve a little further into the arcane and locate the lost ring, recipe, or whatever, Maylene tried to oblige. If they were too stupid or too lazy to trace what had disappeared by negligence or by nefarious means, she was willing to attempt the retrieval, for a price. She was less expensive than Bow Street, less obtrusive than a red-vested Runner, and much more genteel. If the patrons chose to see Maylene's methodical investigations as being spirit-inspired, guided by one of Lady Tremont's eerie evening evocations, that was fine, too. A spine shiver was an added bonus to the addlepates who couldn't find their Adam's apples.

Between locating souls who had gone on to their reward and stuff that had gone missing, the Treadwells were staying out of the poorhouse. They were staying busy, too, needing a logbook to keep the various seekers straight. Between the almost nightly sessions with Max, the afternoon at-homes when callers came to make appointments, and the various searches and information gathering, the ladies had little time for socializing. Even if they had more free hours, invitations cards were not filling the tray on the mantel, since the Treadwell ladies were known to be unable to reciprocate. They were more likely to be invited as the entertainment than as guests, so they rarely accepted the few invites that came their way. Maylene wondered how, then, she was supposed to find Lord Shimpton a bride.

After all, she had not been able to find herself a husband. Just because she enjoyed her freedom and the feeling of accomplishment, just because she could earn an income, unlike most of the females of her acquaintance, did not mean that Maylene wished to remain single all her days. She might not need a husband, but she desired one, nevertheless. She wanted a home and a family of her own, a normal existence, with no interference from the afterworld. Like every other female, living or dead, she wanted to be loved.

Maylene did not need her mother's reminder that, instead of gathering rosebuds, she was perilously close to withering on the vine. Nearing her twenty-second year, she was nearly on the shelf.

Her prospects were as cold as the tea in the pot. Without attending the Season's festivities, the balls and rides in the park, Maylene could not meet eligible gentlemen. Those gullible gossoons who came to her mother's drawing room were not to be considered. Maylene could not respect any of them, so how could she marry one of them?

Campbell interrupted her dismal thoughts as he came to bank the fire to conserve coal. When he was done, the butler pulled his waistcoat down over a prominent paunch that attested to Cook's excellent meals. He cleared his throat.

Maylene set her cup down. Campbell would be wanting to close up the house and retire for the night. The Treadwell House ventures took a lot of everyone's time and effort, loyal staff included.

"A good night's work, Miss May, if I say so myself," Campbell told her as he put the tea tray back on the cart to wheel into the kitchen.

"Ah, Lord Shimpton was generous, then?"

"And Lady Crowley also."

"I thought she might be. I still don't know if she really wanted to speak to that dirty dish husband of hers or just wanted to make certain he was truly gone."

"She seemed pleased enough to know he was waiting beyond. I thought the harp a lovely touch, miss."

Maylene had a terrible thought. "He *is* deceased, isn't he?"

"Indeed. I sent my nevvies to the newspapers, checking obituaries. Gone aloft or out to sea, he's dead."

"That's all right, then. But what are we going to do about Lord Shimpton? Mama almost promised him a bride, and now the chawbacon is eager for leg shackles."

Campbell wrinkled a nose that was equally as prominent as his waistline. "Too bad he's not eager for a bath."

"I shall leave that to Mama and Max," Maylene said with a sigh, leaning her head on the raised back of the sofa. "I've lost track, Campbell. Do you recall who or what is scheduled for tomorrow? Or should I consult the appointments calendar?"

"I believe the morning has Lord Volstead's book room penciled in."

"His uncle's missing will?"

Campbell nodded his gray head. "He expects your mother to chant a spell and find it in that pigsty of a library."

"No, he's merely too lazy to take down every book and search for himself. Besides, the Volstead library hasn't been dusted since before that uncle died, and his lordship does not want to soil his own hands. He's too much the squeeze-crab to hire an adequate staff to see the job done. We do have enough help, don't we?"

Campbell drew himself up, affronted. "Of course, Miss May. My nevvies have arranged for the usual group of youngsters to come. Trustworthy, every one of them."

"And hungry, of course. Make sure Cook lays in an ample breakfast, and hampers for us to take along. The boys work much better when they are well fed." With few chances for honest labor, Maylene's lads, as they were coming to be known, were eager to assist in her investigations in exchange for decent meals and a few coins. They knew she would be generous in sharing any rewards if they were successful, and never out of temper when they were not. None of the crossing sweeps or errand boys had ever had such an employer before. When they were finished, not a speck of dust would be left in Lord Volstead's library, nor a scrap of paper in any book.

"I suppose we'll have to see about a new housekeeper for Lord Shimpton after nuncheon," Maylene said. "An honest one."

"With a touch of superstition to keep her that way," Campbell added, knowing that the promise of an otherworldly overseer could keep most employees on their toes. A hint that the formidable, if former, Lady Shimpton might be watching ought to be enough.

After a visit to the employment agency and the unpleasant task of getting rid of Shimpton's current housekeeper, with Campbell and his burly nephews at her side, Maylene would have to face another interminable afternoon of morning callers, absurd as that was. Cook provided a lavish tea, the callers made appointments with Lady Tremont for an evening's session, and Maylene took notes. She would not even have time for a walk in the park before supper, not if she was to prepare for the evening.

"Everything is ready for Lord Patterson, isn't it?" she asked Campbell. A great deal of effort had gone into the search on his behalf.

"You know it is, Miss May. You saw to it yourself. Sad story, that."

"Yes, but we have a happier ending, if it works." She got to her feet, gathering her shawl and a few straggling hairpins. "I suppose the viscount will return tomorrow evening, also?"

Campbell nodded. "And Lady Crowley, too."

"I'll have to make some notes for my mother then, Campy. You go on to bed. I'll just be a minute more."

Maylene bit her lip when the butler left. A minute here, an hour there, the afternoon, the evening—and she'd be no closer to finding her own heart's ease than she was before.

* * *

They found the missing will halfway through the library search, but Maylene kept her small army of boys cleaning and shaking out the musty tomes. She did not like to leave a job half finished, and they were already covered in dust anyway. She was handling the most ancient volumes herself, saving the brittle bindings from the lads' enthusiasm. A month wouldn't be enough time to put this collection in order, she thought in disgust at the cheese-paring Lord Volstead. In addition to the will, they found two love letters, a handful of pound notes, and an IOU for ten thousand guineas, signed by a well-known gambler from the previous era. The debt must have been owed to the previous Lord Volstead and never called in by the current holder of the title. Maylene didn't know if the voucher was still good, but from the generous check Lord Volstead wrote her, she supposed it must be. The nip-farthing was so pleased, and so impressed by her intuition to keep looking after the will was found, that he added another zero to the amount. Campbell's nephews' hints that she'd been led to the discovery by a higher power did not hurt, either. Her reputation and her purse were greatly enhanced from the morning's work.

The threat of the magistrate, not Max, convinced Shimpton's chatelaine to leave, to be replaced by a kindly older woman with three grown sons of her own. She'd know how to look after the gudgeon, Maylene believed, until they could find him a wife to bear-lead the bacon-brain.

Maylene needed a bath. What she got was a hurried wash in the basin of tepid water left from her morning toilette. Afternoon callers had arrived and, according to the upstairs maid, one young gentleman in particular was asking for Miss Treadwell, not Lady Tremont.

A young gentleman? Maylene put on her newest day gown, a high-waisted sprigged muslin with blue ribbons that matched her eyes. Unfortunately, she did not have time to repin her hair, which had come out of its braid again, so she tied another blue ribbon around what curls she could gather and went downstairs.

Campbell would not have made the error. The young man was no gentleman. He was a solicitor, ill at ease and awkward. Maylene could not decide if he was uncomfortable to be among the titled guests or to be in a house of haunts, but that Mr. Ryan kept tugging at his collar and consulting his pocket watch, with a wary eye on Lady Tremont. He must believe her poor mother was a witch, then.

Maylene took him aside and offered tea. The poor fellow looked as if he could use spirits, of the liquid variety, but their cabinets were not stocked. Perhaps Lord Volstead's contribution to psychical research could extend to the wine cellar.

"You wished to see me, Mr. Ryan?"

"Yes. No." Ryan almost ran his fingers through his red hair, until he recalled that it was pasted across his forehead with pomatum. "That is, I have been sent."

"Sent? By . . . ?"

"My employers, the firm of Hand, Hadley and Choate. They, ah, also handle Lord Volstead's affairs."

And his lordship had wasted no time in consulting his legal advisers on the validity of his uncle's will and the gambling chit. Maylene had known the Treadwell ladies' reputation would benefit from this day's work, though not so quickly. She'd thought Volstead would celebrate his stroke of good fortune when he went to his clubs that evening, and had hoped he'd mention her mother's name.

"His, ah, lordship was very grateful for your, ah . . . "

Divination? Soothsaying? The unfortunate young man obviously labored under the misapprehension that magical forces were involved, ones that could turn him into a frog if he offended. Maylene almost told him not to worry; he was already a toad. Instead, she poured her guest a cup of tea and offered a plate of poppy seed cake. The cup rattled in Ryan's hand as he accepted it, and then the slice of cake he'd balanced on the edge of the saucer wobbled, ready to fall. Maylene held out another saucer just in time. Now Mr. Ryan's face was as red as his hair.

Taking pity on him, Maylene said, "Yes, it was a lucky find, wasn't it?"

"Luck, that's right." Ryan was relieved to be handed a solution. A chap could comprehend luck, by Jupiter. Guidance from above was another matter. "Lord Volstead called you Lady Fortune. And my superiors decided they'd ask your assistance, having nowhere else to turn."

"I see," she answered. "Their last resort."

"Yes. That is, no. Lud, no offense, Miss Treadwell." He took a deep breath. "You see, my employers are men of reason, but their own searches have yielded no results, despite the investigators they have hired and the advertisements they have placed in the newspapers and the reward they have offered."

Munching on her own slice of cake, Maylene heard the fascinating word "reward." "And now?"

"Now they are willing to rely on . . . "

"Luck? Woman's intuition? Or my mother's contacts in the spiritual world?"

The teaspoon flew out of his hand. "Lud, not that, that last. That is, Lord Volstead said as how it was you and some helpers who found his papers. Not Lady Tremont. No disrespect intended, Miss Treadwell."

"No offense taken, Mr. Ryan, but just what is it that your estimable associates are looking for?"

"An heir. If we can prove he is, indeed, the heir. But we have to find him first. Lord Volstead swears you can find anything."

Maylene was getting a headache. "I think I need a tad more information, Mr. Ryan."

He dabbed at his lips. "Yes, of course. Five years ago the Duke of Winslowe died. His son and grandson were both killed in a coaching accident on their way to the funeral. The duke's brother and *his* entire family had succumbed to the smallpox epidemic. A younger brother died, leaving only three daughters, and the oldest male cousin died a bachelor. The next cousin in line had emigrated to the Canadian provinces, where his surviving son became a trapper." Ryan shuddered and took another swallow of his tea. "Hand, Hadley and Choate sent agents across the continent, only to find that the heir apparent had apparently been killed by a bear. You can imagine how long the investigation took. We had to be sure."

Maylene wished she had her pad and pencil handy for taking notes; she'd never keep all this straight in her head. Then again, they were all deceased, and Mr. Ryan seemed to have no desire to communicate with any of them, thank goodness. "So who is the heir?"

"There was a cadet branch of the family in the generation before the last duke. We have been tracing them for the past two years, through Ireland and Wales, searching parish records and registers. My superiors believe that a young man named Joshua Collins from Yorkshire is the new Duke of Winslowe and heir to the estates and fortune. Unfortunately, we cannot find Mr. Joshua Collins, nor even ascertain if he is alive."

"Then you will wish an appointment with my mother to search the afterworld?"

Ryan choked and spewed crumbs across his lap. "Afterworld? Heavens, no. What good would a ghost be to us? We're looking for a music instructor, not a mirage."

"A music instructor?"

"That's what he was until last year, pianoforte and violin teacher in Bath. Then he gave notice to his students and fell off the face of the earth."

"Surely, someone knows where he is. A school, a concert hall if he is a musician, friends, relations."

Ryan shrugged. "We have tried them all. That's why Mr. Hand sent me to you."

"But I have connections in neither Bath nor Yorkshire."

"There is a sizable reward, and my employers are willing to reimburse you for your time."

But she had no information gatherers, no helpful troops of street urchins in Bath. She had no place to stay, and could not leave her mother alone in London for as long as an investigation could take. She already had three inquiries under way, to say nothing of finding Lord Shimpton a bride. And her a husband. To leave London during the Season was to admit defeat. "Perhaps in the summer," she said.

"Did I say there was a very large reward?"

Chapter Four

He'd be handsome and single. There was no justice in this world if the missing heir was already married, Maylene decided. And the starving musician would be so grateful to be rescued from his attic room and handed a fortune that he would fall on his knees, vow his eternal devotion, and offer for her hand in holy dukedom. Holy matrimony, she corrected, then laughed at herself. The only way Mr. Joshua Collins would fall at the feet of Miss Maylene Treadwell was if he collapsed in a faint at her news. She was definitely not the type of female to bowl a man over with her looks or charm at first meeting, although Mr. Ryan had seemed pitifully grateful when she agreed to think about his dilemma. Perhaps he was merely grateful to be leaving a residence where the other callers might be culled from the graveyard.

Maylene had been unable to convince the young solicitor to stay for dinner, much less for her mother's evening gathering. He would have left sooner if he'd noticed the predatory look on her mother's face as Lady Tremont glanced at them in the corner of the parlor, heads together. Mr. Ryan might have had "son-in-law" writ on his forehead, in hair grease. Mama must be growing desperate, Maylene thought, to consider a very junior man of affairs as a suitor for her daughter. Desperate enough to ask Max to locate the old duke, she hoped. Surely, His Grace would know the whereabouts of his own heir.

Not willing to put all her eggs in one very fragile basket, Maylene convinced her great-aunt to write to her correspondents in Bath, and persuaded Campbell to check with his sister's husband's cousins, who owned a tavern outside the resort town. She swore them not to reveal the reasons for their inquiries, as Mr. Ryan feared imposters or duke-nappers almost as much as he feared the supernatural.

She could think of nothing else to do, unless her mother received inspiration from on high. Schools and theaters had already been checked, as had way bills for ships carrying emigrants, every professional orchestra, all the employment agencies. Collins must never read a newspaper, she thought, or else he had a good reason for not answering the solicitors' advertisements, which would make him even harder to find. And the man had been missing for over a year. Meanwhile, she had a gathering of ghouls to direct.

The circle was larger this evening. Lady Crowley and Lord Shimpton were there—and the solicitors thought Maylene was lucky!—as were two other "regulars," Sir Cedric and his lady, who frequently sought contact with their lost soldier-son. Max always told them the boy was at peace, dreaming of them, and they always left relieved. Lastly, Lord Patterson had arrived, pathetically anxious to discover news of his missing Toby. They were all, including Aunt Regina and Campbell the butler, taking their designated chairs at the round table, which Maylene had hastily rearranged so that Lord Shimpton was downwind of her.

When they were all seated, holding hands with nervous smiles as strangers touching each other were wont to do, Lady Tremont directed everyone to stare at the candle in the center of the table, to concentrate their thoughts on their blessed departed.

"Max," she called after a bit. "Max, dear, are you there?"

Then came a knocking. Sir Cedric, at Maylene's side, jumped and squeezed her hand hard enough to stop the flow of blood. His wife screamed.

"Max?"

Max did not rap on the table to signify his presence, Maylene knew. Lady Tremont would not stoop to so theatrical, so common a device. Still, they heard a definite knocking. Lady Tremont frowned. The maid was in the music room, and the young footmen were dealing with Lord Patterson's Toby, so there was no one to attend the front door. "We are already disturbed, Campbell," Lady Tremont told her butler, "so you might as well see what the noise is about."

Campbell disengaged himself from Lord Shimpton with no little relief and left the room. Straining to hear, Maylene thought she detected two strange voices raised in some kind of altercation with Campbell. If she hadn't been so careful of the household accounts, she'd have worried the bailiffs were at the door. After a minute or two, while Sir Cedric and his wife pretended they'd not been frightened out of their wits, Campbell returned to the room. Two gentlemen stood behind him, still in their caped greatcoats. They held their hats and walking sticks, but strode into the parlor very much as if they intended to stay.

Campbell introduced them as if they were guests at a ball, and as if he hadn't been staring at a candle, awaiting a visit from a vapor. "His Grace, the Duke of Mondale," he intoned. "And Socrates, my lord the Earl of Hyatt."

Ignoring the callers, as best one might two large, angry, and determined gentlemen, Lady Tremont addressed her faithful servant. "Tell them I am not at home, Campbell."

Aunt Regina gasped. The Duke of Mondale was one of the most respected men in Parliament, having devoted himself to the nation's welfare after losing his wife some ten years ago. Lord Hyatt was a legend in his own right. Young and wealthy, he disdained Society, preferring his vast country properties. The betting books, when they dared to mention his name, generally held favorable odds of his remaining a bachelor, despite all the lures cast for him. Aunt Regina kicked her niece under the table and hissed, "You are, too, at home, Thisbe."

Since this was so obvious a truth, the older, distinguished-looking gentleman stepped forward and bowed politely. Then he begged Lady Tremont's forgiveness for the intrusion. "My case is desperate, my lady, and I beseech you to . . . to do whatever it is that you do."

Maylene noted that His Grace was indeed pale and drawn, with lines etched in his forehead and cheeks. The much younger earl appeared simply angry, scowling and slapping his walking stick against his highly polished Hessians. Larger, broader, his dark-haired, grim-faced presence seemed to fill the dimly lighted parlor. In the shadows, he looked like a messenger from the netherworld, come to punish poor mortals for dabbling in the spiritual realm. Maylene shivered, and not simply because the usual scant fire was not penetrating the parlor's chill.

"I am sorry for your difficulties, Your Grace," her mother was saying, "but we have already begun the session for this evening. It will be hard enough to recapture the correct mood."

Maylene could have sworn she heard Lord Hyatt snort. Her eyes narrowed. She might have her own opinions of her mama's flights of fancy, but no arrogant aristocrat was going to belittle her beloved mother. She drew her shawl more closely around her shoulders and prepared to stand, to do battle with Lucifer himself if need be. But her mother was going on. "If you wish to make an appointment with my butler, I would be happy to consult with you tomorrow. That is the way of these things, Your Grace."

Mondale ran his hand through silver-tinged locks. "I can only apologize again and beg you to make an exception, Lady Tremont. I am at my wit's end, and when I heard Lord Volstead singing your praises this evening at my club, I knew I just had to come, to ask for your help. He swears you and your, ah, minions can find anything, even if a fellow doesn't know it's missing." He sighed. "Ah, if that were only the case."

Lady Tremont's tender heart went out to the man so patently suffering. "Just what is it, Your Grace, that you are trying to find? Or should I say whom?"

Lord Hyatt coughed in warning, but the duke was determined to get help, no matter that he had to air his family's dirty laundry in so public a manner. "My daughter, ma'am, though I beg you not to mention this to anyone." He bowed to the rest of the company, and everyone nodded their intentions of keeping his confidences. "We gave out that she is visiting an ailing relative, but she never got there. I have no idea where my precious Belinda could be and fear she might have been kidnapped since she is a considerable heiress. Bow Street is trying to locate her, and every man I could hire, but with no results so far. I thought . . . "

"You thought Max might be able to find the young lady," Lady Tremont concluded, nodding.

"Max?" The duke shook his head. "No, although if you have confidence in your own man, I would add him to my payroll."

Her mother laughed. "Oh, Max is not for hire, but sit down, Your Grace, and we will see if we can find any answers for you."

Aunt Regina let out a breath of relief and smiled, showing the duke her new false teeth. "And take your gloves off, Duke." Aunt Regina batted her equally false eyelashes at him. The duke bowed again, handing his coat, cane, and gloves to Campbell.

Already half out of her chair, Maylene stood back and said, "Please take my seat, Your Grace. I will be just as happy to observe from afar tonight." She gathered her shawl and moved to the sofa that was, happily, nearer the fire. She pulled a pad and pencil out from the workbasket set nearby and prepared to gather what information she could.

As he sat, bowing to the others gathered around, the duke told his friend, "You might as well leave, Soc. I might be a while."

When Maylene jerked her head toward the door, Lady Tremont seconded Mondale's suggestion. "You seem anxious to be on your way, Lord Hyatt. Such, um, agitation is not conducive to focused thoughts. The mood, don't you know." And Hyatt's stormy countenance and looming presence were not comfortable, either. If ever there was a nonbeliever, Maylene felt, it was this broad-shouldered, sharp-eyed earl.

If Lady Tremont wanted him gone so badly, Lord Hyatt decided, he believed he'd stay. So what if he had an appointment with Lady Ashford, the most dashing and expensive widow in all of London? Friendship had to come first. Besides, Aurora knew better than to sulk or berate him for his tardiness. But this delay would cost him, he also knew. The bauble—Aurora preferred rubies—he could easily afford. The extra hour of tedious small talk to assuage Lady Ashford's feelings of ill-usage was a far higher price. He was not sponsoring the female's London Season for her conversation, by George, but he was too much the gentleman to rush a woman into intimacy. And Lady Tremont had the nerve to talk about losing the mood!

Then again, he'd wager that Lady Tremont had the nerve to

sell snowballs in hell. Just look at all the fools gathered at her
stage, waiting for her performance. He nodded curtly to his acquaintances, surprised to see such usually rational beings as Sir
Cedric and Lord Patterson at this farcical, fraudulent fortune-
telling. He was not at all shocked to see Shimpton in attendance. The simpleton was liable to believe the moon was made
of green cheese. That was another black mark against Lady
Tremont and her ilk: only a hyena preyed on the helpless. Well,
they were not going to get their fangs into his old friend Mondale, not if Hyatt could help it.

Glowering, he announced that he was in no hurry to leave
and was, instead, actually quite interested in the proceedings.
"I've never seen a ghost, ma'am."

The old lady laughed, but Shimpton's hands were shaking.
"You never said Mama would come back in person!" he
whined.

Lady Tremont glanced uncertainly to her butler and her aunt,
then nodded. "Feel free to stay then, my lord. But not as a par-
ticipant, I think, since I sense a decided aura of skepticism in
you." She also sensed an eligible *parti*. A person could not live
in London, could not read the newspapers, could not listen to
Aunt Regina's chatter without knowing that Socrates Hughes,
Lord Hyatt, was nicknamed the Ideal, and not for any philoso-
phy he might share with his namesake. Well-favored, well-
bred, and well-financed, he was welcomed everywhere he
chose to bless with his presence, especially those households
with unmarried daughters. "Why don't you sit on the sofa,"
Lady Tremont suggested with a wave of her slender hand in
Maylene's direction, "and observe for this evening?"

He'd observe, all right, Soc vowed, then expose these charlatans to his friend so they could get on with a proper search for
Belinda. Mondale was simply too devastated to be thinking
clearly, so Hyatt would do it for him. He made his way to the
sofa, next to the youngish female draped in shawls. A poor relation of one of the other guests, he thought, or perhaps Lady
Crowley's paid companion. The chit was passable enough, he
automatically noted as he got close, except for the pale hair
tumbling every which way out of an inept topknot. If Lady
Tremont was looking for auras, the female had an absolute

corona of curls. She looked like a dandelion. And she was frowning at him.

"Ah, and I was so looking forward to pressing Lady Tremont's bare hand," he said as he sat beside her, staring pointedly at her uncovered fingers. "I don't suppose you'd consider . . . ?"

Maylene hastily hid her ungloved hands in the folds of her skirt. She would not be taking notes this evening after all. "Please be still, my lord. Lady Tremont is trying to concentrate, to unite all the mental energies to reach beyond."

He snorted. "Don't tell me you believe all that poppycock. You don't look like a gullible peagoose."

Maylene drew herself up in rigid affront. "Then perhaps I look like Lady Tremont. I ought to, my lord, for I am her daughter."

The chit did have the same flashing blue eyes, pale hair, and willowy form, Hyatt saw now that it was too late. He felt his cheeks grow warm. *Dash it*, he hadn't blushed in more years than Shimpton could count, yet this baggage made him feel like a jackanapes. No one had made introductions in this havey-cavey household. How was he to know? He ignored the fact that they hadn't been invited, hadn't taken the time for proper social graces. "My apologies, Miss . . . ?"

"Treadwell, if you care," she snapped, still indignant. Now that Lord Hyatt was closer, entirely too close for her comfort, Maylene could see that his dark scowl was made fiercer by the shadows of dark stubble. The cad hadn't even bothered to shave before calling on them!

Following her disapproving glance, Hyatt rubbed his bristly chin. He wasn't half as prickly as this little termagant. Deuce take it, he'd meant to bathe at the town house in Kensington he maintained for discreet trysts with his current mistress. And he'd intended to let Aurora shave him. The widow had a way with soap and warm water that. . . . Well, by the time he got there, Soc would not trust the woman with a razor at his throat. Unaccountably, he felt the urge to make amends to Miss Treadwell, despite having her tarred with the same brush as her mother, in his mind. "This call was not my choice, and witchcraft is not to my taste."

If Maylene were closer to the fireplace poker, she'd hit the insufferable brute over the head. "Witchcraft? That's what you think my mother does?"

"No, I think she dupes susceptible fools into parting with their money. Is that plain speaking enough for you, Miss Treadwell?"

"Quite plain enough and quite enough speaking." She pointedly turned to face her mother, who was instructing the others to watch the flickering candle while she closed her eyes and swayed to her own soft chant. "I can only wonder why you bothered to come at all."

"Mondale is my friend," he answered, "and Lady Belinda and I were about to become betrothed."

Maylene's head snapped around, loosening even more wheaten curls. "The poor girl is engaged to marry you? No wonder she disappeared."

Chapter Five

"Touché," he said, giving her the fencer's salute. So the little dandelion wasn't a mere ball of fluff. "But I assure you, the informal arrangement was—is—to Lady Belinda's liking."

Now Maylene made an unladylike sound. "More to her father's, I'd wager."

Socrates fingered the lace at his cuff. "Lord Mondale is pleased, naturally, but he had nothing to do with Lady Belinda's decision."

An earl and an heiress, marching estates, family friends? Maylene could imagine the pressure brought on the girl to accept this paragon of a *parti*. Why, she herself had all she could do to fend off her family's matchmaking. How could a motherless young girl, more gently reared, dare refuse her father's choice? "Hah," was all she said.

Now that Miss Treadwell was showing her claws, Socrates no longer felt so gauche over his earlier lapses. In this household, the chit was undoubtedly no better than she ought to be, if not an outright lieutenant under her Captain Sharp of a mother. Now that he thought of it, Volstead had been ranting about the daughter's miraculous powers of discovery, guided by the mother's sight. The whole rumgumption smacked of necromancy and medieval sorcery. He would not be surprised to see a dish of entrails wheeled in instead of tea. Except, of course, that the pompous butler would be serving neither the much-needed refreshments nor mutilated chickens; the insolent fellow was serving instead as one of his mistress's fellow conjurors, eyes fixed on the candle. What, was the entire ménage part and parcel of the scheme? Either that or they were all attics-to-let.

"Not that it is any of your concern, Miss Treadwell," he told her in his best depress-the-toadstools voice, "but Mondale would never force his daughter into anything. He quite dotes on the chit, his only chick, don't you know. That's why we are here, grasping at straws."

It took no transcendental powers to interpret the sneer on Lord Hyatt's lips. Maylene could recognize the arrogant earl's disdain and disbelief as if she could read his mind. And wouldn't he hate that idea, too! In what she hoped was an equally patronizing voice, Maylene declared, "One gets out of such experiences what one is willing to put in, my lord."

"And I already put fifty pounds into an ugly vase just to get past that larcenous butler of yours."

So much? Maylene made a mental note to tell Campbell to order a better quality of cognac and brandy, if they were going to be entertaining such top-drawer gentlemen. "And what are you expecting in return?" she wanted to know.

"Honestly? I am expecting a good show. Smoke and mirrors, sleight of hand. Incense and incantations. That kind of jiggery-pokery. Then we can get on with the real search." And he could get on to his dinner, and dessert.

"You'll be disappointed."

He would be if his dinner was cold, as well as his mistress.

"My mother does not employ such ruses, my lord. She uses the candle and the chant for concentration only. Her mental energy is what is at work here, not any magician's bag of tricks."

"If you say so." He was being polite, at least, until Lady Tremont began to pant slightly. Her face reddened, and beads of perspiration formed on her forehead, under the lace cap she wore. "Nice touch, that," he said, smug in his proven assumption. "The gasping might be a bit much, but your mother is very good, miss. I suppose you are going to say she is undergoing an infusion of energy from the ectosphere or some such drivel."

"No, my lord, my mother is having a hot flash. That is why the room is kept so cold. And a true gentleman would not have mentioned the fact."

Lud, Hyatt thought, trumped again, and by a wisp of a witch. If she did have any sorcerous skill, he was sure he'd be having bugs for supper, if any landed on his lily pad. At least Miss

Treadwell did not cast her eyes down and agree with every statement he made, like every other female he knew, proper young lady or paid companion. Socrates didn't know if he liked the new experience any better than the rest of this rigamarole. He turned his attention back to the table, where Lady Tremont had stopped droning and was now grinning like a child in a toy shop. She was murmuring softly, too low for him to make out the words.

"What's going on?" he demanded.

"Ssh. You'll disturb the connection. Mama is greeting Max. See how happy she is? Next she'll be introducing him to the company."

At least someone made introductions around here. Hyatt looked around. "Who the devil is Max?"

"Lower your voice. And Max is not a devil at all. More an angel, I should think, although Mama has never been clear on that. Max is my mother's link to the beyond."

"He's dead?" Hyatt's whisper was loud enough to wake him if he wasn't.

"Definitely dead."

"And you believe she's talking to him—and he's answering her?"

"My mother believes it," she answered evasively.

"Fustian."

"You'd think one bearing the name of a great thinker would at least keep an open mind."

"My parents spent their wedding trip in Greece in their bedroom, not in the libraries there."

Miss Treadwell blushed, and Hyatt was pleased to see how easily he could get a rise out of the little kitten. Then his stomach rumbled in hunger, and she giggled, the hellcat. "How long is this blasted argle-bargle with the afterlife going to take?" he demanded.

"Oh, Mama quite enjoys Max's company. She will chat with him as long as he lingers, or until she becomes too exhausted from the effort."

"Bloody hell."

"You could leave. You could take the side door through the garden without disturbing the others."

He crossed his arms over his chest. "Not without Mondale."

"Very well then, but be quiet, my lord, for Mama is about to ask Max her questions."

The session started right, at least. "Max, dear, do you recall that Sir Cedric and Lady Bannister came last week to ask about their son who went off to war? We've all been thinking about young Ian. Have you been able to speak to the dear, brave boy?"

There was no sound in the room. Even Hyatt seemed to be holding his breath, it seemed to Maylene. Then Lady Tremont nodded and smiled. "He is visiting with his little sisters? How nice that he has family there, Max. Now his parents won't have to grieve that he is so alone, will they? And he feels no pain? How silly of me. Of course he has no body, so how could he be suffering? Yes, dear, I'll be sure to tell his parents that Ian and the little girls miss them, but they are happy."

Lord Hyatt drummed his fingers on the sofa arm and muttered, "Everyone in the world knows Lady Bannister lost three daughters in a row before giving birth to the heir."

"Four," Maylene corrected. She'd done her research.

"Well, it's no secret, so Lady Tremont isn't telling them anything they didn't know."

"No," she agreed, "but look how elated they are to hear that young Ian is at peace. They encouraged him to join up, you know, and cannot help but feel wretched, besides mourning his loss."

"The lad was a soldier. What did they expect?" Still, he could not ignore the relief on Sir Cedric's face, nor the tears of joy streaming down his wife's cheeks.

"All our children are together, Ceddie," she sniffled into the handkerchief Lady Tremont's butler produced. "And we will see them again eventually. Thank heaven."

"And thank Lady Tremont," her husband seconded, patting her hand.

"No, I do nothing," that lady said. "It's Max who is so busy in the beyond. Are you still there, dear?"

Silence reigned again, until Lady Tremont smiled and let out her breath. "Yes, dear, I know you reach out to us for as long as you can, and I do understand how tiring it must be. But Lady Crowley has returned to make her final adieus. Is her beloved husband available?"

"Beloved? Crowley?" The earl was whispering in Maylene's ear, none too softly. "The only decent thing he ever did for this world was leave it."

"You say he is practicing again?"

Oh, heavens, Maylene thought. Not the harp. The earl was certain to march over to the connecting door and catch Nora "dusting." That's why he stayed on, she was sure, to expose them for mountebanks. His toplofty lordship would think nothing of ruining Mama, not when he was doing a service for his friend.

Her mother must have heard Lord Hyatt's asides, thank goodness, for she never mentioned Nora's cue word, "harp." Instead her head whipped from side to side. "He's practicing his flying?" She peered into the corner, then swung her eyes to the door. "Watch out for the— How silly. Of course Lord Crowley would not bump his head on the lintel. He hasn't got a head, has he?"

Lady Crowley was like an owl, trying to twist her head in a complete circle to follow Lady Tremont's darting glances. She put her hands up to the sausage curls that bounced along her cheeks. "My stars! I felt him go by!"

"I felt the breeze," Campbell claimed, straightening the two strands of hair that had fallen onto his forehead, ostensibly from Lord Crowley's inexpert swoops and soars.

Aunt Regina felt it, too. Her false eyelashes were aflutter, and her wig was decidedly lopsided. Her bust enhancer had also fallen askew in her gyrations.

"Pigs will fly sooner than Crowley," Lord Hyatt declared, and Maylene had to bring her hand to her mouth to hide her own smile.

"You keep practicing, Aloysius," his widow called out. Then she muttered, "That should keep the old rip too busy to chase after lightskirts, for the first time in his life."

"He's not in his life," Hyatt pointed out. This time the duke turned to frown at him, but his lips were twitching, too.

"Thank you, Max." Lady Tremont was already going on, reminding him that Lord Shimpton had returned again to chat with his dear mama.

Instead of watching her mother, Maylene watched the earl. She'd seen her mother's transformation, the more rigid carriage, the jutting chin, the piercing nasal whine. "That you, sonny?" her mother finally called in Lady Shimpton's strident tones. "You're late, as usual. And what's that nosewipe you've got draped around your neck?"

The earl was smiling now, the first time Maylene had seen him look less than grim. "She's got the old bat down to perfection. Your mother is a masterful impersonator, I'll give her that."

Shimpton was clutching at the Belcher neckcloth he sported. "It's all the go, Mumsy."

"It should go straight to the dustbin, Frederick. I wouldn't have let you leave the house in such a rig. A proper wife wouldn't have either, I swear. What have you done about finding one?"

"I, ah, it's only been a day, Mums, but, . . . but Lady Tremont said she and Miss Treadwell would help me look."

The earl's scowl returned. "Ah. So that's the plan for the poor sod, is it?" His lip curled. "Drag him in and browbeat the bacon-brain into making an offer, thinking he's pleasing his mother. What, is he the best you can do?"

Maylene raised her own chin a notch. "I assure you I have no ambition to wrest a proposal out of Lord Shimpton, my lord, by any means." She could not speak for her mother. "As for my prospects, they are no concern of yours."

"Except in so far as I am a fellow bachelor who knows what it is like to be hunted for one's title and wealth. Shimpton is too simple even to know he's in your sights."

"A proper girl, sonny, mind you," Lady Tremont was saying in Lady Shimpton's voice. "None of your Birds of Paradise."

"Mumsy, I wouldn't!" Shimpton screeched. "I don't. I mean I never have." His sweat-beaded brow attested that he'd been thinking of it, though.

"Someone here has been thinking improper thoughts," Lady

Shimpton's voice thundered. "I can feel 'em, like worms on my grave."

All eyes immediately swung to Lord Hyatt, whose reputation as a womanizer was almost a legend.

"Deuce take it, am I on trial at a court of cadavers?"

His indignant disclaimer merely confirmed Maylene's suspicions. Rumors and reputation aside, the man nearly defined sensuality, or what she knew of it, at any rate. She whispered, "No, you are a betrothed man, with the morals of a midden rat, that Lady Shimpton can sense your lascivious thoughts through the ether."

"I am not engaged yet, Miss Treadwell, and my morals are no concern of yours, dash it."

"Except in so far as I am a single woman," she threw back at him, "who would like to know that her fiancé was faithful to her. Perhaps Lady Belinda had more reasons than we know for crying off."

"She did not cry off, blast you." His jaw was clenched, and his hands were clutching his knees, almost as if he feared strangling her if they were empty.

"Nor did she confide her destination in you, obviously," Maylene pointed out before turning back to listen to Lord Shimpton promise his mother to try to find a bride of good birth.

"Remember, the dowry don't matter so much as the chit has to be a downy one, sonny."

No dowry? A man would be a fool to take a bride who brought nothing to the marriage, Socrates thought. Then again, Shimpton was a fool, and Miss Treadwell was pockets-to-let. He was right; the pernicious pair was trying to land the looby. "Why doesn't she just toss him your bonnet?"

Because Maylene would rather go bareheaded to church than wed that clunch. She glared at her conniving mother, her complicit great-aunt, and the cork-brained viscount. Then she glared at the self-righteous, rag-mannered rake next to her for good measure.

"There better be some wits in the marriage, Frederick," came the deceased dowager's advice; "else you'll lose your way on the honeymoon and never get home."

"You better put him on a leash, else he'll never find his way to the church!"

Furious that the insufferable Ideal was determined to think the worst of her, Maylene snapped back, "I'll make sure his driver knows the direction."

Chapter Six

So they were out to snabble the vacant-headed viscount. The jade had as much as admitted it. Good, Hyatt thought, she'd be bored within a month of the wedding. Nay, a week, then an adventuress like Miss Treadwell would be ready for a real adventure, and a real man. Hyatt thought he might like to be that man. At least the chit had spirit and sense, two things that would be wasted on Shimpton. Socrates took out his quizzing glass to see what else would be wasted on the paper-skulled peer.

Why, of all the rude, revolting affectations, Maylene decided, pulling the shawl closer around her shoulders so no bare skin showed above her gown's low neckline, this had to be the worst! Of course she never realized that, by pulling the woolen wrap closer, she outlined her figure more revealingly. Lord Hyatt noticed, then nodded a connoisseur's approval of her small but shapely bosom. Lady Tremont and Max noticed, and finished their communication with the viscount with: "And don't be getting any notions to play fast and loose with some innocent gel, sonny. It's marriage or nothing."

Hyatt slipped the looking glass back into his pocket. Lud, the baroness couldn't read minds, could she?

Hoping that Lord Hyatt could not see her red cheeks in the dimly lighted room, Maylene prayed that her mother would move on to the next petitioner, Lord Patterson. At least Mama was not trying to marry her off to the myopic, three-score peer, nor needing to warn him off. Patterson had eyes for nothing but the portrait of his little Toby that lay on his lap, if he could see it at that distance.

Lady Tremont took a sip of water from the glass in front of

her while Lady Crowley patted Shimpton's trembling hand and loudly whispered, "I like your neckcloth, Frederick, no matter what the old witch— That is, no matter which style your dear mother might have preferred."

Campbell cleared his throat to gain everyone's attention. Then he stamped his foot. "Leg cramp, don't you know."

Maylene knew that was the signal for his nephews in the next room to get ready. Lady Tremont nodded and asked if Max was not too tired for a few more questions. "For Lord Patterson has come back three times, dear, hoping for word of his precious Toby. Have you seen Toby, Max?"

A scrabbling sound came from the next room, and Lady Tremont's voice grew stronger, to cover the noise. "You have? Not, not in the beyond, I pray, Max, for poor Lord Patterson would be quite bereft without his little Toby."

"What's he saying, ma'am?" Patterson cried. "Never tell me Toby is gone aloft."

"You've found him for us?" Lady Tremont said in a higher pitch, giving an excited squeal. "What's that, Max? You are speaking so fast, and there is so much yip-yap that I cannot make out . . . Oh, there was an accident, you say? A runaway carriage? Oh, dear!"

"That's what I was afraid of!" Patterson wailed. Sir Cedric's wife was weeping, and even Aunt Regina was squeezing out a few fake tears.

"But he didn't die? He lay at death's door until we started calling him back, you say? Lord Patterson's love and devotion brought him right back from the gates of the Happy Hunting Ground? Oh, Max, that is good news indeed."

"But where is he?" Patterson shouted. "Where's my laddie? How can I find him?"

In her own voice, Lady Tremont told him, "Max says that dear Toby might be a little different than you remember him, but that's because he has been so close to the Light."

"Yes, yes, but where?"

"He will find you. Call him, my lord. Let us all call him. Toby! Toby!"

Maylene called him, as did Lady Crowley, Aunt Regina, and

Campbell. Shimpton asked if they were going to call his mother back next, and should he take his neckcloth off first.

"Just call, you twit," Patterson screamed. Sir Cedric and Lady Bannister joined in, and the Duke of Mondale shrugged his shoulders and called, too. Soon "Toby" filled the room, with one "Mumsy." In all the noise, no one heard the connecting door open, nor saw the little fox terrier shoved into the parlor. He was the spit and image of the dog in the portrait, which happened to have been painted some six years earlier. Toby hadn't looked so chipper in years, not before and definitely not after the runaway carriage. In all of London and the outlying areas there had not been a single aged fox terrier with the appropriate markings for sale.

The pup hesitated in the doorway, likely terrified to hear his new name being shouted by so many strangers. Then he unerringly bounded for Lord Patterson's chair—which had been introduced to a lamb chop before the guests' arrivals.

"Toby? Toby, my boy, is that you? Why, look at you, my fine lad! By George, you are a handsome fellow. Ah, how I have missed you." Patterson was on his knees, tears streaming down his cheeks, as he hugged the curly-haired little dog he could barely see.

The only dry eye in the room, in fact, belonged to Lord Hyatt. His hazel ones saw very well indeed. He saw a confused young dog, a delighted old fool, and a satisfied smile on Miss Treadwell's misty-eyed face as she surveyed her handiwork. Gammon, that's what it was, but how could he denounce the minx and her mother in front of Patterson's so-evident joy? At least his friend Mondale wasn't taken in, for the older man was smiling despite his own woes, and even winked at their underhanded hostess.

Lady Tremont suggested that Lord Patterson and Toby take their leave, as Max's voice was growing weaker in her head, and they still had some queries to put to him. One of the footmen came when Campbell pulled the bell cord, ready to assist with a new braided leather leash. The other footman was sent to fetch his lordship's carriage. From the parlor Maylene could hear Campbell's discreet cough as they passed the Chinese urn, and Patterson's, "Of course. Dash it, Toby, stop wriggling whilst I make a donation. Down, sir, I say, so I can open my purse. Devil take it, Campbell, keep the whole thing. I'd have paid anything to get my laddie back."

Campbell's nephews and the other lads would get a bonus, Maylene decided. And perhaps Treadwell House could afford to keep a carriage again. Her fingers itched to make lists of the current account balances, but that would have to wait till the large suspicious gentleman next to her had gone. For all she knew, he was merely waiting for morning to set the magistrates on them. For now, her mother was chanting again.

"Let us focus our mental energies once more." Lady Tremont addressed the air above her as soon as the room was restored to silence, murmuring to the somewhat smaller circle. Lady Cedric was wrinkling her nose, but Maylene could not tell if she was getting a sniff of the lamb chop or of the viscount. "Max, dear, I can feel your fatigue, but do try to borrow strength from our collective thoughts for a few moments more. We have two small questions, if you would be so kind."

Mondale sat forward in anticipation. He was going to be disappointed, Maylene knew, because her mother never changed the order of her proceedings. New requests were made in the order they were received. Maylene had passed on news of Mr. Ryan's search that afternoon, so her mother would direct her thoughts, and Max's, there first.

"Max, dear, we are searching for a young gentleman named Joshua Collins. All we know is that he is sandy-haired, slightly built, and musical. There might be an element of danger involved. I do hope he has not gone aloft, but you could save us a lot of effort by telling us if he has. Oh, and Max, dear, Maylene wanted me to tell you that there is a most generous reward for locating him. As if you care about such things now. What would you do with money, anyway?"

A reward? Were these ninnyhammers hunting wanted men now? Lord Hyatt frowned. He had never heard of a Joshua Collins, and did not care to wonder why there should be a bounty on his head, musical or otherwise. Was there no end to these females' foolishness? Prying among the criminal elements was far more dangerous than dabbling with the dead. Then he relaxed. From what he'd seen, any supernatural search was liable to produce nothing more than a few memories and a new mutt. Besides, why should he worry over the connivers? The Treadwell women were as deceitful as any cardsharps preying on the ignorant and unwary. Lud, he despised dishonesty.

A small part of his mind, the part connected to his lower organs, likely, was meanwhile mulling over the chit's name. Maylene, was it? Volstead had said some such, but Socrates hadn't been paying attention, too busy trying to dissuade Mondale from calling on Volstead's sorceresses. Hyatt could understand the man's desperation, and damn the selfish chit Belinda for causing her father so much grief, but to call on the thaumaturgists at Treadwell House? They'd have done better to consult a Gypsy fortune-teller, for the Gypsies might even have an idea to Belinda's whereabouts. Miss Maylene Treadwell did not.

May. The first violets and the unfurling ferns, pushing through a cover of last year's leaves. Yes, it suited her, bursting with life, exuberantly awakening from a winter's rest. Shimpton would only put her back to sleep. That, too, was none of his concern. Aurora Ashford was. He consulted his pocket watch. "Damn, there'll be the devil to pay," he muttered.

"No, only the Fund for Psychical Research," Maylene told him, fully aware of what kind of appointment his lordship must be anticipating. "And you've already made your contribution."

Socrates had to bite his lip to keep from laughing. He would *not* find this farouche female amusing. There was nothing amusing about Lady Tremont's asking Mondale to describe his daughter, either.

"She . . . she is about shoulder height, with soft brown braids that she keeps in a knot. And her eyes are the blue of . . . of an autumn sky, a bit grayish, wouldn't you say, Hyatt?"

Socrates shrugged. The lady had blue eyes. Two of them. They were not the startlingly clear mountain lake color of Miss Treadwell's. He would have remembered that.

"Can you think of anything else that might help, my lord?" the shrew asked him now. "As a man about to become engaged, surely you can give a better description than brown hair and bluish eyes."

In the face of her disapproval, Hyatt was tempted to say that

Lady Belinda's bosom was more rounded than her own, or that Belinda never had a hair out of place, and she would not be caught dead in a threadbare, faded shawl. He held his tongue. "You should have brought the miniature, Duke."

"Next time."

Next time? Over his dead body, Hyatt swore. He'd give the fakers this one night, at considerable cost to himself, incidentally, but no more. He was not going to see Mondale sucked into a whirlpool of greed and guile, not by this group of gull-catchers.

Lady Tremont was asking Max to look around. "Not that Lady Belinda has departed the mortal plane, dear, but perhaps someone knows where she has gone. You can see so much more from your vantage point. And His Grace is so unhappy at her disappearance, Max, that surely you and your friends will take pity on him, won't you? We all know what it is to lose someone so beloved, don't we, dearest? Even a short while is too long. And the dear earl is sorely missing his promised bride."

Whose eyes he cannot describe, Maylene added to herself. And who was certainly not the reason he kept checking his watch. The Ideal might be a magnificent representative of manhood, but he'd make some poor girl a wretched husband. Perhaps Belinda had concluded that herself.

"So, Max, dear, you will let us know if you discover anything? Perhaps in a few days? I know that is soon, but thank you, dear, for trying. Good night." Lady Tremont sank back in her seat and reached for the glass of water.

"Two days?" His Grace cried. "That's much too long! Belinda is in trouble, I know she is, else she would have come home or written me. I cannot wait two more days!" With shaking hands, he accepted the glass of wine Campbell poured out for him as Lady Tremont tried to soothe his impatience.

"I can try tomorrow if you wish."

Hyatt was growling next to Maylene. "Never. You will not get your claws into him. Surely the man is suffering enough without your machinations. Instruct your mother to tell him what he wants to hear, for heaven's sake, and let him be on his way. You've had your payment, now give him his money's worth."

"It doesn't work that way," Maylene insisted. "Mama knows nothing about Lady Belinda"—how could she when they had done no research?—"and won't know anything until Max tells her. As she tried to explain, the beyond is a large place, with millions of souls. One cannot simply throw a name into the ether and have answers returned."

"You don't believe that humbug any more than I do."

"I believe in my mother."

"Bah! You believe you can feather your nest on Mondale's grief."

Maylene *had* been thinking of a new bonnet, with an ostrich feather.

"Very well, if I cannot appeal to your nonexistent sensibilities to another's sorrow, I'll appeal to your avarice. I'll toss another hundred pounds into that monstrosity in the hall if you get your mother to say that Belinda is alive and waiting for Mondale to find her. That's all she has to say, and it's most likely true."

"I pray it is so. But I cannot put words in Mama's mouth, not for any amount of money. Only Max can do that. And even if I could get her to try to reach him again, she is much too drained." Maylene gestured to where her mother was slumped in her seat, trying to hold her head up until Campbell brought the tea cart. "Anyone can see that she is exhausted from her labors."

"Anyone can see that Lady Tremont is a consummate actress. She could have made her fortune on the boards."

Maylene had had enough. She stood, forcing Hyatt to his feet also, in a belated effort at civility. Her eyes were like sapphires, spitting icy bolts of blue lightning his way. Her hands were on her hips, allowing the dowdy shawl to fall open to reveal a stirring view of heaving bosom. With the mop of pale curls around her head transformed into a halo by the fire behind her, Miss Maylene Treadwell looked like an avenging angel. The only thing missing, Socrates thought, was the flaming sword. Her tongue, however, could flay a man alive.

"You have come into our home and insulted us at every turn. In your narrow-mindedness, you refuse to consider other views, other possibilities. We might not have helped find Belinda any-

way, for any girl forced into marrying an ogre such as you de-
serves not to be found. Why, I'd help her stay missing rather
than bring her back to such a fate. So leave, Lord High-and-
Mighty Hyatt, and take your friend with you. Take your filthy
money, too, for you cannot buy truth any more than you can
buy love. Go, my lord, and do not come back."

Mondale was bending over Lady Tremont's limp hand,
thanking her for her efforts, swearing to return the next evening
in case she was up to another effort, or to inquire as to her
health if she was not. Socrates would have dragged the man
away by force, but he could see his efforts would be wasted.

"I'll be back, Miss Treadwell," he said through gritted teeth.
"Count on it."

Chapter Seven

W hat did you think of him, dear?" Lady Tremont drifted into the book room the following morning, where her daughter was busy with lists and logic, trying to deduce where Mrs. Ingraham could have mislaid her husband's journals. Maylene was also trying to imagine what the shriveled old prune thought was written in those ledgers to make finding them worth the king's ransom the barrister's widow was offering. Maylene was getting nowhere with either problem, so she did not mind her mother's interruption.

"Think of whom? Oh, *him*. I thought he was ruthless and rude and arrogant beyond measure." And as handsome as the Devil, which he was. But handsome is as handsome does, Maylene told herself. In that case Lord Hyatt was as ugly as sin, which he also personified.

Lady Tremont took a seat across from Maylene's desk, gathering together papers that Maylene had carefully laid out in piles. "Rude, dear? I thought His Grace everything refined and dignified. And not a bit high in the instep. No, not condescending at all."

"His Grace?"

"And such concern for his missing daughter. Why, the dear man is even willing to forgo a lifetime of beliefs to get his only chick back. I find that touching, May, do not you?" Lady Tremont reached across and tried to push some of her daughter's unruly curls back under the hair ribbon Maylene wore. "Why, I know how I would feel if you were missing, dearest."

His Grace? Maylene hadn't thought of the duke at all, not once in the hours she'd spent awake after last evening's encounter, not once in her restless, dream-filled sleep. The man who was still strolling through the corridors of her mind, to her dismay, had long dark hair, a shadowed jaw, and a knowing look.

"And his friend," her mother was going on. "So elegant, so well turned out."

Well, she'd tried to turn the dastard out. "I'm afraid he'll be back, Mama."

"Of course he will, May. He wants to find the poor missing girl as badly as his friend."

No, he wanted to prevent them from helping the duke—or from earning a living. She did not want to upset her mother with the notion that Lord Hyatt was just as likely to have the lord high sheriff with him when he returned. Instead, she said, "I found Lord Hyatt to be an insufferable boor, Mama."

"Truly, dearest? I suppose a gentleman such as Lord Hyatt cannot help being a bit full of himself. When a young man comes into such an elevated title and such a handsome fortune at so early an age, people quite dote on him. And to be given the sobriquet the Ideal, why, it would be amazing if his lordship was not a tad puffed up."

"A tad? The man is so full of his own conceit it is astonishing that his hat still fits on his head."

"And a very handsome head it is, too, dear, didn't you think?"

"No," Maylene lied. "I found his eyes too cold"—they saw too much—"his mouth too full"—of cynical comments—"and his nose too prominent." He'd been sniffing out a hoax all night.

Her mother ignored the obvious taradiddle. No female in her right mind, from seven to seventy, would find the earl anything less than heart-stoppingly attractive. "You know," she said, " 'tis an accepted fact that he disdains the social world."

"The beau monde, Mama, not the demimonde. The man has a terrible reputation as a womanizer."

Lady Tremont went on as if her daughter hadn't spoken. "And I would not have supposed that such a sophisticated gentleman would be interested in exploring the afterworld with us, yet there he was at our little gathering."

"He is only interested in exposing us as shams and having us barred from crossing Polite Society's thresholds entirely."

"But he said he was coming back. He was very adamant about that, too."

"He is only returning to defend his friend Mondale from our clutches, Mama, nothing else."

Her mother clucked her tongue and fluffed the lace at Maylene's collar. "Perhaps his lordship has another reason, darling. He did seem to admire your, ah, gown."

"He stared down my neckline, the cad!" Maylene now stared at her mother, aghast. Mama could not be considering Lord Hyatt as a prospective suitor for her spinster daughter, could she?

"You know," Lady Tremont was saying, "I do not believe it is a love match between Lord Hyatt and Lady Belinda."

Yes, she could. Maylene's "hah!" scattered half her papers across the desk. "The man loves nothing but his own consequence and his own pleasures."

"Aunt Regina says he is devoted to his grandmother, who raised him, don't you know. So he must have some tender sensibilities, dearest, under that . . . that commanding presence. And it is not like you to be so critical." Her mother straightened the papers again.

"And you would find redeeming qualities in a slug, Mama." If he were single. That Mama and Aunt Regina had already discussed Lord Hyatt meant the case was serious indeed. Good heavens, her mother truly was dicked in the nob. Maylene knew she had to nip this awful idea in the bud, on the instant. "Next you are going to tell me that he is kind to children and dogs," she protested. "Save your breath, Mama, for the earl is of the breed of gentlemen who believe that women are inherently inferior, lacking in both intelligence and honor. You may be assured that the arrangement between Hyatt and his future wife is more in the nature of a bank merger than a love affair. They will blend titles and fortunes, land and power, not hearts and souls as the poets would have it." And as Miss Maylene Treadwell would have it.

"Do you know," Lady Tremont mused as if she were speaking with Max instead of her fuming daughter, "the engagement has never been announced. I believe we will have to find Lady Belinda and ask her wishes in the matter."

Lady Belinda's wishes did not matter a whit to Maylene. If Lord Hyatt were not promised to a duke's daughter, he would be seeking the mother of his heir among the highest ranks of the *ton* at Almack's; he would not be courting any impoverished ape-leader, at afterlife assemblies. And as for Maylene, well, she would rather marry Lord Shimpton.

"No wonder she ran away."

That's what the Treadwell chit had said, and it rankled. Socrates Hughes, Lord Hyatt, had been pursued by marriage-able misses since his sixteenth birthday ten years ago. He'd never entertained the idea that the one he finally chose might reject his suit. He didn't find the notion entertaining at all. And Mondale's chit? He'd known Belinda since she was in pinafores, and the girl never had anything but sweet smiles for him. It wasn't as though she could look much higher for a match either, for there were deuced few eligible dukes around, and most of them were affianced to their second cousins. Dash it, though, now she'd disappeared, and here was the Treadwell twit blaming him. That experience did not please Socrates either.

Was it true? He could not believe that Belinda could shame him this way, haring off rather than make their engagement formal. No, there had to be a rational explanation for her disappearance, and it was not to be found at Treadwell House on Curzon Street. Rational, hell. 'Twould be more like that rackety, frizzy-headed female to leave a man waiting on the church steps. At least Belinda was too well bred to do that. She'd gone to a house party with a group of friends a fortnight ago, but left the party on her own after a few days, saying she'd received a note that her dearest aunt was ailing. But she hadn't gone in any carriage of the duke's, she hadn't arrived at her relative's in Wales, and her aunt was in the pink of health.

Hyatt had *not* given her a disgust of himself. Hell, he hadn't even attended the house party—or any of the other inane festivities of a debutante Season. Giving up his bachelorhood was enough of a sacrifice.

Belinda'd been a success, of course. A pretty duke's daughter with a pretty dowry could not be anything less than a Toast.

But she hadn't favored any gentleman above the others, according to the widowed cousin who acted as her chaperone. That woman was no help, prostrate with grief at having lost her charge, and most likely her position, too.

Mondale feared foul play, since Belinda was a considerable heiress. But a ransom note would have arrived by now, Hyatt reasoned. And if some dirty dish had abducted her to force a marriage—and a hefty marriage settlement out of the duke—then Mondale would have received notice by now, with demands for her dowry.

The earl could not believe she'd simply eloped under the casual eye of the cousin. Belinda was too refined, too aware what was due her name and his. She never had a hair nor a word out of place, never wore an article of clothing nor held a belief that was not in the highest kick of fashion. He would not have offered for her otherwise. If he had to have a wife in the interests of securing the succession, Hyatt would make dashed sure she wasn't the type of female to cut up a man's peace. Unlike Miss Treadwell. His mind wandered of its own accord to that misfortunate miss, with her ugly shawls, moppish hairdo, and outspoken, outré opinions. He pitied the poor devil who took that termagant to wife. To bed was another matter. . . .

No, Lord Hyatt wanted a well-bred mother for his heirs, that was all. He had competent housekeepers and experienced mistresses for everything else. He did not want the begetting of those heirs to be a burden, naturally, so he'd made sure Mondale's girl was pleasant to look at, with a modicum of intelligence. Lady Belinda suited him, Hyatt told himself again. And she had understood the nature of the arrangement before she'd shyly smiled and agreed.

He had not frightened her off, either. The chaste kiss he pressed on her sweet lips was almost avuncular, telling her without words that he'd not make undue demands on her.

He couldn't help wondering how Miss Treadwell's lips would taste, if they were not pursed in disapproval or issuing cutting remarks. Well, he had a few things to say to her, too. Thanks to her and her mother's cozy party of ghost-gabblers, Belinda's disappearance was about to become public knowledge. Oh, they'd all agreed to respect Mondale's need for secrecy. The missing chit would be ruined if any of the *ton's* high sticklers discovered she was not where she was supposed to be. Hyatt, however, did not trust a one of the spirit-seekers not to share the tidy tidbit of gossip over tea: Hyatt's filly had done a flit. Soc didn't give a rap for Society's opinion of him—his of them was not high, either—but neither did he relish becoming a laughingstock at his clubs. An earlier announcement of the engagement would have to be made, he decided, to stop the rumors. Until Belinda was found, however, nothing could be done except try to keep her disappearance quiet. Which meant he had to try to dissuade Mondale from returning to Lady Tremont's spectral sitting room.

"You cannot believe that gammon, Duke," Lord Hyatt said over a brandy at White's. There were no further reports from Bow Street or the hired investigators, and the man was looking more haggard than ever.

Mondale raised his glass, but merely stared into the dark swirls. "What, that old Crowley was skimming past our heads or that Patterson's pooch returned to life ten years younger?" He managed a half smile. "No, I did not believe those clangers. Yet there is Volstead's story. You cannot deny the man came into a fortune. I saw him repay a gambling debt to you with my own eyes."

"They searched his book room. I'm sure there are misplaced papers and lost letters in every library in London. It only takes time and effort to find them, not the hand of God—or Lady Tremont."

"Yes, but there is something. Call it women's intuition or whatever. I remember that my Araminta had a knack for knowing when I'd be returning from a journey. No matter how many days early or late I arrived, my favorite meal would be waiting for me. She said she just knew. That's it!" His Grace set his untouched glass back on the table between them and leaned forward excitedly. "I'll ask Lady Tremont to try to contact Minty. Surely she'll know where our only girl's gone."

Lord Hyatt finished his drink. Then he finished the duke's.

Chapter Eight

"I have come, Miss Treadwell, to invite you for a drive in the park."

If Lord Hyatt had said he'd come to sack Rome, Maylene couldn't have been more surprised. In fact, if the large, haughty gentleman had declared war on some small country, challenged Max's ghost to a duel, or accused them all of heresy, she would be less astounded than at this polite offer. The fact that the Earl of Hyatt was in her mother's drawing room that afternoon, with no ducal friend to protect and with no séance scheduled, was amazing enough. And he was perfectly shaved. "A drive?"

He bowed his head ever so slightly. "A drive. In the park. You and I."

So now he thought she was stupid, besides greedy, grasping, and felonious. Maylene put down her pencil, which rolled off the desk. "You and I, my lord, have nothing to say to each other."

The earl bent to pick up the pencil, leaning over her closely enough to be heard by the other guests. "On the contrary, Miss Treadwell, I have a great deal to say. And I believe you would prefer to hear it in the relative privacy of the park rather than here."

Since the drawing room was filled with spirit-seekers, curiosity-seekers, and just plain seekers, Maylene had to agree. She'd been at the writing desk in the corner, taking notes, but now she could feel all of the company watching her. "Actually, I prefer not to hear whatever it is you feel inspired to say. I'd wager it will prove to be as unpleasant as your company last evening."

Studying the point on her writing tool, Hyatt drawled, "*Au contraire*, Miss Treadwell, my company last night was everything delightful."

Maylene could not miss his meaning. The man was a libertine! The sooner he was gone, the better for her pulse rate. "Good day, my lord."

The chit was going to refuse his invitation out of hand? In front of a pack of gullible gossipmongers? By George, she'd accompany him out the door if he had to drag her by that ridiculous mop of hair. The ribbon threaded through the blond curls was having as much effect as a rock had on a flowing river. "Has no one told you that it is discourteous to reject an invitation without a good excuse?"

She took out a fresh sheet of paper. "I am busy, and I do not like you." And she would not fuel her mother's aspirations. "Is that sufficient excuse?"

Hyatt sucked in his breath. "You are the most unmannerly chit I have ever met."

"And you, sir, are the most arrogant man I have ever encountered."

The pencil snapped between his fingers. "No wonder you are still unwed."

"How dare you! Especially since you are equally unmarried. Recall that it wasn't my betrothed who fled, my lord, but yours." She pulled out a drawer to find another pencil, but tugged too hard in her annoyance, and the drawer and its contents went flying. "Now see what you've made me do!"

Every other conversation in the room had died. Campbell gestured for one of the footmen to fetch a dust pan, but no one else was budging, waiting to see what happened next. Maylene was mortified. His lordship's previously pristine white shirtfront and brocaded waistcoat both had spots of ink on them. Heavens, now he would think her clumsy in addition to the rest of her faults, and deem Treadwell House a rag-mannered residence. At least the butler was not taking tea with the guests as he had last night.

Her traitorous mother came toward them, close enough to wipe an ink stain off Maylene's cheek. She was nodding her approval. "Wasn't that lovely of the earl to offer you a ride through Hyde Park, May? He asked my permission first, naturally. Such courtesy. I told him you would be delighted with the treat. You know you've been wishing to get out more, dearest, and the weather is quite perfect, for once."

"But Mrs. Ingraham's journals . . . "

"Have been missing this long, dear. They can stay lost another hour or so. Besides, I feel certain Max will have some information about them for us tonight. Or perhaps tomorrow." Lady Tremont floated across the room in a cloud of lavender gauze drapery, pausing to make an appointment with one lady and to answer questions about Max for another.

Maylene knew there was nothing for it but to accept the earl's invitation, not without making a scene, and she'd already done that. She could stall, though. "Perhaps we can go later, when my mother would be free to join us. She could use the fresh air and exercise also."

Socrates jerked his head toward the window, where Maylene could see a groom walking a pair of sleek chestnuts hitched to an elegant rig. An equipage like that hadn't been seen in front of Treadwell House since her father died. No, not even before. Baron Tremont never had enough blunt for such pricey horseflesh, and never had a good eye for it. Maylene was sorely tempted.

"Lady Tremont can come another time," Hyatt was saying. "But the horses cannot be left standing much longer. Furthermore, I brought the curricle today, and there is only room for two."

"Then I cannot come." Maylene was disappointed and relieved at the same time. "Such an excursion would be highly improper. I do know how Polite Society works, my lord."

"Then you should know that is perfectly acceptable for a young lady to ride with a gentleman in an open carriage in full view of the others. My groom will be chaperon enough, standing behind the seats."

Maylene waved her hand at the gathered guests. Unfortunately she was still holding the opened ink bottle. Now Hyatt had spots on his cheeks and chin. She blushed, but set the bottle down. "I cannot leave my mother to entertain alone, my lord. I shall have to refuse your so-kind invitation."

Hyatt reached across her to replace the drawer, his sleeve

brushing the bare skin on her arms. "I never took you for a coward, Miss Treadwell."

He might think her foolish, feckless, and fraudulent, but Maylene would be damned before she'd let the Ideal think she was afraid of him. "I shall go fetch my bonnet, my lord."

Good, he thought, wiping his hands and face with the towel Campbell brought him. Then he wouldn't have to worry about a bird mistaking her hair for a nest.

Maylene was impressed despite herself. The proper groom, the high-bred horses, the masterful way Hyatt held the ribbons, all combined to drown out her misgivings. Best of all, the earl was concentrating so hard on getting his spirited cattle through the city traffic that conversation was impossible. Without Hyatt's habitual sneer to ruin her pleasure, Maylene could almost imagine herself as a fashionable young lady taking the air with a handsome beau among the rest of the nobility. For once she could pretend to be a marriageable miss whose greatest talent in life was painting pretty watercolors or playing the pianoforte.

Of course her gown was last year's style. While Campbell tried to remove the ink stains from Hyatt's waistcoat, Maylene had managed to scramble into her favorite Pomona green day dress, with Nora's help. The new jonquil ribbons hid the gown's worn spots very well, they'd agreed. Nora's arthritic fingers were hopeless with Maylene's hair as usual. One of these days she was going to cut it all off, Maylene swore, and be as scandalous as Caro Lamb with her shorn locks. For today, her chip straw bonnet, with its matching yellow ribbons, hid most of the unruly curls.

In all her finery, she looked the veriest dowd next to Hyatt, of course. His fawn breeches and form-fitting coat labeled him cock of the hill, whilst she was nothing but a mud hen. Still, the sun was shining, and he was not scowling—yet.

Once they reached the park, Hyatt tipped his hat or nodded to various acquaintances and pointed out notables to her. He never stopped the carriage to make introductions, which would have pleased her more, but she contented herself with thinking that he was minding the horses, not ashamed of his companion. He'd invited her, after all.

Hyatt took his cattle at a trot through the park, headed for less congested areas. While the *ton* came to promenade, to be seen and to see who was in whose carriage, he was hoping no one recognized the atrocious female in his. He had almost reached the shelter of a stand of trees, however, when they were accosted by a rider on a swaybacked gray gelding.

"Halloo, Miss Treadwell," Lord Shimpton called.

The earl cringed, and not just for the way the booberkin bobbled about in the saddle. With enough sawing on the reins, Shimpton managed to turn his old hack—and everyone else's attention—in their direction. As soon as they came to a stumbling halt, the gray put its head down to nibble at the grass. Shimpton would have gone over the beast's neck, except for the death grip he held on the saddle.

"I say, Miss Treadwell," he called over, "what a surprise to find you here. That is, Lady Tremont did say you were out driving with the Ideal, but I thought she must be imagining things. Not that I think she does, as a rule, no matter what some others might say. I may be slow—Mumsy always said I was dumber'n dirt—but I'm not stupid enough to believe a bouncer like that. But here you are."

Shimpton's neckcloth was tied high enough to hide his weak chin, but it was therefore high enough to impede the movement of his neck. This was not, perhaps, the best arrangement for a bruising rider. For Shimpton, it made no difference. The horse knew its way home and would get there when it got up enough energy.

"Er, yes," Maylene replied. "Here I am. Did you want something?"

"Wanted to discuss marriage with you."

Hyatt was choking, and not because his own neckcloth was too high or too tight. Refusing to look at the earl, Maylene addressed Shimpton: "I think such a discussion ought to wait until we are more private, don't you, my lord?"

"Oh, right. Wouldn't want the Ideal dangling after the same female. I'll see you tonight, shall I, then? And you too, Earl, what? You'll be back at Lady Tremont's, won't you?"

If he weren't afraid of giving Shimpton's gray heart failure, Socrates would have taken his riding whip to the whopstraw. The dunderhead might as well have announced in the broadsides that the Earl of Hyatt was as balmy in the brain box as the rest of Lady Tremont's cabalistic coterie.

One quick glance at him and Maylene nodded. "Yes, tonight. But for now you mustn't keep your horse standing. I will see you in Curzon Street, my lord. Good day."

Without a word, Hyatt set his horses to a trot, putting as much distance between him and the vapor-minded viscount as Hyde Park would allow. He did not stop until they'd reached a narrow track that bordered the Serpentine. He pulled up and told Jem Groom to go to the horses' heads. With any luck, he thought, no one else would be around to identify the quiz in his curricle.

"Let us get down a bit, Miss Treadwell, and commune with nature. I realize you are more used to communing with the dead, or Shimpton, which is almost the same, so this should be a pleasant change."

In charity with him for once, for the day truly was delightful and she was not spending it with the viscount, Maylene accepted his hand and stepped down from the curricle. "Although Mama does prefer to call the deceased 'dematerialized.' 'Dead' sounds so permanent, don't you think?"

"Oddly enough, most people do believe that death is permanent. Of course you believe in angels and such, Miss Treadwell. Or is it ghosts and goblins?"

"And things that go bump in the night. Yes, I believe such things are possible, after we pass from this plane. Of course we'll never know until we get there, so I choose to keep an open mind. What do you believe, my lord?"

"I believe we should walk along the water's edge. The view can almost make you imagine you're in the country."

Maylene believed he didn't want to share his feelings or opinions with her. He was quiet as they walked, picking their way across the wet grass between muddy tracks and horse droppings. Maylene's toes were already feeling damp. He'd said a drive, so she'd worn her slippers, not boots. They'd be destroyed. Hyatt, of course, was wearing high-topped Hessians and wouldn't notice if they waded through a stream. The scenery was almost worth the sacrifice of a pair of shoes, though, she decided, for ducks and swans floated on the quiet waters, and children played along the embankment. Two boys had a sailboat on a string, and a toddler threw bread to the birds under the watchful eye of his nursemaid.

"How charming," Maylene said. "Thank you for bringing me."

"My pleasure," Hyatt lied. Deuce take it, it was no pleasure at all. If he wanted to be in the country, by Jupiter, he'd go to the country. He owned enough of it, where he wasn't tripping over some friend of his grandmother's or an old schoolmate. He was in Town now for Mondale's sake, though, so he would get on with it.

"I brought you here to discuss last evening with you, Miss Treadwell. I realize we may have gotten off on the wrong foot"—he ignored her "humph" of agreement—"and thought that if we had a little chat, a friendly coze, you know, we might come to terms."

Maylene stopped in her tracks. "Terms, my lord? Are you attempting to buy us off again? I told you bribery won't work. My mother gets her inspiration from Max, not money."

"Come down from the boughs, Miss Treadwell," he said, tugging her onward, toward a bench by the water's edge. "I thought that you might explain to me your mother's theories, so I could understand more fully. For instance, who the devil is Max?"

"Max is no demon at all, as I said. I do not know what to call him, other than a spirit. Mama never likes to speak of him, for she finds his absence too sad. His visits give her great joy."

"Your father?"

"No, my father's name was Maynard, hence my Maylene. And I am sorry to say neither found any joy whatsoever in the marriage. Theirs was an arranged match that suited no one except their parents. I hardly knew him, for he was always at some race meet, house party, or hunting box. He drank to excess, gambled to ruin, and rode untrained horses. He kept mistresses, and Mama kept waiting for him to kill himself. She won."

"You are very open about your past." No other female of his acquaintance would admit to such a sordid family history, common though it might be.

"The failure of my parents' marriage is general knowledge; why should I try to hide it? Besides, Mama has nothing to be ashamed of. She led a blameless life in the country, although she would have been within her rights to . . ."

"To take lovers?" Her blush told him Miss Treadwell was not as comfortable with such modern views as she pretended. She'd change her tune if she married Shimpton. "But Max?"

"I think Max must have been the child she miscarried before my birth. She always says that only great love can bridge the beyond, so that seems the likeliest answer."

"Very well, so Max speaks to her. But Lord Crowley doesn't?"

"No, only Max."

"What about Shimpton's mother? The *ton* breathed a sigh of relief when that dragon stuck her spoon in the wall. I cannot fathom why anyone would wish to bring her back."

"Lady Shimpton, ah, speaks through Max. I am not quite sure how that works. I don't believe Mama understands it herself. When that happens, she is more exhausted than usual."

As were all actresses after difficult performances, Hyatt thought. He had kept enough of them to know.

"And do you think such activities are good for people? Calling up their dead relations?"

"I do not believe it hurts anyone."

"Only their pocketbooks?"

Maylene was silent, watching the swans. She'd never approved of her mother's hobby much either, but loyalty to her mother, and necessity, were strong influences, too.

"Tell me," Hyatt said, steel in his voice, "do you not feel the slightest remorse for fleecing the poor sheep who come to you?"

So much for a comfortable coze.

Chapter Nine

The buttons were off the fencing foils.

"I feel sorry for those who have lost loved ones and cannot go on with their lives without some comfort from strangers. If my mother provides that comfort, fine." Maylene turned to go back to the carriage, but was prevented by Hyatt's hand on her arm. The ground was too slippery to struggle.

"What," he asked, "is your perfidy now a public service?"

Miss Treadwell did not spar by gentleman's rules. She went straight for the throat. "And what of you, Lord Hyatt? What do you do to serve the public welfare? You gamble and drink and wench, just like my father."

"No, I win. Furthermore, no one depends on me for the roof over their heads except my tenants, and they are well provided for."

"And they in turn provide the wherewithal for you to live the life of the idle rich. You are nothing but another mindless pleasure-seeker, just like the others of your sort."

Hyatt could not defend the indefensible any more than Miss Treadwell could. He despised the wasted, wastrel existences most of his fellow peers enjoyed, which was why he seldom took part in the social Season. "At least I conduct myself with honor," he insisted. "Which is more than you and your little band of parasites and predators can say. Bloodsuckers all, and it makes no difference to you if your victim is bled dry. You'll go on to the next innocent, unwary pigeon."

Now Maylene did push against his arm, but the earl was not ready to release her. "How dare you," she gasped. "As if you were truthful when you invited me for a friendly drive! Next you are going to say Aunt Regina is a villain because she wears false teeth."

"And false everything else, too."

"So it gives her pleasure to look younger than her age. Who is hurt? I ask again. And who gave you the right to sit in judgment of us lesser mortals, my lord High Hat?"

"Why, you little shrew. I'll—"

Whatever his intentions, they were interrupted by a call from the opposite bank.

"Miss Treadwell, Hyatt, isn't it?" Lord Patterson peered across at them. "I thought so, but wasn't sure until I heard your loud voices. Good day to you." He was throwing a stick for Toby along the water's edge. "Lovely day, what?"

The day was positively ghastly. Maylene wished it were over. She could not offend the elderly peer, though, not when he had been so generous, so she called back, "And how are you and Toby going along?"

"Fine, fine," Patterson said, coming closer, despite Hyatt's muttering about doddering old fools who doted on dogs. "But, you know, I think something is wrong with Toby."

Maylene could see that Toby was in the pink of health and happiness, dancing at Patterson's feet, barking at the ducks, rolling in the damp, muddy grass. "He looks fine to me, my lord."

Patterson bent to scratch the little dog's ears. "Oh, he is well. But the thing is, I don't think he is my Toby after all. Don't tell your mother, Miss Treadwell, but this little fellow stole my kippers this morning, right off my plate. My Toby would never have reached across the table that way, no, he wouldn't. And I think I always knew my own laddie was gone; he would have come home else. And if he had returned, I'd only lose him again soon, for he was growing old."

Too old to be chasing runaway carriages, obviously, Maylene thought.

Patterson went on. "But I am not complaining, mind, nor criticizing your mother and her friend Max. In fact, you folks did me a good turn. You see, I'd never have replaced the lad on my own. Now I have this fine little chap. He's not the same, but he is lovable in his own way. I think Toby would be happy for me."

"I'm sure he would. And this, ah, Toby is very similar in looks."

Patterson nodded. "Except that my Toby had been gelded. Coming back from the dead is one thing, but . . . " He shrugged. "We'll come to terms about the kippers, see if we don't."

"Of course you will," she said, waving as he hurried after the little terrier, who was trying to steal the toddler's ball.

Maylene turned back to Hyatt, who seemed to think it uproarious that the old Toby had been neutered and the new one was intact. And that their deception had been discovered. At least he wasn't storming at her. But Maylene, too, felt vindicated. "You see," she said in triumph, "we made the lonely old man happy. Perhaps we did bend the truth a bit, but it was for his own good. And who is to say that Max didn't send just the right dog for him when we went looking?"

The touch of humor about his lips disappeared. "And what will you do for Mondale? Find him a brown-haired six-year-old in an orphanage? He's missing his daughter, for God's sake, not a dashed dog! I insist you leave the poor man alone! Play off your tricks on fools like Shimpton and Patterson, not any friend of mine."

Maylene stamped her foot, then regretted it immediately as mud squelched into her thin slippers. "Who are you to insist on anything? To dictate my actions?"

"Who? I am the one who has enough power to ruin you and your mother. One who can make sure that women like Lady Crowley and Sir Cedric's wife never cross your doorstep. I can shred your reputation so badly that even Shimpton won't have you, or destroy your credit with the banks and merchants. In other words, I am the one who can see you forced out of London if you do not leave Mondale alone. Tell him you cannot help and let him go, or I'll make sure that dead dogs are the only company you'll ever have. Neutered ones, by gad."

Hyatt could to it, Maylene knew. Their social standing was already shaky and their financial credit uncertain. She was disappointed to think that he *would* do it. "You disgust me. If my betrothed was lost somewhere, I'd be scouring the countryside.

But instead of trying to help the duke in his search, you are spending your time browbeating innocent women."

There was nothing innocent about this female, except perhaps in the technicalities, Hyatt thought. He was right to be concerned, he knew he was, for the Treadwell House troop meant to bewitch poor Mondale with their cork-brained cosmology. Otherwise the chit would have backed down by now. A man would have, rather than tempt Hyatt's powerful right arm or his deadly aim with a dueling pistol. Any other female would have capitulated long ago. Any other female would be in hysterics by now, not standing with her arms on her hips, her foot tapping in a pile of duck droppings, and sparks flashing from her blue eyes. If looks could kill, he'd be lying there alongside the foul fowl stuff.

But he was an earl, by Zeus, a man. And a man did not retreat, not from a frowsy young female who looked like a green hornet in a bonnet. The only problem was, he couldn't think of what else to do. If he weren't a gentleman . . .

"Ho there, Hyatt," someone called out.

This someone was definitely not a gentleman, and definitely not someone for Miss Treadwell to know, no matter her failings. She was still a lady, and he was responsible for her welfare since he'd brought her to the park. So Socrates grabbed her elbow again and spun her around, turning Miss Treadwell's back to the dirty dish Finster. He shook her when she protested, and pulled her closer against his chest.

Maylene could barely breathe, except for the scent of Lord Hyatt. Pressed to his superfine coat, she pounded on him with her free hand. How dare he! This was the outside of enough! First he shouted, then he manhandled. Why, the man was a positive menace! And he smelled good, all citrus and spice. "Unhand me, you cad!"

Then she heard, "Ssorry to interrupt, Hyatt, can ssee you're busy."

Could he be trying to protect her? Maylene peeked over her shoulder under her bonnet's rim. And stopped trying to get out of Hyatt's sheltering hold. The man who was speaking had pointed teeth, what there were of them. He had a scar down one sallow cheek, under the pockmarks, and his once-white linen was the color of the dishwater it should have been soaking in. Good grief, the man looked like a footpad. A not very successful footpad at that. And Lord Hyatt knew him?

"Finster," he curtly acknowledged.

"Heard you wass here."

While Finster paused to spit tobacco juice through the filed front teeth, Hyatt muttered, "Is there anyone who doesn't know?"

"And heard you wass going to the witch's ssabat tonight."

"Bloody hell."

"I've got a message for Lady Tremont. Tell her that if Ingraham's journals are made public, she'll be at the other end of the sséancess."

"The other end?" Maylene whispered.

"Beyond," Hyatt told her softly, still trying to keep her face averted from the loose screw. Then he surprised Maylene even further by saying, "The lady is a friend of mine, Finster. I take threats against her personally."

Finster spit again, somewhat closer to Hyatt's boots. "And I take hanging personally. You tell her." He slithered away to where a bare-ribbed roan was standing, mounted, and disappeared through the nearby stand of trees.

"Thank you for warning that creature off, Lord Hyatt," Maylene started to say, "and for trying to shield me. What an unpleasant man."

"Unpleasant?" he shouted. "Unpleasant? The man is a maggot! He's a bastard, literally and figuratively, who's been thrown out of every club and gaming house for cheating. He's been caught rigging horse races, and there were rumors that he fired early when some poor fool challenged him to a duel. Of course the fool couldn't bring charges because he was already dead. And you find him unpleasant? Is that an example of your intuitive powers, Miss Treadwell?"

"You seem upset, my lord."

Socrates had been angry at this young woman before. He'd been irritated, possibly even irate. Those were like summer breezes to the cyclone of rage that was blasting through him. He felt that he was about to explode from the blood boiling within. "No, Miss Treadwell, I am not upset. I was upset to think you were running a thimblerig on my friend. I was upset that you lied to Patterson, and I was upset that you are trying to trap Shimpton into marriage. Now I am outraged! Your mutton-headed metaphysics was bad enough; now you are mucking about with makebaits like Finster, and I am going to have to get involved! Are you such an imbecile that you cannot see how dangerous a game you play? Do you have any idea at all what you and your mother are dealing with? I suppose you'll tell me that Max will protect you from maw worms like Finster."

"It is no concern of yours," Maylene tried to interject.

Hyatt wasn't listening. "By all that's holy, Ingraham knew the truth of every criminal case for the last fifteen years. He was barrister to half the high-born defendants, and got most of them acquitted. The information in those journals could ruin a good portion of the *ton*. They're not lost, you ninnyhammer. Mrs. Ingraham is broadcasting their disappearance to extort more money from her dead husband's clients."

"You cannot know that, my lord."

"What, do you believe she simply misplaced evidence that could be worth a fortune in the wrong hands? Damn, I never thought to find anyone stupider than Shimpton, but you win the laurels. Lud, if you two do marry, I pity the children you'll have—haystacks for hair and elephant ears, with not an ounce of intelligence between them. Just what the world needs, blast you."

It was beginning to occur to Maylene that she had nothing to fear from Finster; she wouldn't live long enough to face him. She took a step backward, but Hyatt's hands clasped her shoulders that much harder. "My lord, you are beginning to frighten me."

"At last something does!" Socrates was so angry that she was so addlepated—he would decide why later—that if he didn't shake some sense into her, he deserved sainthood. So he wouldn't rattle what brains she had, he kissed her. He'd decide why that seemed like a good idea later, too.

Maylene stopped struggling. Then she stopped thinking of anything but the earl's lips on hers. She rose on tiptoe, getting closer, not even feeling the mud ooze in her shoes. She felt nothing but his lips. She *was* nothing but her lips, touching his.

She'd have to remember to tell her mother that there really was a Paradise. But then she remembered her mother, and her mother's teachings. She wasn't a lightskirt, and this was no simple token of affection. This kiss wasn't Cousin Grover the Groper's damp lust, nor that curate's chaste salute when she was seventeen. This was raw sensuality, an expression of Hyatt's anger, meant to punish, to dominate, to subordinate and subdue.

So she slapped him. Maylene hauled her right arm back and let it fly with all her might, connecting with his left cheek with an impact that brought tears to her eyes from the pain of her palm. What it did to Lord Hyatt was another story.

The earl's head snapped around from the force of her blow, and he jerked back, off balance, into a patch of duck detritus. And his high-shined boots skidded in something less than a champagne polish, to be followed by his buckskin breeches, his burgundy Bath superfine coat, and his long black hair, in that order. He bellowed a curse and started to rise, lost his footing again in his own skid marks, then tumbled backward down the inclining embankment, straight into the Serpentine, with its stagnant waters and weeds.

"There," Maylene called over her shoulder. "You wanted to commune with nature, my lord. Commune."

She marched toward the carriage without another look back, not stopping till she passed Hyatt's groom, hurrying to his master's aid. "I wish you to drive me home," she told him.

"Aye, miss, but his lordship . . . "

He ran past her, but she halted him with one sentence. "If you do not drive me home, I shall drive myself."

His master or his cattle? Jem scratched his head, then chose to save the horses. Lord Hyatt was already broken and blown.

Chapter Ten

Oh, dear, I do hope you haven't dampened the earl's enthusiasm."

No, Maylene didn't think she'd done that, precisely. Her mother was distressed to see her daughter arrive home in a temper and in a hired hackney, without an escort. Lady Tremont wasn't half so distressed as she'd be if she heard what really happened, Maylene knew, and saw no reason to mention that she'd left Hyatt with seaweed streaming off his shoulders and curses streaming from his mouth. And that she'd practically commandeered his curricle. At least she hadn't left Hyatt to make his sodden way through the crowds of promenaders in the park. She'd made his groom set her down just outside the gates, where she could hire a hackney, freeing Jem to go back and retrieve his master.

"I thol you you hab windmilth in your head, Thithbe." Aunt Regina was testing out her new cheek pads. She removed them to say, "Of course the gel gave Hyatt a disgust of her, Thisbe. I told you you should have taught the chit to flirt instead of letting her bury her nose in all those books. There's nothing about her to appeal to a buck like the Ideal, not when females like Aurora Ashford are ready to kiss his feet."

They wouldn't be this afternoon, Maylene told herself, looking down at her own ruined slippers.

"Why, she'd do better with a touch of the hare's foot," Aunt Regina was going on, "than any highbrow education. A bit of kohl for her eyes, a dab of color on her lips . . ."

Of course, Maylene told herself, wishing she could go upstairs and throw herself on the bed. A little face paint and Hyatt would forget she'd planted him a facer. When water ran uphill.

"No," her mother defended loyally with a mother's blindness, "our May is perfect the way she is. And where would we be without her clever head for figures and such? Besides, we would not want your false colors to give any of the gentlemen the notion that our girl is fast."

No, then they might kiss her in the park. Maylene was developing a headache so severe that it had a name of its own—Hyatt. Before she went to her room, however, she had to warn her mother about the Ingraham journals. "Have you done any thinking about Mrs. Ingraham's inquiry, Mama?" she asked.

"Why, no, dear. I was hoping Max would be able to offer us a clue, since you haven't uncovered anything."

Maylene had searched every likely cranny and cubbyhole. "Do you think it's possible that Mrs. Ingraham has hidden them away on purpose, that she intends to extort money for their nonappearance? I gather that there might be some incriminating material in the journals, material that her husband's associates might not wish brought to light. That does not sound like the type of thing one would casually misplace, does it?"

"What, and she would use our activities in the afterlife to further her evil intentions? Oh, dear."

Maylene was hoping that her mother regretted their involvement, not that the money was going elsewhere. "I'm beginning to think such might be the case, Mama."

Aunt Regina was nodding, setting the fake bangs to bob at her wrinkled brow. "I always thought there was something havey-cavey about the woman. Second wife, don't you know, and Barrister Ingraham's fortune going to the children of the first wife. She might need the blunt."

"I'm more concerned that some of those mentioned in the journals might think that we have something to do with the scheme, Mama. They might turn out to be unsavory types, you know. Mr. Ingraham did represent criminals, after all."

Lady Tremont tossed her embroidery back into its workbasket at her feet. "We'll just have to see what Max says about it, won't we? Dear Max would be quite angry with someone leading danger to our doorstep."

Then Max should be positively livid at Lord Hyatt.

Having done her best in the Ingraham matter for now, Maylene was not up to discussing the Duke of Mondale's daughter. She'd let her mother figure how to tell the worried parent that they couldn't help him find Lady Belinda. That should satisfy Hyatt, not that such was a concern of Maylene's, but they did, in fact, have no clues as to the heiress's whereabouts. There'd been no hint of an affair in the gossip columns, not the slightest mention of the lady's name being linked with anyone her father might have favored less than Hyatt for his daughter's hand. Lady Belinda might have favored her horse more, for all Maylene knew. So they would be finished with another investigation. Perhaps then she could convince her mother to take a trip to Bath, to look for the missing music instructor. They could go if they economized and did not spend their recent windfalls on the wine cellar. Then they would not be in London to face Finster and his ilk—or Hyatt.

In her bedroom at last, Maylene did not burst into sobs as the huge lump in her throat seemed to presage. Instead, she sat at her dressing table, staring into the mirror to see if she was the same girl who'd set out this afternoon. Never in all her days had the old Maylene behaved so irrationally, so outrageously. Never in all her days had she known such emotion, such anger—or such remorse. Striking a gentleman was bad enough, but sending him flying into the river was beyond the pale, even if she'd been provoked. She had never seen a gentleman so incensed, no, not even her father when he'd lost his hunting box on that horse that fell down dead at the starter's pistol. Lord Hyatt would ruin them for sure now.

She supposed she'd have to send him an apology, the dastard, not that she expected his forgiveness, the devil take him. The rake had been as much at fault as she, Maylene told herself, with his insults to her intelligence, her honor, and even her looks. Haystack hair indeed! Then he'd assaulted her virtue. She'd write the apology, Maylene swore, because she was a lady. But she wouldn't mean a word of it. Nevertheless, she'd write it, she vowed, as soon as she finished lopping off her long, tangled curls.

She might look like a tasseled lampshade when she was done, but there. And there. And there. Maylene kept snipping,

even the back that she couldn't see. Now if she could only cut
away the memory of his kiss so easily.

Hellfire and damnation, he knew he'd have to apologize to
the infuriating female. Socrates couldn't imagine what had gotten into him, before he'd gotten into the water. After that, he
was sure he'd swallowed a gallon of the murky stuff, and a
minnow or two. He'd managed to free the little boys' boat from
the entangling weeds while he was still immersed, so he had an
excuse to offer to passersby, after he saw his curricle and prize
horses pass by. The wench had stolen his rig, by Zeus! She'd
sent it back soon enough, granted, before he was forced to drip
his way through Rotten Row, but the twenty minutes he spent
sodden on a bench seemed like an eternity.

But before that? What the devil had possessed him to kiss the
woman? He was a grown man, by George, not some green
youth given to impetuous emotions. And he was a betrothed
man, besides, or as near as made no difference in his own eyes.
Miss Treadwell was a lady, or as near as made no difference in
the eyes of Society. That alone should have made her safe from
improper advances. Besides, he did not even like her! She was
unscrupulous, ungoverned, and unwilling to listen to advice. So
why, Socrates asked himself again, as his valet poured the third
can of hot water over his head to try to eradicate the stench of
stagnant water, why had he kissed her?

Because Aurora Ashford hadn't waited for him last night?
No, he'd been more relieved that there wouldn't be a scene over
his lateness than regretful over his unsatisfied physical needs.
Hyatt had a ruby and diamond pendant sent over this morning
to appease the widow. If the bauble was not large enough to
turn the trick, well, there were scores of other Diamonds for
him to mine.

He'd kissed Miss Treadwell because he was upset, he recalled, and he was upset because Finster was threatening to
carve the ladies up for breakfast. Socrates couldn't even give
the excuse that he was acting on Mondale's behalf when he
threatened that loose screw in return. Mondale would turn his
back on any female involved in so sordid an affair. Hyatt had
turned into a stag in rut.

Thunderation, he'd kissed Miss Maylene Treadwell. And deuced well enjoyed it. The female must be a witch after all, he decided. Yes, that was a good explanation for his outlandish behavior—she'd ensorcelled him. Now all he had to do was convince himself he believed in witches and magic.

His conscience demanded he apologize. Diamonds came cheaper. Socrates would rather swim in the Serpentine again than spew out his regrets for such lamentable conduct. So he sat in his tub until his skin shriveled. Then he took twice as long as usual to shave, for the second time that day. He decided to create a new neckcloth style, then spent another twenty minutes thinking of a name for the knot. Philanderer's Fall? The Disoriental? The Trone d'apology?

Not wishing to hear any of the day's damp *on dits*, the earl changed his mind about dining at his club. His kitchen was unprepared, naturally, so he caught up on some correspondence while his expensive French chef tore his hair out, trying to turn out a creditable meal. In appreciation, Socrates ate every bite— slowly.

He was ready, damn it.

The reflections from Aunt Regina's necklaces, bracelets, and rings couldn't have been more brilliant if they were real. The old lady had emptied her jewelry box in honor of the duke's return, every piece of Austrian glass a different color. The reason no one was blinded by the sight of her refulgence in Lady Tremont's little parlor that evening was that they were all staring at Maylene.

As soon as Maylene entered the room, her mother, in her usual lavender gauze, started fanning herself with the gloves she'd just removed. Campbell's mouth was ajar, so he could not announce her arrival. No one said anything, in fact, until the duke, in his old-fashioned, courtly manner, said, "Very fetching, my dear."

Lady Crowley, nervously patting her own thick sausage curls, echoed, "Cropped curls are all the crack, Miss Treadwell."

Mrs. Ingraham muttered, "Scandalous," at which Aunt

Regina made a rude noise. Bobbed hair wasn't half so bad as blackmail.

Lord Shimpton was aghast. "Mumsy would not approve. No, I am certain she would not."

"Your mother wouldn't approve of any girl she didn't select herself," Aunt Regina said and snickered at him. "But her opinions don't count, Shimpton. She's dead, remember? And I like your new look very well, May."

So did Maylene. The short curls had dried almost instantly by the fire, and took no time to comb through. The pink ribbon she'd wound through them was more for decoration now, matching her gown, and less to keep order, making her feel younger and prettier. Without the weight of her hair and the worry of it coming loose, Maylene felt a new sense of freedom.

Another weight was lifted from her shoulders. *He* was not present for her mother's gathering this evening.

"Yes, well, this seems to be everyone now," Lady Tremont announced. "Shall we begin?"

Campbell helped the guests take seats around the small table, placing the duke on Lady Tremont's right this evening, Lord Shimpton on her left. Lady Crowley and Mrs. Ingraham raced for the chair next to Mondale, but the barrister's widow won. Maylene took up her own seat on the sofa near the fireplace, out of the circle.

Lady Tremont was starting the ritual of directing her companions' thoughts to the candle in front of them and to their beloveds above them when they all heard the sound of the front door opening and closing.

Maylene's heart sank to her feet, which had finally warmed from their muddy trek. How did one face a man when one had acted with such abandon, then abandoned him? All the demons in hell could not fill Miss Treadwell with more dread than having to meet the Earl of Hyatt after his Hyde Park dousing. She closed her eyes, praying for the floor to open up and swallow her. As her mother always said, all things were possible if one set one's mind to them. She set her mind to disappearing.

"I say, Cuz, you are looking deuced ill. Not going to swoon, are you?"

Maylene's eyes snapped open. The sight that met her eyes

wouldn't gladden the heart of many a maiden, but Cousin Grover had never looked so good to Maylene. Granted he had less hair on the top of his head than the last time she'd seen him and more sprouting out of his ears, as well as the usual drip of moisture at the end of his nose. But he wasn't Hyatt.

He was, however, employing the same obnoxious affectation, surveying her through his quizzing glass. "Dash it, I never heard you were sickly, but the physicians must have cut all your hair off to relieve the fever. Why wasn't I called if the case was so serious?"

"I am fine, Cousin. Truly, I am not ailing."

"No? I heard you'd left the park in a demmed skimble-skamble manner. Thought you must be stricken with the influenza or such."

"And you called to inquire into my daughter's health? How kind, Cousin Grover. However, Maylene is in the pink of condition, as you can see." She was in a pink frock, at any rate. "And we are about to begin this evening's meditations. So if you will forgive us, Cousin . . ."

"Well, I won't, if the chit ain't sick, and that's a fact, Cousin Thisbe. I won't tolerate it a'tall, m'cousin gadding about with a known rake, acting the hoyden for everyone to see. I am head of the family now, by Jupiter, and I won't hear of it."

"If you won't hear of it," came a low, slow drawl from the doorway, "then perhaps you should not listen to gossip. Miss Treadwell is a lady, and I beg leave to differ with anyone who says otherwise."

Chapter Eleven

Hyatt was here, and he was defending her? Maylene thought she must have prayed too hard. Now she was hallucinating.

"There was nothing improper about Miss Treadwell's conduct in the park," Lord Hyatt stated unequivocally, almost daring the pasty-faced baron to contradict his word.

Cousin Grover was not well pleased that his stirring of the scandal broth was not causing more of a stink. That malador was Shimpton. Disappointed, Grover waved a scented handkerchief in front of his dripping nose. He'd thought to use the rumors to advance his suit for Maylene's hand, claiming an engagement announcement was necessary to prevent further slander of the family name. He did not think he wished to partake of pistols for two with the Earl of Hyatt, however. Grover knew full well who'd be having the breakfast for one.

"I, ah, didn't mean to impugn your lordship's honor, heh heh. Just looking after m'dear cousins, don't you know."

"Admirable, I'm sure." Socrates was sure of no such thing, seeing Ingraham's widow at the table. If he had any care for his kinswomen's safety, the baron should have tossed Sophie Ingraham out of the house, rather than berating Miss Treadwell for her behavior. Hell, Tremont should be calling *him* out, for his misdeeds. Then again, if the clunch had any influence with the Treadwell House ladies, they wouldn't be in the oracle business. Mrs. Ingraham could conduct her extortion at her own house, and Socrates could resume his affair with Aurora Ashford, instead of having lascivious thoughts about a larcenous little mophead—who was looking like a street urchin with her raggedly shorn curls, or a sleep-tousled angel. No, he would not think of Miss Treadwell in the same breath as sleep, beds, and rumpled sheets. He was a promised man. Bloody hell, he hadn't even thought of Belinda and her disappearance all afternoon, only the maddening Miss Maylene Treadwell. A few more hours in her company and Socrates feared he'd be as want-witted as the rest of these widgeons. "Why don't we let Lady Tremont get on with her, ah, musings, shall we?" he asked.

"Never say you subscribe to that fustian. I don't believe it."

"You can believe I am here." Hyatt's one raised eyebrow told Tremont that he could also believe the earl would plant him a facer if he didn't take his leave.

One of Campbell's nephews showed a disgruntled Grover out, no closer to possession of Treadwell House than before. The earl took his seat next to Maylene.

"You do not wish to join our circle?" Mrs. Ingraham asked hopefully. "Campbell won't mind moving over."

Socrates would rather sit next to a scorpion than the black-clad, blackmailing widow. "No, I am simply an interested observer. Please do not let me interrupt." While Lady Tremont was refocusing her group's concentration, he whispered, "A word with you afterward, Miss Treadwell?"

After his defense, Maylene could only nod. Besides, Lady Crowley or Mrs. Ingraham would be too happy to carry tales of any confrontations. She smiled for their benefit. She wished she had a glass of wine, for her nerves' benefit. Instead, she took up her pad and pencil, ready to justify the Fund for Psychical Research with her notes, ready to ignore the earl. The restless drumming of his fingers on the back of the sofa near her ears made both of her tasks harder.

Lady Tremont must have made contact with Max, for Maylene recognized the delighted smile on her mother's face. "Good evening, dear," the baroness said. "I am so pleased you could visit with us tonight. We have a lot of company on our search for answers. Can you feel their energy? Their love, reaching across the ether?"

Max must have felt something, for Lady Tremont nodded. "Yes, dear. First our good friend Lady Crowley has returned, hoping to speak at last to her beloved husband."

At the word "beloved," Hyatt sneered. "The man was a dirty dish, and she is better without him."

Maylene agreed, but told him to shush anyway.

"Yes, dear, it's her last good-byes she wishes to make. Lord Crowley died so suddenly, you recall, that she never got a chance."

Hyatt did not refrain from commenting: "He was in his cups, and in the arms of a doxy, else he wouldn't have wrecked the curricle on the bridge. They never did find his body, did they?"

Maylene did not answer.

"What's that, dear? Lord Crowley is too busy to converse with us again? He's practicing, you say?"

Lady Crowley glanced around. "I don't feel him flying about the room."

"Not his flying?"

Not the harp, Maylene hoped.

"Oh, he's singing with the choir? How lovely, dear."

Hyatt whispered, "He'd have done better to practice his swimming."

"Why, I can almost hear him!" Lady Crowley cried, cupping her hand to an ear.

Maylene and the earl could almost hear him too, a soft baritone humming.

"Why, I never knew Aloysius could sing." He'd done nothing but shout during their married days. "And he has such a lovely voice!"

"Which sounds remarkably like that of the young footman who opened the door for me this evening," Hyatt noted in a low aside meant just for Maylene's ears.

"Lady Crowley is pleased," she replied just as softly. And indeed the widow of nearly two score years was smiling as gayly as a girl of seventeen. "Aloysius singing with the heavenly chorus. If that don't beat all. Ah, well, perhaps he'll stop by to chat with us another time."

Lady Tremont passed on the request, and then asked if Lord Shimpton's dear mama was free to speak to her grieving son. After a few moments of swaying, indecipherable murmurings, and odd facial contortions, the attractive baroness transformed herself into a frowning, jaw-jutting gorgon. "You here again, sonny?" she squawked. "Why ain't you at some ball, doing the pretty with the gels? You ain't never going to find a wife this way, holding hands with old Crowley's widow."

"A ball, Mumsy? Me?" Shimpton would rather face his mother's disapproval than a roomful of debutantes. Lady Crowley handed him her handkerchief to dab at the sweat on his forehead. "But . . . but you know I can't dance."

"Then ask Miss Treadwell to teach you. She won't mind."

Maylene groaned. She minded very much. Hyatt chuckled, but her mother, or Shimpton's mother, was going on: "Decent sort of female, don't you know. Clever and capable. Pretty, too."

At least no one could see her blushes in the candlelight, Maylene prayed.

The viscount was confused, a not unusual state. "Thought you'd be mad 'cause she looks like Caro Lamb."

"She looks like a lamb lamb, you clunch—an adorable little baby sheep."

Maylene had her hands over her eyes by now, mortified. The earl's laughter did not help. The spirits were not through with Shimpton yet, though, for that rasping voice next demanded that the viscount retire his gray gelding. "You ain't never going to impress a female on that decrepit old nag. No, you'd do better to get yourself a landau so you can take a gel and her mother for a drive in the park. That's the way it's done, sonny. Mind, you let the coachman drive, Frederick, not you."

"At least they're not setting a hazard loose on Hyde Park," Hyatt commended, still smiling. "The idea of that rattlepate at the ribbons is alarming."

He did not think it so funny when Shimpton stuttered, "But, Mumsy, I cannot go buy a coach and pair. You always did that for me." And the voice answered, "Don't worry, Frederick, Lord Hyatt will go to Tattersall's with you."

"Bloody hell."

Maylene laughed now, especially when everyone turned in the earl's direction, various degrees of hope and amusement in their expressions. He nodded in scant courtesy.

"There, that's settled, sonny. Just see he don't introduce you to any loose women on the way."

Maylene could hear the earl's teeth gnashing. "Your mother is skating on very thin ice," he said.

Her mother was already undergoing another transformation. This time when she emerged from her trancelike state, one side of her mouth hung lower than the other, and her eyelids drooped. She spoke in the rusty, wheezing voice of an old man. "Are you there, Sophie?"

"Ingraham?" The barrister's widow gasped. "Is that you?"

"Whom were you expecting, wife, Lucifer? He'll be calling on you soon, you follow the path you're heading."

"Path, Ingy?"

"You know, Sophie, those journals. They were never meant to be seen by anyone. That's why I made you swear to keep them locked up tight."

"But, I . . ."

"Couldn't leave well enough alone, eh?" The voice took on strength, the measured cadences of a practiced orator. "I left you a handsome jointure, Sophie, whereby you could live well if you aren't extravagant. You are getting greedy, wife. Know this, then"—the voice rose to a crescendo—"if you choose to disobey my wishes, then my wrath will be upon you!"

Shimpton was shaking, and Lady Crowley gave a little squeak. Aunt Regina shrank down in her seat.

"That's Ingraham to the life," the Duke of Mondale whispered to no one in particular. "I heard him at trial a few times. Damn if I don't expect to see his white wig next."

Mrs. Ingraham, however, did not seem fazed at all, not even when the clap of thunder boomed through the parlor, shaking the very walls and leaving the scent of brimstone behind. Maylene could not help her involuntary start, and even Lord Hyatt was impressed. "Very dramatic, if a tad overplayed. Gun powder down the chimney?"

Maylene shrugged. Campbell had thought it a good idea; she hadn't.

"Nice try, but too bad the widow isn't affected," Hyatt said, noting Mrs. Ingraham's composure. "She doesn't believe a word of your mother's playacting, and it will take more than a cheap parlor trick to discourage that one from her villainous intentions."

Lady Tremont was not finished, however. Still in the barrister's voice, she loudly declaimed, "Hear this, Sophie. If you try to use those journals for immoral gain, I shall have my own revenge. I'll tell everyone what your father did for a living—and what your mother did for hers. I'll make sure everyone knows that you cheat at silver loo, and that you pass wind when you are nervous."

Even Lord Shimpton was wrinkling his nose. She was nervous, all right.

Mrs. Ingraham leaped to her feet and shouted, "This is nonsense, and you are all a bunch of fools!" then fled the room.

"I hope she made her contribution on the way in," Hyatt commented. "You and the others have earned it. I doubt you'll be troubled by the likes of Finster after this night's work, thank goodness."

"Was that a touch of approval I detected in your voice, my lord?" Maylene wanted to know. Not that she wanted his approval, of course.

"What, for your mother's performance? She could have put Sarah Siddons to shame. It's too bad acting on the stage is not considered respectable for females of good birth. Lady Tremont might have made an honest living."

As opposed to what she was doing now, he implied. Maylene turned in her seat so her back was toward the earl, to listen to her mother.

"Max, dear, I received an affecting letter from a young man who could not be here this evening, although I am hoping he will attend our little sessions some time soon. He was kind enough to make a generous donation to our research, in hopes we might discover the answer to a question that is plaguing him."

Hyatt was back to tapping his fingers on the back of the sofa. The man was not a restful sort, drat him, Maylene thought—nor a forgiving one. To occupy her mind with anything but their coming conversation, she wrote down the name of the man her mother mentioned, Lieutenant Canfield, although recovering what the lieutenant was missing was beyond her woeful talents, or anyone's.

"The dear lieutenant was a gallant officer, Max, until he was struck by a nasty cannon ball during the Peninsular Campaign. Talavera, I believe he said. He was fortunate enough to survive, unlike Sir Cedric's youngster, but the brave boy did lose his leg there."

While Lady Tremont wiped a tear from her eye, Hyatt exclaimed, "Good grief, Toby's ballocks were bad enough. Never tell me your mother is going to try to bring Canfield's leg back!"

His voice was loud enough that Lady Crowley's complexion turned somewhat green. Or perhaps she'd been holding Shimpton's hakelike hand too long.

"Don't be absurd, my lord," Maylene told him. "My mother is neither a grave-robber nor a resurrectionist. If you'd only listen, you'd hear that she is trying to help a troubled young man."

A disabled veteran would be helped more with the offer of a position, Hyatt knew, than any higgledy-piggledy in the hereafter. There was little enough work for able-bodied ex-soldiers, much less one so handicapped. The earl made a mental note to check with the War Office. If the lieutenant was in difficulties, he'd see what he could do. It wouldn't be the first time.

"The dear boy is wondering, Max, if he and his missing limb will be reunited in the beyond, since it was buried on foreign soil. He thought we might have an answer for him. What's that, dearest? You'll ask Admiral Nelson? What a downy idea! Of course the hero of Trafalgar would know if all his parts were gathered together. I am sure the admiral is much sought after, but do you think I can tell our dear lieutenant to call next week, Max? Yes, I am sure he will feel much better if he starts getting out and about, rather than staying close to home. Perhaps we can introduce him to some likely young ladies, too? Why, yes, the right female would never notice his missing limb, Max. How very clever you are!"

And how devious her mother was, Maylene thought, in getting another eligible gentleman into her daughter's vicinity. Canfield would be invited to tea before the cat could lick its ear.

Hyatt could also see the martial light of matchmaking in her mother's eyes, for he leaned closer and whispered, "At least, Miss Treadwell, you won't have to teach Lieutenant Canfield to dance."

Chapter Twelve

Max, dear, do you recall that we asked about another young man, Mr. Joshua Collins? We would be so pleased if we could help find the dear boy."

Maylene fancied they would be so wealthy from the reward that she could stop worrying over the bills. She might even set some of the money aside for a small dowry, to make herself slightly more eligible on the Marriage Mart. She smiled to think that some gentleman might wish to wed her for her money, since none had come forth for her looks or her mind. Even Cousin Grover wanted the house and a wife who could not refuse his advances.

Socrates wondered about this Collins fellow. When he'd checked with Bow Street this morning, he'd asked about the man and the reward Lady Tremont had mentioned last night. None of the thief-takers knew of Collins, so Hyatt had to wonder who wanted him and why. Lady Tremont wasn't saying, he noticed, and Miss Treadwell grew dreamy-eyed at the mention of his name. Hyatt's hand clenched into a fist.

"So are you able to tell us anything at all, dear? What's that? I cannot hear you, for the music."

"What music? I don't hear any music," Lady Crowley complained. "Is Aloysius practicing again?"

Maylene wrote the word "music" on her notepad, although that did not tell her anything. The missing heir was a music instructor, after all. She'd expect him to sing or play. Maylene did pencil in "What kind of music?" because sometimes her mother's later recollections were good places to begin an investigation.

Frowning, Socrates watched Miss Treadwell scribble. This was what the Treadwell House ladies called research? The

Royal Society for the Sciences would laugh them out of Town, if any of those august gentlemen had a sense of humor.

"Do speak up, Max. Yes, that's better, dear. Mr. Collins is not beyond, you say? Why, that is wonderful news, Max. Yet? He's not there yet, but might be soon? Oh, dear. Is that blood I see?"

Lady Crowley gasped and clutched her throat. Lord Shimpton leaned closer to her, and she gasped again. Maylene wrote: "Blood. Near death? Injured? Accidentally or on purpose?"

"And someone else is looking for him, too? Oh, my. Can you try a little harder, Max, because it sounds as if the dear boy needs our help, if we can find him in time."

Hyatt wished he knew what the deuce the flea-brained females were up to now. No, he told himself, he didn't want to know. He was already hiring injured veterans, helping a jackass at the horse auctions, and defending Miss Treadwell from her own cousin, by Jupiter. Next thing he knew, he'd be assisting at the dance lessons.

"We'll try again tomorrow, Max, dear. I know you are growing weary, darling, for your voice is growing faint, but we have one more question. It's His Grace of Mondale, come looking for his precious daughter, who's been missing over a sennight. The naughty chit's got her father all upset, Max, so can you tell us where dear Lady Belinda is?"

Hyatt sat up straight, both fists clenched now. Gone was the restlessness, replaced by angry intensity. "If you witches make Mondale suffer any more . . ."

"What did you say, Max? That music is still playing, so you'll have to speak up. We'll ask about Mr. Collins again next time, dear. We really need to know about the young lady now, for her own sake and for the dear duke, who is so concerned. And for Lord Hyatt, of course, who is going to marry her, unless she has eloped, as our Maylene thinks."

Hyatt glared at Miss Treadwell. "Dash it, she did not run off!"

Maylene was listening for something to write, so she did not answer, but her shrugged shoulders gave eloquent testimony to her opinion. She'd run as fast and as far as she could, Maylene decided, rather than wed such a beast. Why, she'd rather make for the border with Shimpton this evening, than make her apologies to Hyatt later. Besides, he was going to ruin them anyway, no matter how she begged his pardon for the park episode. Wasn't he looking like thunderclouds already? Some women might find that dark brooding look attractive; Maylene found it frightening. She wrote down "music" again, then crossed it out.

"Have you found anything for us, Max?" her mother was asking again.

"He's found a rich purse in Mondale," Lord Hyatt muttered.

"You haven't? Well, I suppose that is good news. I didn't get the feeling that Lady Belinda had gone aloft, either, but I am sure His Grace will be pleased to hear that you agree. Have you any glimmers of where she might be, then?" Lady Tremont's brow furrowed in concentration. "There's that wretched singing again. Max, if that is Crowley's choir, they need a great deal more practice."

"Do you hear the singing?" Viscount Shimpton whispered loudly to the duke, who was listening intently. His Grace shook his silvered head.

"No," he said in disappointment. "Dash it, I was hoping for more. A sign, a clue, even a wild guess. That would be better than what I have now."

"You have Thisbe's word that the chit is alive," Aunt Regina hissed across the table, "and that's better than Bow Street could do for you."

Maylene could see that her mother was growing weary, or perhaps she was disappointed that they'd have to tell the duke they couldn't help him. Having a duke at their gatherings was a coup. Maylene would miss his largesse, not his large friend.

"Do you think the duchess would help us, dear?" the baroness asked. "His Grace was hoping you might ask her, if you happen to come upon Lady Araminta, of course. A mother always knows when her child is in trouble."

"Damnation," Hyatt swore. "That means we have to come back."

"And what's that, dear—he should bring a handkerchief of Lady Belinda's when he returns?"

Lady Tremont was confused. Maylene was horrified. Hyatt was outraged. "This is going to go on forever, isn't it? Now that you have the poor man in your coils, you'll just keep finding new ways to keep him coming back. Until he runs out of blunt, or Bow Street finds Belinda. Confound it, I should have gotten him drunk at White's."

"Now there's the perfect solution," Maylene bit back, as upset as Hyatt by the news that this torture was to continue. "When all else fails, resort to the bottle. That's sure to bring his daughter back to the duke."

"As much as a bunch of numbskulls nattering to nomads of the next life."

That apology was growing harder and harder to make. Maylene wrote down the word "handkerchief."

"Or one of her gloves? Whatever for, Max?"

Hyatt swore again. "Because your boggarts have decided to turn bloodhound now, I suppose," he said under his breath.

Lady Tremont smiled suddenly. "Alex is going to help? Oh, how lovely, Max. Now I am sure we can find Lady Belinda."

"Alex? Who in tarnation is Alex?" Hyatt asked Maylene.

She hunched her shoulders under the shawl. "He is one of Max's friends, I guess."

"You don't know?"

"Well, he might be a brother."

"Dash it, woman, don't you know how many brothers you have? Or had?"

"I was an only child. And my mother does not like to speak of it."

"No, she only likes to speak of what cannot be proved. Now she's got two pet ghosts to hoodwink Mondale with."

"Max isn't a ghost. That's an unhappy entity that has not gone beyond because of unfinished business or a curse. Max is quite content."

"He can be dancing on his cloud for all I care. I tell you this, though, whoever the devil Alex is, ghosts cannot smell!"

Socrates had become so irate that he'd forgotten to lower his voice. Lady Tremont sagged in her chair, the contact broken. She stared around vacantly until her eyes found his. "They can if they are dogs."

Maylene dropped her pencil.

"Alex is a dog?" Mondale asked for them all.

"Well, he was."

Hyatt threw his hands in the air. "Now I have heard everything. Come on, Mondale, let us get out of this lunatic asylum before they lock the doors."

The duke, however, seemed amused by the discussion raging around him.

"Dogs don't go to heaven," Lord Shimpton insisted.

Aunt Regina asked, "How do you know, if you haven't been there?"

"My mother always said they were dirty, heathen animals. She'd never let me have one of my own."

"She never let you have an idea of your own either," Aunt Regina told him, reaching for one of the glasses that Campbell was passing around.

"Maybe I'll get a dog then. Always wanted one. If Max can have one . . ."

"No, my lord, you need a wife, not a dog," Lady Tremont said, sipping at her sherry and musing aloud. "And if that soldier can be reunited with his leg, I don't see why a dog cannot be reunited with his master. Why should a poor animal wander through eternity without his best friend?"

Hyatt wanted to scream at them all. He wanted to leave. He wanted a brandy. But he had to make his apology for attacking the unfortunate Miss Treadwell this afternoon in the park first. Lud, it was his wits that had gone wandering.

Miss Treadwell was still sitting apart from the others, hunched over her notepad. Socrates brought a glass of sherry to her, then just stood staring, as Campbell and the footmen went around lighting the oil lamps. His right hand—without volition, by Jupiter—reached out and touched one of the short golden curls that caressed her cheeks.

"Good grief, you didn't cut it off because of something I said, did you?"

Maylene coughed, then took a hasty swallow of her wine before she answered. "Gracious, no, I'd been meaning to do it this age. I had an appointment with Monsieur Vincente for a fortnight now." She named the premier coiffeur to the *ton*. "Cropped hair is all the fashion, don't you know."

He raised one eyebrow, but one side of his mouth was raised also, as if he were trying not to smile. The dowdy chick dressed in last year's style was instructing him about fashion, was she? "And is the uneven length à la mode also?"

"But of course. Symmetry is so boring, don't you know?"

Well, Miss Treadwell was never boring. "I, ah, was wondering if I might have a moment of your time, in private."

Such a polite invitation to her execution. Maylene's knees were shaking. "In private? Mother would never let me . . ."

Her mother would let her go to dinner with the Devil if he was single, and they both knew it. "That is, my mother needs me. These sessions quite drain her of all energy."

Since Lady Tremont was happily sipping her sherry and chatting with the others, Maylene shifted her focus to her greataunt. "And Aunt Regina finds them wearying also. At her age, you know, one cannot be too careful, so I always assist her up to her bedchamber. Isn't that right, Auntie?"

Aunt Regina just looked at her as if she'd sprouted a second head. Maylene stepped closer and whispered in her aunt's ear: "If you don't come with me now, I'll tell everyone that Mrs. in front of your name is as false as your jewelry."

Aunt Regina drooped over Maylene's arm and moaned piteously. They made their hurried farewells and almost escaped, except that Hyatt stopped them at the door. "Coward," was all he said.

"No, that's Howard, your lordship." Aunt Regina drew herself up to her five feet naught on her elevated heels. "Mrs. Howard."

As they left, Maylene could hear Lord Shimpton complain that a dog was easier to come by than a wife.

And he wouldn't have to dance with it.

•

Meanwhile, the music kept playing. Raucous voices were lifted in a rude song in the taproom, while upstairs at the run-down inn, in a shabby room, another voice was raised in desperation. "Don't you leave me, Joshua Collins. I don't care what that drunken surgeon said—you have to live. We have our whole futures together, you promised. I swear I'll never forgive you if you die!"

Chapter Thirteen

The black phantom was chasing Maylene to the edge of the precipice. She looked down to the bottomless pit, and there he was, the same dark specter, ready to catch her. The dream did not make a lot of sense, but, then again, it was a dream and easily interpretable. Drat the man for cutting up her peace, Maylene thought, even when she was asleep, which had not been for nearly long enough. His promise to call the next day had kept her awake long into the night, wondering where she could go to be from home all day. When she'd finally fallen asleep, the dastard had invaded her dreams. And then, much too early, the maid Nora had shaken her awake.

"That Monsieur Vincente fellow is here to cut your hair, Miss May. Says as how he's sorry he forgot yesterday's appointment."

"I made no—" But she knew who did. She pulled a pillow over her head. "Send him away. I cannot afford to pay his exorbitant prices anyway."

"The Frenchie told me to tell you that the hairdressing will be for free, since he missed your appointment."

Artists like Monsieur Vincente never did anything for free. Someone must have paid him, and paid him well to get him to Treadwell House at this time of the morning. So his lordship felt guilty for insulting her hair, did he? Too bad. "You may tell monsieur that his services are no longer required. I found someone else to do the job."

"Pardon, Miss May, but I'd be reconsidering, was I you. Lessen, of course, you don't mind looking like a ewe what got shorn by the sheepdog instead of the shepherd."

So Maylene had her hair trimmed and styled off her face with matching tortoiseshell combs the coiffeur produced. "*La Cherubim, à la Vincente,*" the genius proclaimed, kissing his fingertips. "Mademoiselle will have all the gentlemen at her feet, no?"

No. She had one gentleman, on her feet.

Lord Shimpton arrived for his dancing lesson before Maylene could have breakfast, much less escape the house. The viscount brought part of his own breakfast with him—muffin, eggs, jam, coffee. Unfortunately, they were all on his neckcloth and dribbled down his shirtfront. Lady Crowley had come along to play the pianoforte for them, so Maylene did not even have that excuse for avoiding the mutton-head.

Two pairs of slippers ruined in two days. At this rate, she'd be barefoot by week's end. At the rate Shimpton was learning, she would not be able to walk by week's end. The complicated quadrille was hopelessly beyond him, and Maylene would not get close enough to him for the waltz. The jigs were too strenuous, Maylene declared to herself, for someone who perspired so profusely, and the contra dances were too hard to teach without other couples in the set. He'd never find his next partner in the figures, not without a map. So they practiced the minuet. Bow, point, point, step. Bow, step, step, point. Shimpton could walk his way through that, Maylene decided, if she did not mention turns, twirls, or crossovers. And she could tell him that her occasional hops and skips were part of the dance, not efforts to rescue her toes.

She finally sent him home with Lady Crowley, hinting that a gentleman changed his clothing after such vigorous exercise.

"What, that little bit of prancing? Thought it would be harder, don't you know. Of course, I'm liable to forget it all by tomorrow. Usually do. Better have another lesson before I have to dance with a real lady."

And this was the man her mother wished her to wed?

Not necessarily, now that there were other choices.

The scene in Lady Tremont's drawing room that afternoon was enough to gladden any hopeful mother's heart: one unmarried daughter, four unmarried gentlemen. Why, the place was practically awash with possibilities. Except for Shimpton, who hadn't.

Of course Cousin Grover was missing his hair, Lord Shimpton his brains. Lieutenant Canfield was minus one leg, and Lord Hyatt, certes, had no heart. Maylene despaired, but her mother was beaming at them all over the tea tray, insisting they stay longer than the usual fifteen or twenty minutes. Cousin Grover needed no urging, since he was determined to keep one eye on the woman he intended to marry, and one eye on the tea cakes.

Lieutenant Canfield had reluctantly answered Lady Tremont's invitation to tea, anxious to hear what she had to say about his lost limb, but hesitant about making such a public appearance. He need not have worried, for Aunt Regina took him in hand after he limped in on his crutches, pulling forth handbills advertising carved wooden peglegs, ivory prostheses, even a cloth contraption that could fill out his pantaloons. And Lady Tremont was everything warm and welcoming, pressing more poppy seed cakes and raspberry tarts on him. Lord Hyatt mentioned various mutual acquaintances and hinted at possible business arrangements. Viscount Shimpton was ecstatic that Canfield once owned a dog and begged the lieutenant to help him select a pup. He hadn't liked Maylene's suggestion that she take him to where they'd found Toby. He did not want a dead dog.

"Besides," he said, "Miss Treadwell is already helping me find a wife. Wouldn't want to ask her more than that."

Miss Treadwell made Canfield feel at home, too. She did not hover over him or show pity, but saw him seated comfortably, served his tea, then took up her sewing next to him. She also bade him remain once the usual calling time was expired. Miss Treadwell was a deuced attractive female, too, the soldier thought. If a dasher like her wasn't revolted at his missing leg, he thought, then perhaps there was hope for him after all. Maybe he'd go home to Hampshire and put his luck to the test with Becky Haverhill. Yes, he was glad he'd come, and agreed to be introduced to Max that evening, whoever Max was. Perhaps he was someone else who might know of a position for a one-legged man.

The only one in the room who was not polite and friendly to the young veteran was Tremont, who was eying him suspiciously, but Canfield could not decide if the balding baron was more jealous of his position next to Miss Treadwell, his thick head of hair, or the last raspberry tart Lady Tremont was putting on his plate.

The gentlemen seemed determined to outstay each other, even after the last slice of cake was gone. Canfield did not want to make his awkward exit in front of the elegant earl, and Tremont didn't want to leave his flighty cousin alone with the Corinthian. Shimpton wouldn't go for fear his new friends would forget about helping him find a wife, a carriage, and a collie. Or perhaps a poodle. Maybe a mastiff. Lud, how was a chap to decide when his brainbox was already filled with the minuet? He sucked on his lower lip, wondering if he should ask his mother.

Finally, Socrates had enough. He stood and invited Miss Treadwell for a ride in his carriage, since the day's rain had ceased.

"What, you are willing to try that again?" she blurted. "I mean, no thank you, my lord. I have correspondence to catch up on, and must gather last evening's research notes. Then I have to inform Mr. Ryan about our search for Joshua Collins."

"She'll go," her mother declared. "Campbell, fetch her wrap."

"Think I'll fetch m'horse and toddle along with you," Shimpton offered. "Get some pointers about coaches, don't you know."

Maylene could have kissed him. Well, not quite, but she was grateful, nevertheless. "I know," she said, "why don't we all go? You have not been outside all day, Mama, and Aunt Regina does so like to visit with her cronies in the park. We can send round to the livery for a carriage, and Lieutenant Canfield can accompany us, too." Cousin Grover could sit up with the driver or ride with Hyatt in his curricle. He wouldn't pinch either of them.

Hyatt would not hear of their hiring a coach, not when he had a carriage house full of them. He sent one of Campbell's nephews off to his lodgings with a message for his own stables, and another for Mondale's. Somehow, and Maylene was not quite certain how it came about, she found the others bundled into an elegant brougham, except her mother, who was with the duke in his landau, while she herself was back in his lordship's curricle, with his lordship's thigh pressed uncomfortably close to hers. Very well, she thought, she'd make her apology and then walk home.

Somehow, and this time she was fairly certain the earl had engineered it, their carriage became separated from the others after they entered the string of vehicles in the park. When he suggested they get down for a walk, however, Maylene claimed a sore ankle. After a morning trying to teach Shimpton to dance, that was not so farfetched. Instead of winning her a reprieve, though, her excuse merely made Hyatt direct his groom to get down and wait near the entrance for them.

Once more he drove away from the crowds, but not along the waterway, Maylene noted. Obviously, he was about to give her a bear-garden jaw and distrusted her temper near the Serpentine. Hyatt also held tightly to the reins, most likely fearing she'd make off with his curricle again.

The blasted female was sitting as far away from him as possible on the driver's bench, Socrates noted. B'gad, did she think he was about to ravish her in broad daylight in the park? "I am not a rakehell, Miss Treadwell." That was not what he meant to say, either. Deuce take it, this impossible chit with her angel's cap of golden curls was robbing him of his wits as handily as she was robbing Mondale of his blunt. She and her mother were adventuresses, he reminded himself, vulgar mushrooms, outright cheats, or Bedlamites. He, however, was a gentleman.

"I deeply regret—" he therefore began.

Maylene had gathered her courage and started her own apology. "I am dreadfully sorry that I—"

"Excuse me."

"No, you were saying . . . ?"

"I was trying to beg your pardon for my behavior in the park yesterday, Miss Treadwell. Although I have no excuse for taking such liberties, I wish you to know that I am not in the habit of mauling young women about or making crass public displays. I swear such a thing will not happen again. That is what I wished to say."

The horses seemed to take all his notice, for he was not meeting her eyes, which was fine with Maylene. Staring at the glossy backs also, she launched into her own prepared speech. "And I wished to apologize for shoving you into the river and then making off with your horses and driver. I am not in the habit of . . . of mauling gentlemen about either, nor of creating commotions."

"But I provoked you, Miss Treadwell, so I take full blame for the episode."

"You were only trying to protect your friend, my lord."

"No, I was high-handed and arrogant, just as you said. I have no business dictating your actions or threatening you and your mother. No matter what I may think."

He had her full attention now. What was almost a handsome apology and a suspension of hostilities was sounding more like the earl Maylene knew, and wished she didn't. Her eyes narrowed. "Just what do you think, my lord?"

"Come now, Miss Treadwell, you know how I feel about your mockery of people's grief and your enriching yourselves on their sorrow. Just as I know your opinion of 'pleasure-seeking peers,' as I believe you called me and my friends. We have been through this and must agree to disagree. To avoid any further contretemps, we shall simply avoid each others' company in the future."

"And you shall not try to destroy our standing in London?"

"If you don't try to destroy Mondale."

"We have never tried to destroy anyone, my lord."

"You did a fine job on my clothes yesterday. My valet almost resigned. But you showed excellent science. Perhaps you should be giving Shimpton lessons in the manly art of boxing instead of the ballroom."

"Don't let my mother hear you, or she'll have us both tutoring that tottyhead. She is trying to help him, you know, the same as she is trying to help the duke, in the only way she can."

"I would like to believe that. Your mother is a lovely woman, even if I cannot ascribe to her beliefs."

"Oh, that never bothers Mama. She knows you'll believe when you get to the beyond."

"Then we have a truce, Miss Treadwell?"

"Pax," she agreed, holding her hand out to seal the bargain. Instead of shaking it, as she expected, he brought her gloved fingers to his lips. "And . . . and thank you for sending over Monsieur Vincente this morning. I shall repay you, of course, but it was very thoughtful."

"No, I won't hear of it. I owed you for my boorishness. Besides, it was worth every penny, for the curls are delightful."

Maylene colored at the compliment, then recalled that he was still holding her hand. "My lord, we really ought not be stopping here like this, apart from everyone else."

He sighed, but released her hand after pressing a light kiss to the palm. "That's right. I am not a rake."

"And I am not a light-skirt."

They both sighed. The earl gave the horses the office to start, then cursed. "Dash it, I am no monk, either." And he reached over, pulled Maylene closer, and kissed her.

The earth moved. No, the curricle moved. The highbred cattle had been given their orders and were stepping out smartly— right into the path of a high-perch phaeton. With her eyes closed, savoring the forbidden feelings, Maylene did not see the other vehicle. Neither did the earl until the other driver started shouting and the horses tried to veer off the track. The grounds were still muddy, however, so the earl's curricle slewed onto the wet grass, and kept going, sideways, into a tree. Maylene screamed, the horses screamed, and Socrates swore. Then the curricle splintered.

Hyatt tried to break Miss Treadwell's fall by grabbing for her, but only succeeded in landing atop her in the mud. Then everyone was shouting and running in their direction across the park, just what neither Socrates nor Maylene wished. They were not hurt, nor were the horses, merely mired and mortified. Pushing Hyatt's not inconsiderable weight off her with her mud-covered gloves, Maylene scrambled to her feet and surveyed the ruin of another pair of shoes. At least it wasn't her neck that was broken. "I can only imagine what would have happened, my lord, if you *were* a rake."

Then the rest of their party was there, exclaiming, commiserating, finding handkerchiefs, and making room in the other vehicles. Lord Shimpton was relegated to riding at the back of

Mondale's rig, standing at the groom's position, since Canfield couldn't and Grover wouldn't. The viscount muttered, "Don't s'pose I'd ought to be asking the earl's advice about m'carriage after all."

Chapter Fourteen

Lady Tremont declared that there would be no session that evening, due to the drama of the day. The ladies needed time to recover, she said. Dear Maylene needed a long soak in a hot tub, lest she be stiff, besides black and blue. And Lady Tremont needed to recover her equilibrium, after the shock of knowing that her only child could have died in the accident. She sympathized with the duke more than ever at his temporary loss of Belinda, but would be no help to him in her emotional state. So she took up the new gothic novel from the lending library and disappeared into her bedroom.

Aunt Regina decided her own nerves were so frazzled that, since the brandy Maylene ordered had arrived that afternoon, she needed a restorative—or two.

As a result, Maylene had too much time alone, time to feel every bruise, time to think. She tried thinking of finding the lost heiress, but only found herself wondering if Lord Hyatt kissed Belinda so fervently. Then she took out her notes on the missing teacup to Lady Pritchard's prized set. One of the servants undoubtedly broke it, but Maylene did not wish to cost some poor maid her job. How much, she wondered, would Mr. Wedgewood charge to repeat the pattern? And would Lord Hyatt repeat his?

Teacups be damned, why in the world did the man keep kissing her? Was he mad? That or he must think she was a high flyer like Aurora Ashford, and he was about to offer her carte blanche. Well, she wasn't, and she would never accept such an arrangement, even if she did accept his kiss. And that was another conundrum: why she let a nearly betrothed, clearly bullying man kiss her, twice. Maylene could have stopped him this afternoon, she knew, well before things—things like the reins—got out of hand. But she hadn't stopped him, had shared in the earth-shaking embrace, and that hurt more than any bruise.

Hyatt was not precisely a gazetted rake, just as he'd said. He'd never been accused of debauching an innocent, and his name was not linked to every Bird of Paradise in the demi-monde, only a select, discreet few when he came to town for Parliament. And the choice had to be his, for the number of hopeful misses trying to trap the Ideal into marriage was second only to those trying to tempt him into trysts. Or so Maylene heard from Aunt Regina.

They were all fools. Oh, he was wealthy, and she could attest to his generosity. And he was very well built. Maylene could attest to that, too, having felt every hard plane of his firm build when he landed atop her. He was attractive, beyond doubt. But the Earl of Hyatt was so stubborn, stiff-rumped, and sure of himself, that lesser mortals were as dirt beneath his boots. No self-respecting woman should ever think of allying herself to such a tyrant, either in marriage or in a less sanctioned liaison.

Maylene decided she would not think of him at all, in any way, shape, or well-built form. So she went in search of company. Aunt Regina was snoring in the parlor, and Campbell had retired for the night with the rest of her opened bottle. Some spirits lasted forever in this house; others did not.

Thinking of spirits, Maylene scratched on her mother's door. As soon as her mama had set aside her novel and patted the place next to her on the bed, Maylene settled back upon the pillows and asked, "Mama, just who is Max?"

Lady Tremont fiddled with the lace on her frilly nightcap, not looking at her daughter. "Why do you ask, dear?"

Her mother was blushing, by heaven! Maylene's suspicions were strengthened, if not confirmed. "I always assumed he was one of your infants, lost at birth. You love him so much and seem so close to his memory."

"Oh, yes, dear. I will never forget my Max."

"But, Mama, if Max died as an infant, he wouldn't have a dog of his own, would he? I mean, Canfield might easily meet up with his lost leg some day, but how can Max have what never was?" For that matter, now that Maylene thought of it, how could a baby speak to those other souls? How could he speak to Lady Tremont?

"Oh, Alex was Max's dog, all right. They went everywhere together. Why, Alexander died trying to pull Max out of that burning inn. That's why they were buried together, you know. Actually, I think it was because no one was sure which bones or ashes belonged to whom, but no matter. They were close in life, close in death, so it only figures that they would be close in the beyond. And Alex has been a great help to our investigations, you know."

Maylene didn't know. A dog was guiding Mama's way through the hereafter? A dead dog? Good grief. "Then Max is not an infant, not one of my brothers."

"Why no, dear, he is your father."

"My father?" Maylene felt as if a huge weight had fallen on her, knocking her breath away, for the second time that day. "But my father's name was Maynard, and you said you never wished to speak to him again, in this life or the next."

"Yes, dear, but Maximilian Treadwell was Maynard's brother. His younger brother, I am sorry to say. He had no money of his own, and no prospects. My parents refused the match, although we had loved each other forever, it seemed. Then Tremont offered for me, out of spite, I always supposed, and jealousy of his brother. He was always a small-minded man, you know. My father accepted his suit."

"But you and Max . . . ?"

"Oh, we ran away, of course. What else were we to do? But my father and Maynard caught up with us before we reached the border. Not before we had spent the night together, though."

Lady Tremont shook her head, setting the lace on her cap to fluttering. Not as violently as Maylene's heart was fluttering, of course. "Then . . . then I am a bastard?"

"Oh, no, Maynard said it did not matter, that he was vowed to have me for his wife. Only a selfish man could have done such a thing, don't you think? But my father agreed, for he'd already spent a portion of the marriage settlements. So the baron and I were married that week, and then you were born. You have my hair and eyes, dearest, but you have Max's sweet, loving nature. You could not be the child of that ogre, Maynard. Max and I are quite agreed on that."

"But what happened to Max? Did he ever marry?"

"Oh, yes, a pleasant girl he met on his travels. Max always liked to go exploring, don't you know. They had no children, unfortunately, before the dreadful fire, or we would not be saddled with Cousin Grover now, of course."

"And you didn't mind?"

"What, that Grover would inherit your father's dignities? Tremont had already bankrupted the estate, so it made no difference to me."

"No, that Max married someone else."

"Oh, no, for his wife made him very comfortable. I loved Max far too much to wish him a lifetime of loneliness. And I had you, dear." Lady Tremont reached over and stroked her daughter's cheek. "It wasn't the same, but it was enough, so it was only fair that Max have someone, too, besides Alex."

"And then he came back to you, after he d— went aloft?"

"Yes, his love reaches out and touches me. Now I have both of you. Isn't that perfect?"

Perfect, when one of her mother's loves was dead and the other was an illegitimate daughter? But the arrangement seemed to make her mama happy, so Maylene did not voice her concerns. She kissed her mother good night and returned to her own room, thinking about a love that could last for decades, through separation and through marriages to others, through death itself.

Maylene believed in such an enduring love as much as she believed that Max wasn't a flight of her mother's fancy, born out of regret and loneliness. But, oh, how she wished such a love were possible, and hers.

Early the following morning an enormous bouquet of roses was delivered to Maylene, along with an even larger ham.

"A ham?" Aunt Regina asked. "What kind of beau sends bacon?"

Maylene was reading the note that was written in a dark, bold hand on crested stationery. "It's from Hyatt, to beg our pardon for his ham-handed driving. He asks if he can call, to reassure himself of my well-being after the accident."

"Very handsomely done," her mother approved.

Aunt Regina didn't. "He could have sent a side of beef, then. You know, because he wasn't steering right. I don't like ham. It sticks in m'choppers."

"You have given me a delightful idea, my dears. Why don't we have a dinner party this evening? You know we never get to entertain, and this will be perfect. The dear duke can use something to brighten his days, and we can show the earl that we have no hurt feelings."

No hurt feelings? Every bone and muscle in Maylene's body hurt, no thanks to him. "They'll already have engagements for dinner, Mama. You know that the Quality never eat at their own tables."

"*We* are Quality, and do not forget that. We can ask. Yes, and we'll invite Lord Shimpton, too, and Lieutenant Canfield. And Lady Crowley and her niece, who is having her come-out soon. Perhaps she'll do for Shimpton, since you are so determined not to have him. At any rate, he can use the practice of speaking to other young ladies. And dear Canfield needs to see he is accepted in Society. I suppose we shall have to invite Tremont to round out the numbers."

"Oh, not Cousin Grover, Mama, please."

"I'm sorry, dear, but he is head of the family, you know. Besides, I believe Lady Crowley's niece will have a handsome *dot*. If Lord Shimpton does not appeal to her, she might just take a shine to Cousin Grover."

"The only thing that shines about that ninny is his bald pate," Aunt Regina said. "I offered to take him to my wig-maker any number of times. Still, he'll come to dinner, if only for the ham. And turtle soup." When Maylene gasped at the expense, she added, "Mock turtle soup, then. But we absolutely must have turtle soup if a duke is coming."

Lady Tremont and her aunt started debating courses and covers, while Maylene started calculating costs. In view of their obvious delight to be entertaining again, even on such a modest scale, Maylene could not protest. Instead, she started writing out invitations for Campbell's nephews and the other lads to deliver and wait for responses, so she knew how much food to order.

Everyone accepted, so Treadwell House turned into a beehive of activity. As in a beehive, the queen retired to her bedchamber to get ready for the evening; Lady Tremont had to catch up on her beauty sleep so those ugly blue shadows under her eyes—caused by worry over her daughter—disappeared. Aunt Regina had to polish her ivory teeth and her paste pearls and her own silver-plated epergne, a huge monstrosity with elephants and monkeys and palm trees sprouting in all directions. Filled with Hyatt's roses, perhaps it wouldn't look so terrible, Maylene decided, although its height would make conversation impossible. Considering the mismatched company, however, that was not necessarily a drawback.

While her mother and great-aunt were preparing themselves, having declared themselves not at home to callers, Maylene prepared the house. She consulted with Cook over the menu and Campbell over the wines. She went to Gunter's to order ices, and to Covent Garden flower market to purchase ferns to sit on the bare spots of the dining room carpet. She worked with the maids to wipe the good china, and with the footmen to clean the chandelier. The little-used dining table needed rubbing with beeswax, and the windows needed scrubbing. By the time the candles—wax, not tallow—needed lighting, Treadwell House was glistening, and Maylene was groaning. She was exhausted, she ached, she only wanted her bed. Instead, she got her mother, her great-aunt, and Nora fussing over her.

"What do you mean, you're not ready?" Lady Tremont shrieked. "You've had all day to prepare!"

At least her hair would not take ages, and she had only the one gown suitable for evening, a celestial blue lutestring with an ecru lace overskirt. It wasn't entirely out of style, and one of the earl's roses tucked in the neckline was a nice touch, they all decided, since she refused to wear any of Aunt Regina's glass beads. Maylene did let her great-aunt apply the hares-foot to cover a slight bruise on her cheek from yesterday's fall, and a bit of rouge to give her some color.

She need not have bothered, for none of the gentlemen noticed her, not with Lady Crowley's niece in the room. Miss Isabella Tolliver-Jones was a Diamond of the first water, a petite brunette with rounded shape and dimples. She smiled through lowered lashes, she giggled, and she lisped. Her gown was figured white satin, with three ribboned flounces, and she wore a crown of white rosebuds in her perfect ringlets. Maylene felt old, ugly, and out of fashion. Then she felt worse for being mean-spirited. Miss Tolliver-Jones was a charming young lady, and if she wanted to bat her big brown doe eyes at short-in-the-upper-storeys Shimpton, can't-dance Canfield, or bellows-to-mend Baron Tremont, Maylene wished her well. Miss Tolliver-Jones, however, had eyes for no one but the Earl of Hyatt.

"He's engaged, you ninny," Maylene wanted to shout. "And he is too old, too bold for a dainty spun-sugar morsel like you." But she didn't, of course. And if her own blue eyes were turning green with envy at the sweet compliments he paid the girl, bringing an adorable blush to dewy cheeks that needed no enhancement or camouflage, well, no one was noticing her, so Maylene didn't have to worry. She didn't have to worry about the epergne hindering conversation, either, for Shimpton was totally tongue-tied in the beauty's presence, Canfield grew morose when he couldn't rise to his feet to kiss her hand or escort her in to dinner, and Cousin Grover was silently staring at her through his looking glass with the same avidity he'd bestowed on the raspberry tarts. Only Hyatt seemed undaunted, offering his arm and his charm with equal polish.

He didn't care for Lady Belinda at all, Maylene thought, angry for the missing heiress's sake.

And Maylene didn't care for ham, either. And the mock turtle soup tasted bitter.

Chapter Fifteen

Socrates couldn't decide which was less conducive to good digestion: the gruesome epergne or Miss Treadwell's glower. What the deuce did the female want from him? Here he was doing his best to be polite to her odd companions, and all he received back was dagger glances. If looks could kill, he'd be as dead as one of the elephants on the centerpiece. But, devil take it, he'd almost killed the female, so he was conscience-bound to attend her peculiar gathering and be an accommodating guest. Hyatt would never sit down to dinner with such a parcel of peahens otherwise.

He still could not figure out how he'd lost control of himself and the reins, though it had to be Miss Treadwell's fault. The blasted chit kept making him act like a schoolboy. Well, that would end after tonight. In the morning he would set out to find Belinda himself, no matter what Mondale said. He'd start at the house party in Suffolk and not stop until he'd found the lady. Then he'd marry her. The earl had waited because she was so young, when he should have wed her for that very reason. Socrates knew he could have kept her safe from danger then, and safe from buffle-headed notions, if that was what had sent her haring off. They should have at least announced the engagement; no one would dare interfere with Hyatt's chosen bride. Now Belinda was missing, and Socrates was sitting game for silly twits like Miss Tolliver-Jones.

The persistence of pudding-heads like the little beauty was the reason he eschewed Polite Society, the reason he did not do the Season, the reason he'd offered for Mondale's chit in the first place. As his grandmother was constantly reminding him, now that he was nearing thirty, he needed to set up his nursery.

Mostly though, he needed to be free from the endless, every-where pursuit.

Perhaps that was why Miss Treadwell constantly set him off balance. She was the one female of his acquaintance who did not wish to wed him or bed him. She loathed him, which was refreshing in an admittedly muddle-minded way. Lud, for all her sins, he'd never have forgiven himself if she'd come to harm in his curricle. And he'd hate like hell to try explaining his lapse to Max, or Max's dog.

The thought brought a smile to his lips, which caused Miss Tolliver-Jones to simper. Miss Treadwell never simpered. She did, however, glare like a Greek goddess sending thunderbolts. Maybe one would hit the epergne. Dash it, would this dinner never end? He wished he'd sent a book, instead of a ham.

After dinner, the men shared a tolerable port, and Hyatt discussed with the duke his intentions of starting his own search.

"But I have had experienced men search every inch of a forty-mile circumference of the spot. No one saw her. No, if she were there, my men would have found her."

Not in the hedge tavern she'd landed in, they wouldn't. And not when Lady Belinda had gone many miles more than forty, traveling in a ramshackle hired coach, with a scarf over her hair and a rough cloak over her rich clothing. No one noticed such commonplace carriages and their working-class passengers—no one except the villains who'd held them up to steal the fine leather trunks tied behind, along with her purse and all her jewels. Now she couldn't have afforded to send a letter to her father if she wanted to. Besides, mentioning her father's name in such surroundings would see her held for ransom, or sent back for the reward she knew the duke would offer. And she could not go home.

Still undecided about leaving London in the morning, Hyatt was not inclined to linger at Treadwell House. There was not even going to be one of the baroness's bogus journeys beyond for entertainment, due to Miss Tolliver-Jones's presence, the earl understood. She was deemed too young and too delicate for such an experience. She was also too flighty altogether to be trusted with the personal aspects of, say, Canfield's inquiries, or Mondale's. Instead, there was to be cards. The elder Treadwell ladies, it seemed, adored playing and rarely got the chance. Hyatt would never ordinarily sit to dinner with such an ill-favored group, much less game with them for chicken stakes. He could not, however, like the way that loose screw cousin was ogling Miss Treadwell and the rose at her neckline—his rose. Socrates agreed, therefore, to make up one of the two whist tables.

The duke, Lady Tremont, Lady Crowley, and Lieutenant Canfield were already discussing their modest stakes. Mondale seemed relaxed for the first time since his daughter's disappearance, the earl noted, and the soldier was at last at ease, out of the presence of the younger females. Mrs. Howard, who insisted everyone call her Aunt Regina, invited Socrates to sit at her table. Tremont gave up his leering to dive for the seat opposite her though, leaving Hyatt to partner Miss Tolliver-Jones, whose aunt had taught her the rules last week. Lud. He set out to forfeit a polite amount, wondering how much blunt he would have to lose before tossing in his hand. He also wondered why Miss Tolliver-Jones kept shifting in her seat as if someone, some balding libertine, was pressing his leg against hers under the table. Pretending to drop a card, Hyatt looked.

"Why don't you shift your seat an inch or two, Miss Tolliver-Jones?" he asked. "Then the light won't be shining so directly in your eyes."

The chit gratefully slid her chair closer to Aunt Regina, while Hyatt gave Grover a dark glance. If Grover moved his own seat so much as an inch, they both understood, he'd be answering to the earl. Grover did not like the question. "Aren't we ever going to play?" he whined.

Maylene was on the sofa, next to Lord Shimpton. No one would play with the doltish viscount who could barely count to twenty with his shoes on, so it was left to Miss Treadwell to entertain him. She was not a gambler and would not have minded sitting out if the company were more stimulating. The footstool was more stimulating than Shimpton. Happily, she had recalled a book about dogs in the library, a children's book, with a lot of

pictures. While Shimpton was trying to sound out the German
dachshund and the French *chien* and the English d-o-g, Maylene
was free to watch the company and free to see how solicitous
Lord Hyatt was of Lady Crowley's pretty niece.

The chit would have her head turned for sure, Maylene decided. She was too young to see past the practiced smile, the
casual flirtation, the way Maylene could. Miss Tolliver-Jones
would think Hyatt meant all the pretty compliments, and then
her heart would be broken. Besides, she'd forever after com-
pare all the nice young boys she'd meet to the Ideal, and they
would not measure up—not even halfway up. So poor Miss
Tolliver-Jones would never be happy with a likely lad, and
she'd end up an old maid or, worse, in Maylene's opinion, married to a man she could not love. Before the chit's life was ir-
reparably ruined, therefore, Maylene had to separate the two.

She let a few more hands of cards go by before she stood and
walked around the tables, offering a glass of wine here, a dish of
comfits there. She arrived behind Hyatt's seat in time to hear
him compliment Aunt Regina on her playing. This was no Span-
ish coin, for a huge pile of good English coins sat in front of the
old lady. Hyatt was losing without even trying, and losing
plenty, paying his partner's shot, too, of course. If they hadn't
been playing for pocket change, he'd have lost a fortune. "You
are amazing, ma'am. You could take your place with the finest
whist players at White's."

Aunt Regina puffed out her enhanced bosom. "Why, thank
you, my lord. But I cannot take credit. It's my talent, don't you
know. All the females in the family have some gift or other.
Thisbe has an affinity for the afterlife, Maylene is a finder, and
I win at cards."

"She cheats," Maylene whispered in his ear as she reached
over to place another deck of cards on the table, this one not
marked. "That's why Grover is always so eager to be her partner. Perhaps he'll be able to dine at his own board this week,
thanks to you."

Hyatt almost dropped his cards. That sweet old lady? he
thought. The one with her false hair, teeth, eyelashes, and who
knew what else? In this house? Why not? Now that he thought
to look, he spotted an extra spot or two on the backs of the

cards. And Mrs. Howard's gown had long, loose sleeves, with more than a scrawny old arm up them, he'd wager.

But he wouldn't wager with any Captain Sharp, not even for pennies a point. Socrates yawned. "I think I had better quit before I lose High Oaks." That was his country estate outside Brighton. "And it grows late." It was so early, most Londoners had hardly begun their evening revels. It was so early, in fact, a fellow could still get into Almack's, if he wanted to be latched onto by limpets like Miss Tolliver-Jones. She wasn't at that hallowed altar of matchmaking because she was not yet out, of course, but it was Wednesday. Why was Miss Treadwell not attending the Marriage Mart? Perhaps, he pondered, she was not invited. Perhaps the Treadwell House trickery outweighed the title in the minds of the starchy patronesses. Good. At least *some* poor devils were safe from making cakes of themselves.

Finishing a hand at the other table, Lady Tremont called for tea. It would be gauche to refuse, Hyatt knew, but he'd be damned if he'd listen to Miss Tolliver-Jones's giggles for another half an hour. "Do you play, miss?" He gestured toward the pianoforte in the corner. Since most debutantes were expected to perform, that was a safe bet, the only one of the night.

"Like an angel," the chit's aunt cooed, shoving her niece in the instrument's direction. "Show him, love. There is talent in our family also." Lady Crowley giggled, the same annoying high-pitched titter as Miss Tolliver-Jones. No wonder her husband wouldn't talk to her from the thereafter.

Socrates did not offer to turn the chit's pages, to at least two women's disappointment. Instead, he strolled across to where Miss Treadwell and His Grace were deep in conversation. Whatever tomfoolery the witch was pouring in Mondale's ear now, Hyatt didn't like it.

The duke seemed to. "Miss Treadwell has been suggesting a new avenue of investigation, Soc. She believes one of Belinda's friends has to have an inkling of her whereabouts."

"We've asked and asked, Your Grace, and none of them was the slightest help. Besides, any more questions and everyone will know that the lady has disappeared."

"I don't care anymore, and the news will be out soon, when

she does not return from her aunt's in Wales. What is a little gossip compared to my daughter's safety?"

Hyatt cared. The chit would be ruined unless he married her, and he was no longer so certain he wished to be leg-shackled to such a flighty female. "They would have said something if they'd known."

"To you, my lord?" Maylene asked. "Break a friend's confidentiality to her own fiancé? Did you try? I can imagine how far you got, if you were wearing such a scowl."

"Of course I did not interview the chits myself. I don't go to their dos and I don't even know which girls were her bosom bows. We hired investigators. And I do not scowl."

Maylene was not about to let herself be intimidated by the scowl he was insisting he did not wear. "You don't know her friends and don't know her interests, but you think you can find her?" The scorn dripped from her lips.

"What, you think you can? Or Max, whoever the deuce he is."

"He is a longtime . . . friend of my mother's." No one needed to know how long or how friendly. "He, at least, seems willing to try."

"Yes, by letting his deceased dog show the way. You never said—is Alex a pointer, then, or a scent hound? A retriever? Perhaps we should consult Shimpton's book."

Mondale quickly put in: "Miss Treadwell thinks that a female might be more effective at getting answers out of Belinda's friends, Soc, and I agree. Besides, if Miss Treadwell is willing, how can I refuse? We were just deliberating how best to make the introductions before you came."

"Why, I should think all of Lady Belinda's friends would be at Almack's, husband-hunting," Hyatt drawled. "You could simply go there, Miss Treadwell." Then he added, "If you have vouchers, of course."

His tone indicated that he'd believe Princess Esterhazy would tie her garters in public before she allowed the likes of Maylene Treadwell through the sacred portals. Her chin came up. "I do not attend Almack's, my lord, because I am not hunting for a husband."

The earl pointedly looked around the room at all the single gentlemen. "Your mother is."

Ignoring him, Maylene continued, "And I do not think that is the appropriate venue for quiet chats, not under the glare of all those eyes and expectations."

"But you do have vouchers?" Dash it, he'd make Mondale see the chit for what she was, one way or the other.

She was furious now, at his belittling tone. "Of course I do, Lord Hyatt. What I don't have, my lord, is a new gown to wear every week, or a carriage to carry us there. The other thing I do not have, which you very well know, sirrah, is a dowry to attract the sprigs of the nobility who go there seeking brides. I choose not to waste their time or mine!"

Chapter Sixteen

Lud, he'd made a mull of it again. Instead of revealing Miss Treadwell to the duke as the scheming harpy she was, Socrates had made himself look base. Now his old friend was frowning at him, and the chit had tears in her blue eyes. Thunderation, how was he to know old Tremont had left them in such extremely queer straits? And there were plenty of other poor females at Almack's. Of course they were to be found sitting against the walls, dash it. Hyatt would be damned if he'd apologize yet again though. And he surely would not send round another dinner.

"Be that as it may," he said, "you do not travel in the same circles as Belinda's friends, so they have no reason to confide in you."

The duke was nodding. "He's correct my dear. Belinda's friends are a silly lot, barely out of the schoolroom, but I cannot imagine any of them betraying a secret to a stranger."

"Oh, I am not expecting them to tell me where she went, if they know. I merely wish to find out her interests, her hobbies, which museums she might have visited, with whom she corresponded. That type of thing." She turned back to Hyatt. "Unless you can tell me that, my lord. After all, as her betrothed, you should know the lady better than anyone. Which modiste did she patronize, for instance? She might have ordered a warm cloak, a domino, or a traveling costume—something that might tell us her intentions, if not her location. Dressmakers are prodigious gossips."

"How the deuce should I know where she had her clothes made? I told you, I did not follow her about through the Season. That's for debutantes and green boys."

"And men who wish to win the hearts of their ladies. I do not believe you care for Lady Belinda at all."

"Of course I care for her! I've known her since she wore pigtails and pinafores."

"And I have known Grover Treadwell, Lord Tremont, since he wore hair. That does not mean I wish to marry him. And if you care so much, then why are you doing everything possible to prevent me from looking for her?"

"Because you haven't a chance in hell. Or heaven, or wherever your pet ghosties reside."

"I don't know, Soc," the duke said. "A woman's got a different outlook. I never thought to send someone to ask at the dressmakers', for instance. If her supposed chaperone wasn't prostrate with grief, she might have thought of it. Then too, if she weren't such a pawky creature, she might not have let Belinda go off to that house party with her friends, instead of her or her maid. Still, Miss Treadwell has some good ideas. I can check the modistes' bills for addresses, and look through Belinda's desk again for any letters."

"And find out which lending library she subscribed to, Your Grace. If she was a frequent customer, the clerks might recall if she purchased any guidebooks, or if she met anyone clandestinely between the book stacks."

Maylene hurried to find her notebook and pencil. Thinking aloud as she wrote, she put down "dressmaker," and "lending library." "Milliners, her favorite museums, anywhere she might have met someone."

"What, your intuition tells you she's run off with another man?" Hyatt demanded.

"No, I am merely thinking what I would do, should I find myself almost betrothed to an ogre."

The duke coughed, but Hyatt said, "Belinda isn't like you, thank goodness. And she never objected to the match." He was shouting by the time he'd repeated himself. "She never objected, by all that's holy."

"And it was a suitable arrangement," Mondale added.

Maylene shouted back at Hyatt, "If the lady was so eager for the engagement, my lord, where is she? And I beg to differ with you, Your Grace."

Having heard loud voices, Lady Tremont left trying to feed
the lieutenant another slice of lemon cake to join the trio by the
fireplace. She thought her daughter's ideas for finding Lady
Belinda were excellent, unless Max sent them searching in another direction tomorrow night. "But if dear Max cannot help
us, then I am sure Maylene can. She is quite talented at this sort
of thing, you know."

Studying the lists of establishments Miss Treadwell wanted
him to locate or investigate, the duke could only agree. "If Bow
Street were half this thorough, I'd have my girl back by now."

"Maylene says it's all a matter of logic and reasoning, but I
always believe there's another force guiding her, a talent. What
do you think, Your Grace?"

"I think that however she manages it, my money is on your
daughter, ma'am."

Maylene was still thinking, chewing on the end of her pencil. "The money. That might be a problem, Your Grace."

Aha, Hyatt thought, the money. Now the minx would show
her true colors.

"You see, all these people on the lists are working folks, Your
Grace. They cannot take time to talk to me without being rec-
ompensed. And bribes, if you will, can loosen the tongues of
even the most taciturn of gatekeepers or mantua-makers." She
stared at her pad. "I am afraid I have not the resources."

How guileless she seemed, the earl thought, lowering her
eyes at being forced to confess her financial embarrassment.
She'd be asking Mondale for an abbey next.

She did not need to ask; the duke offered, or as near as made
no difference. "Of course not, Miss Treadwell, and I would not
think of allowing you to expend your own blunt. I'll have my
secretary send over a draft on my bank in the morning. You'll
tell him how much, and when it runs out, just speak to me."

Hyatt was livid that Mondale would trust the chit—with his
chit. She'd take his blunt, and they'd be no nearer to finding
Belinda. Just as he'd thought, this had been Miss Treadwell's
goal from the first, to milk Mondale of every shilling she could.
Socrates would be willing to wager that nary a tuppence got
into the outstretched palm of any clerk, carriage driver, or
clothier.

Lady Tremont was smiling at the duke as if he'd volunteered to make their mortgage payments, which in Hyatt's opinion was what Mondale's carte blanche amounted to. And she was not satisfied with that, he realized, when the older woman said, "But I think Maylene's original idea of speaking to Lady Belinda's girlfriends is our best chance, if we can arrange for her to meet them on social terms, not as your emissary, come to snoop out their secrets."

Mondale nodded. "I can see it done. There is to be a ball next week that I know Belinda was looking forward to. I'll see that both of you, and your aunt, of course, receive invitations. All the Season's debutantes will be there as Lady Belvedere is firing off her younger sister, a school chum of Belinda's."

"That sounds perfect, Your Grace. And if you can introduce Maylene to some of them, it's a fine start. Lady Crowley might know some others, and I am sure to recognize a few of their mamas, although I have been out of the social swim for years now."

"Society's loss, ma'am." Mondale's gallantry brought color to Lady Tremont's cheeks.

"And the dressmakers truly are a font of information," Maylene reminded him.

"Especially," the duke added, "when they are gaining a grateful new client. Some of the blunt could go to a new gown, Miss Treadwell. In fact, it should, as required armor to face the *belle monde*, don't you know." He held up a hand, so the light glimmered off the ruby signet he wore. "No, I insist. The *ton* will be at its most splendid, and you will feel better outshining them, my dear. My wife always said nothing gave a woman confidence like a costly new gown. And no need to worry about a carriage, either. I'll come for you myself."

Exclaiming over His Grace's graciousness, Lady Tremont led the duke off to discuss with Aunt Regina who else would be attending the Belvedere ball. The Earl of Hyatt and Miss Treadwell were alone in that part of the room.

"I see what this is all about," he accused as soon as the others were out of hearing. "You want the brass, of course. But the chance to weasel your way into Society again, that's the real purpose behind your efforts to win the duke's trust. You want to

meet Belinda's friends. Hah! They are nothing more than a
bunch of chattering monkeys. They barely know their geography, much less where Belinda might be. No, despite what you
say about remaining single, your ambition is to join the Quality
at play and snare yourself a *parti*, like every other shallow
jade."

Maylene wished there were a nearby body of water she could
shove him into, and to the devil with polite manners. "How
dare you come to my house, eat my food—very well, your
food—and insult me and my mother at every turn. First we are
mercenary, now we are social climbers! Climbing to what, I'd
like to know. Your rarefied atmosphere where you can insult
and offend everyone below? No, thank you."

Hyatt accepted a glass of wine from Campbell, who was
clearing his throat to remind them that the rest of the company
was not all that far away, and the room was not all that large,
for angry words.

The earl pasted a false smile on his face, took a sip, and lowered his voice. "No, first you are charlatans, then you are card
sharps. Vulgar mushrooms come next. Money-grubbing is at
the root of it all, of course."

"You . . . you toad! My mother and I feel sorry for the duke
and want to help him. Can you not understand that? Must
everything be done for ulterior motives?"

"What, like wringing an invitation to the social event of the
Season? Not that I blame you, if this"—he waved his hand at
the gentlemen gathered near Miss Tolliver-Jones and the pianoforte—"is the best you can do for suitors. I'd recommend
you take Canfield, of the three. His prospects are not as good as
Shimpton's, and there's no title like Tremont's, and of course
there's the missing leg, but he seems a steady chap with a modicum of intelligence."

"I'd take a man with no legs, no prospects, and no name if I
loved him. But that is beyond your understanding, isn't it, my
lord? At first I was willing to excuse your behavior because I
concluded you must be overwrought with worry about Lady
Belinda. Now I do not believe you have ever spared a single
thought for her; you are simply mean. I daresay when you decided it was time to set up your nursery, you looked about for a

likely breeder and settled on your neighbor's daughter because she was close to hand and you wouldn't have to exert yourself to win her."

Since that was approximately what had happened, Socrates took another drink of his wine and went back on the attack. "Oh, I must have been mistaken then. You are going to Lady Belvedere's merely to speak with Belinda's friends. Of course you wouldn't dance and flirt and mingle with the young men at all."

Of course she would. Since that was approximately what she'd planned, Maylene took a large bite of the biscuit a frowning Campbell offered. So angry was she that she swallowed wrong and choked.

"Should I slap your back?" Hyatt asked.

"I'd be afraid you'd stick a knife in it," she gasped, catching her breath.

He slid another glass of wine off Campbell's tray and offered it to her. "You might as well have a good time, for the young girls will never talk to you, and the duke will see that you are only using him."

"What, do you think they will speak to a great brooding troll like you who is always shouting and sneering? Come try, and we'll see who gets better results."

"Very well, I will." Socrates had decided to go the instant Mondale had issued the invitation, to make sure that the Treadwell trio did not batten on his friends. Though how he was to keep a watch on the susceptible young sprigs, the genteel gamesters, and the gullible guests, all at the same time, he did not know. "The infants will speak to me because I am a friend of Belinda's family."

"Ah, but the young ladies will speak to me if they think I am interested in finding out if you are free or not."

"Why the deuce would you care?"

"Oh, I don't, but I'll tell Belinda's friends I am interested in you for myself. If they are as foolish as you say, they'll believe me."

Now he choked and the wine spilled. "Miss Treadwell, you are the most devious, dishonest, deceitful female it has ever been my misfortune to meet."

"And you, sir, are an insufferable cur."

"Cur?" Lord Shimpton demanded, coming between them. "What kind would that be?"

Maylene was brought back to her duties as hostess, and back to her senses. She knew better than to argue with this man who had the power to ruin them. And she knew better than to argue with any man, creating a scene in public. She also realized that the room had grown quiet enough that everyone could hear their brangling. "Where is Miss Tolliver-Jones?" she asked. "She's not at the pianoforte."

Shimpton flipped through the pages of his dog book some more. "Oh, I think she toddled off to the library for a book of her own. Tremont went to help her find one."

"Grover? Oh, no." Maylene rushed off to the library, followed by Hyatt out of curiosity and Shimpton out of habit. Things were as bad as she'd feared. First they heard giggles before they reached the book room, then a squeal. As the three pushed open the closed door—a closed door, by heavens! How could that cad?—Grover jumped back, dislodging his hair, both of them, and Miss Tolliver-Jones staggered, as though she'd just lost her support. Maylene pointed her finger at her cousin, then at the door. "Get out, you dastard."

"I say, Cuz, there's no need to be jealous."

"Jealous? You think I am jealous, you conceited coxcomb? I am outraged, yes, outraged, that you thought to seduce a gently born female under your own cousin's roof. What, did you think to compromise Miss Tolliver-Jones into a hasty marriage? It won't wash, you fool, for she is underage and her father will never release her dowry to a dastard like you."

Grover sniffed, then pulled out a handkerchief to wipe his nose. "Harsh words, Cuz. I only wanted to chat with the gal. And she was willing, weren't you, miss?"

"She is seventeen!" Maylene yelled. "What does she know?"

"Oh, stubble it, Cousin May. No harm's done."

Now Hyatt stepped into the room from behind Maylene. "No harm except to a lady's reputation. I've half a mind to call you out over this."

Maylene turned her angry glare on him. "You don't have half a mind to spare if you think a duel will do anything but bandy

Miss Tolliver-Jones's name about in all the men's clubs. There will be no challenge here, do you understand?"

She was right, so Hyatt nodded, vowing to thrash the licentious lord, even if he had to drag him into Gentleman Jackson's.

Maylene went on, "Nothing happened, and no one needs know. Do you understand?"

She addressed all of them, but it was Lord Shimpton who answered. "What did happen?"

"Nothing," three voices told him.

"And you, miss," Maylene told the younger girl, "have learned an important lesson. Now wait to find out about kisses and such until you find the right man, and never go alone off with one of them until you do." She glowered at Hyatt. "For none of them can be trusted." The girl ran out of the room.

At the mention of a duel, Grover had started edging for the door and escape. Hyatt called after him, "If you cannot act civilized, stay away from decent people, or answer to me for it, you dirty dog."

"I say," Shimpton asked, "do dogs need baths then?"

In accord for the first time that evening, Maylene and Socrates answered simultaneously. "Not as badly as you."

Chapter Seventeen

People prayed on Curzon Street. They said their nightly blessings, they said grace over their meals, they went to church on Sundays. Rarely, however, did they pray *in* Curzon Street. At least not before the Treadwell ladies had taken up their research in psychical phenomena.

As if Maylene did not have enough in her dish the day after the dinner party, Nora had awakened her before seven in the morning with the news that a Reverend Bernard Fingerhut had taken up a vigil on the roadway.

Maylene fumbled with her robe, then fumbled with the catch on her window. She leaned out and, sure enough, a man in a clerical collar, Bible raised on high, was right outside the fence that surrounded the grounds of Treadwell House. Quite a crowd of milkmaids and butchers' boys were gathered around him, listening as the reverend harangued the populace against evil, against Satan, against raising the dead.

Maylene lowered the window. "I deal with fanatics only after breakfast."

Her mother, however, also awoke to the report of a man of the cloth holding forth outside her door, shouting about hellfire and damnation, godless necromancers and witches. So she invited Reverend Fingerhut inside for kippers and eggs.

"For speaking with the Lord is hungry work," she told her astonished daughter in the breakfast room.

"Mama, don't be absurd. That raving lunatic wants to see us burned at the stake. He is not speaking with the Almighty."

"He must be, dear. How else could Reverend Fingerhut presume to know what our dear Lord wishes? I personally think He must have given me the talent to use as best I can to help the rest of His flock. But God Himself never told me so, of course. Only Max."

She sounded disappointed that God was too busy to attend her séances, like Lady Crowley's husband. Maylene realized fanaticism before breakfast was nothing new, not in Curzon Street. But, Lud, she hoped her neighbors slept late, and soundly.

Reverend Fingerhut would not have entered such a house of wickedness, but for his calling. And for Cook's steak and kidney pie, which was also calling out to him. By the time every dish on the table was empty, he was quite taken with Lady Tremont, or her cook, and promised to pray for Lady Tremont's soul, instead of for her trial as a heretic.

"And pray for those others we are trying to help, also, my dear reverend," she asked him, making sure Cook packed up enough bread and cheese to see him through a day of kneeling on the cobblestones. "Who knows who might be listening to such a righteous, religious man as you."

Half of London, that was who, Maylene calculated. She could not force the cleric to leave, for he did not appear to be doing anything illegal. Besides, Campbell had already tried. The man could not be bribed or threatened, it seemed. He could only be fed. If his mouth was full, she reasoned, he could not continue his diatribe against devil worship. Maylene added a jug of cider and some buns to the sack. Then she took out the cider and replaced it with a bottle of the new brandy.

Reverend Fingerhut was not as loud after that—whether from the food and drink or the fact that his congregants had to be about their errands, Maylene was not sure. He was not discouraged enough to leave, though.

"I say, Miss Treadwell, do you know that there is a drunken man on his knees outside your gate?" The young solicitor had returned, hoping for results from Maylene's search for Mr. Joshua Collins, the missing heir to a dukedom. Ryan's red hair was once again neatly parted down the middle, then pasted there with pomatum, as if daring a breeze to ruffle one iota of his dignity.

"Yes, I do, Mr. Ryan. It is all the fashion, don't you know, for every neighborhood to have its own religiousist. That way everyone gets a chance at salvation."

Mr. Ryan tugged at his neckcloth. There were no missionary ministers in his block. "But this one is shouting about blasphemy and sacrilege."

"Yes, well, the best of the lot gets assigned to Grosvenor Square, I suppose."

"But, Miss Treadwell, the man is claiming that you call up the dead."

"Oh, then it must be time for luncheon. I'll just tell Campbell to invite him in. You are invited also, of course."

To take lunch with a Bible-pounder and a Bedlamite? "No thank you, Miss Treadwell. I was just wondering if you had any notions as to the missing heir we spoke about."

Maylene wished she had more to tell him. She wished for that reward more than ever. "Well, we do not think he is dead."

"Now that is good news, ma'am. Have you any proof?"

"Proof?" Good grief, didn't the man realize he had come to a spiritualist, not a scientist? "Of course not. I thought you understood that my mother works more with, ah, intuition than hard facts." She did not feel like discussing Max with the stiff-necked solicitor, not with the evangelical outside.

"Oh, then you have no idea where Mr. Collins is?"

He sounded so disappointed that Maylene mentioned they thought there was music, which had Ryan eager again. "What kind? For if it's violin music that he was playing, we can concentrate our search on string quartets, orchestras, that type of thing."

"I'm sorry, I just cannot say."

Ryan seemed to deflate again, so Maylene added, "I wish we had been able to be of more help." She would love to go to Bath and try to trace Mr. Collins's route for Ryan—and for the reward. She knew she could think of lines of inquiry his paid agents might have missed, but such a trip was impossible now, especially since accepting the duke's offer of escort to Lady Belvedere's ball.

"It was a gamble." Gloom weighed as heavily as hair oil on the solicitor's shoulders. "I suppose I'll have to report still another failure to my superiors."

"Well, they cannot be angry at you if their own investigators did no better."

"But if they lose the trusteeship of the duke's estate, they mightn't be able to pay my salary, so blame does not matter."

"Why should they lose their client if they have managed the estate all these years?" Maylene asked.

"Because the entail is dissolved at the end of the year, the title is extinguished, and the properties go to charity. Some church the late duke supported."

"But you had mentioned Mr. Collins might be in danger." She saw no reason to mention Max's report of others calling out to him. "Surely the church would not do him harm, to guarantee the inheritance?"

"It is a great deal of money, Miss Treadwell."

She thought of the maniac minister on her doorstep, and meant to ask Mr. Ryan the name of the church that was the beneficiary of the Duke of Winslowe's estate. Before she could do so, however, her cousin burst into the room. Ignoring Ryan as if the man were a servant or a piece of furniture, Baron Tremont started shouting. "That is the outside of enough, when I am laughed out of my clubs because of some perishing preacher at my cousins' doorstep!"

"Good morning to you, too, Cousin Grover. This is Mr. Ryan, of Hand, Hadley and Choate. And I thought you'd been barred from every gentlemen's club in London for not paying your gambling debts."

Grover inclined his head the tiniest fraction, enough to dislodge the perpetual drip at the end of his nose. "Rumors! Vicious rumors, Cousin May."

"Just like the one about Reverend Fingerhut." Even with the solicitor present, Maylene made sure to stand near the door, where she could call for Campbell if need be. At least Grover was too angry to take her hand as he usually did, leaving it damp and dirty.

"He's no rumor. I saw him myself just before I arrived, spouting about sin and witches' sabbaths, in the street. And I won't have it, do you hear? As head of the family, I insist you and your mother cease your ridiculous fits and starts, so that windbag outside will go on about his own business."

"Oh, he won't go away, Cousin Grover, for sin is his business—preaching against it, at any rate. He'll merely begin on greed and lechery next, after he scours the neighborhood of blasphemers. Shall I call him in now so you might have a private sermon?"

Grover reached up to make sure his hair was in place in its one thin strip across his pate. "This levity is thoroughly unbecoming, Cousin Maylene. Your mother's ill-conceived escapades have cost you your place in Polite Society, and your own intransigence is liable to cost you a respectable future."

If that meant Grover would not be importuning her about marriage any longer, Maylene could only be thankful. On the other hand, she did not like to see her mother disparaged. "To the contrary, Cousin, we lost our standing in the *ton* when my father lost his fortune at the gaming tables. As for the future, our prospects have never looked brighter. Why, we've been promised invitations to the social event of the Season, Lady Belvedere's ball. Who knows what might come of that?" If she was taking advantage of the duke's offer, who could blame her? Only Hyatt, and he was close to blaming the fog, the price of wheat, and the King's ill-health on her, so he did not count.

Grover could count his chances of wedding his cousin and gaining Treadwell House good-bye if she took to socializing with the likes of the Ideal, he knew. And the likelihood of his receiving an invitation to the ball was about as good as his odds of growing a new head of hair. He would not even be invited to tea this afternoon, for Cousin Thisbe's cook was too busy feeding the maggoty missionary to do any baking. Furious, Grover marched back to the street, managing to kick some dirt on the kneeling, black-clad figure as he passed. Then, while Fingerhut was rubbing his eyes, Grover lifted two shillings from the donation plate at the priest's feet.

Maylene apologized to Ryan for her cousin's behavior, then saw the solicitor to the door after promising to try once more for inspiration and insight into Mr. Joshua Collins's disappearance. "Yes, I believe we will be having a session tonight," she said from the open door, waving to Reverend Fingerhut.

With the minister in the roadway, traffic to Treadwell House thinned considerably. Some would-be clients were frightened off by the threats of hell or heresy; others were afraid of having their own sins enumerated. There would be no new patrons making appointments with Lady Tremont for inquiries, fiend seize Fingerhut. On the other hand, perhaps Hyatt was also discouraged from calling. Lud knew the man had sins enough, pride being foremost in Maylene's mind. Or the reverend's accusations might have given him a final disgust of them, on top of his distrust and dislike. He might have decided to stay away finally anyway, after last evening. Good, she told herself, sending another bottle of brandy out to the brimstone-bellower on her doorstep. Very good. Excellent. She'd be thrilled never to see his overbearing lordship again.

No decree of damnation could keep Lord Shimpton away, of course. He couldn't understand half the words the chap on the street was saying, he told Maylene, but he did wonder if the fellow knew anything about dogs.

"He's nattering on about the Hounds of Hell, so I got to wondering what breed of dog they were. Thought your mother could ask Max for me. And Max could ask his friend Alex. I meant to ask Hyatt myself, until he cracked his curricle into that tree. Thought he was a downy cove, the earl. A'course, having a female aboard can make anyone clumsy, I s'pose. If he ain't here, I'll toddle round to the clubs to ask him. 'Less you think the bloke with the Bible really does know what kind of canine they are. Wouldn't want one for a pet, don't you know."

Maylene thought Fingerhut wouldn't know his own name after one more glass of brandy. At least she hoped so.

Chapter Eighteen

Since there was no company, Maylene took up her account books. That way she would not have to think about the company that wasn't coming, for which she was glad, of course. The columns of figures never yielded the same sum twice, though, and she found herself staring out the window on the back garden more than at the ledgers. That was how she happened to notice Aunt Regina and her mother scurrying out the service entrance and around the corner, intent on finding the latest fashion magazines or the least expensive silk warehouse, without encountering the reverend. They were going to a ball, by the stars, and meant to make the most of it. Maylene knew she ought to get back to her columns, for, despite the duke's offer, she could not permit him to pay for new ensembles for them all. She'd find the money somewhere, since the prospect of new clothes had both the older women in alt.

Maylene was not so thrilled. Oh, 'twould be lovely to have a real ball gown and attend a fete with the glittering throngs, but what if they all looked at the Treadwell House ladies askance? What if her mother was laughed at or cut? What if no one invited Maylene to dance? She supposed Shimpton would be there to partner her, so perhaps she should not waste money on new slippers. And she did have a mission, to meet Lady Belinda's friends. But Lady Belvedere's ball might be Maylene's last chance to meet the man of her dreams. After that, she'd buy herself spinsters' caps and a pug dog—and bury those dreams deeper than the debts her father had left them.

With such dismal thoughts, Maylene was pleased when Campbell scratched on the library door to announce a visitor. The butler wasn't wearing his full-pocket smile, so Maylene knew the visitor wasn't—well, wasn't anyone who was not coming back, and whom she would refuse to see if he did.

"Not Reverend Fingerhut?"

"No, miss, that one's in the kitchen, seeing what Cook is preparing for dinner." Campbell stared past her left shoulder. "I don't rightly think you ought to be home, Miss May."

"Mama and Aunt Regina know more about fashions than I, Campy, and I really needed to work on the accounts."

"No, miss, I mean I don't know as you ought to be at home to this caller."

Technically, she had not ought to receive gentleman callers without a chaperone, at least until she donned those cursed caps. "Tell Nora to step down, then." Campbell's brow was still furrowed. "Ah, he's not a gentleman, then?"

"Not a lady, more like. Though she did say as it was a matter of importance, and needing to make an appointment with Lady Tremont."

"A client? We could definitely use another paying customer, Campy, especially if Mama and Aunt Regina have their way about the ball. Do you think she can afford . . . that is, does she believe in supporting the Fund for Psychical Research?"

"She says she's willing to pay anything if you can help her."

"And you've kept her waiting? Send her in, Campy, and see if Cook can produce something for tea."

The woman who followed the butler into the library was decidedly not a lady, not with her rouged cheeks and darkened eyes. She might be nearing sedate middle age, but her hair was the color of sunset, and her figure was that of a moon goddess. She wore a gown of primrose sarcenet, or most of a gown, Maylene concluded, parts having evidently been dispensed with in the interests of . . . certainly not economy, for where the gown wasn't, were magnificent necklaces of diamonds and rubies. They made Aunt Regina's glass gems look like colored pebbles. The caller's expanse of bosom made Maylene's chest look like a paving stone.

The woman was making her own inspection, noting the faded carpet, the frayed drapes, and the frumpish hostess, Maylene was sure. "Won't you please be seated, Mrs., ah, Miss . . . ?"

"Mademoiselle Lafontaine. Fleur Lafontaine. But you ain't Lady Tremont."

And Fleur Lafontaine was as French as Yorkshire pudding. "No, I am her daughter, but I act as her secretary." She gestured toward the ledgers on the desk. "And make all the arrangements for Mama's gatherings."

"Good. Then it's you I want to talk to. How much will an investigation cost me? Lord Volstead says you and your mother are the best."

"I am sorry, Miss Lafontaine, but our services are not for hire. We conduct scientific research, not detection work."

"La, don't go getting niffy-naffy on me. I know you nobs think talking about money is common, but that's what I am. Your man already explained about your fund, in that ugly urn out in the hall. I just want to know how much of my brass will get the thing done right." Miss Lafontaine waved an immaculately manicured hand in the air, displaying a collection of rings that could outfit a harem.

Maylene hid her own ink-stained fingers under her skirts. "Why don't you, ah, explain the situation, and I can better decide if my mother can help you."

"You ain't missish, are you?" the older woman asked. Maylene was able to reassure her caller that, despite the high-necked, out-of-style gown devoid of all ornamentation, she was not at all missish. She couldn't afford to be, but that's not what she said.

"Good, for the story ain't for any schoolroom chit's ears. Then again, I didn't suppose old Tremont's gel would be a milk-and-water miss."

"You, ah, knew my father?" Maylene hoped her voice did not express her dread that Miss Lafontaine knew her parent in the biblical sense.

"Everyone knew your father. A connoisseur of the theater, don't you know."

Her father was a womanizer who'd haunted the green rooms. "Then you are a, um, thespian?" Maylene asked, actresses not being held in high esteem. Thespian sounded more polite; Cyprian sounded more accurate.

"Retired. Come into a bit of the ready, don't you know."

The ready visited Rundell's regularly, it seemed. Maylene nodded. "But you have lost something?" She was hoping to avoid any further mention of her father.

"Not exactly lost. There's no wrapping it in clean linen, Miss Treadwell. I bore me a child nine years ago."

"Not to my father?" Dear heavens, and to think that she'd often wished for a brother or sister! If they were skirting the borders of respectability now, Maylene could not imagine the social stigma of an illegitimate half sibling.

Miss Lafontaine waved her hand again. "Old Maynard? Lud, no. And the father doesn't matter."

It did to Maylene, who started breathing again.

"The thing is, I gave the baby, a boy, up for adoption. A nice young couple, the solicitor said."

"And now you want him back?"

"No, I still don't lead any kind of life to raise a child in. But now I can pay for his schooling and see that he's hosed and shod, don't you know, if that young couple cannot. Or I can make other arrangements if they ain't treating the boy right. The only thing is, I can't find the little blighter. The solicitor who handled the papers died, and his partners handed his files to some jumped-up clerk who won't let me see the records. Not for any price. Ryan must be the only honest lawyer in all of London. Can't even bribe his assistants."

"Ryan? Of Hand, Hadley and Choate?"

"That's the one. Oily chap, ready to jump out of his skin if you say boo. Do you know him?"

"Yes. He had an inquiry for my mother also. But we are not on such terms that he would divulge privileged information."

"Didn't expect that. I thought you might have other ways to get the records."

"You are not suggesting I break into his office, are you?" That had been the first thought that entered Maylene's mind, too. She could not do it, of course, more's the pity.

But no, Fleur was an honest woman now. If she'd wanted a cracksman, she'd have hired the best. Instead, she was hoping that Lady Tremont would have some insight.

For the weight of the purse she tossed on Maylene's desk,

Miss Lafontaine could have insight, hindsight, oversight, and underbite. Maylene took out her pad to make notes.

Could one catch insanity by association, the way one could contract the pox by proximity? That was the only answer Lord Hyatt could think of for his behavior. By everything holy, he was delivering invitations for Lady Tremont and her family to attend Lady Belvedere's ball. He did not want the shabsters to attend, did not want them associating with decent people, did not want to so much as see Miss Treadwell and her silly curly head again. Yet his feet were definitely pointed toward Curzon Street, and he had the invitations in his pocket.

Called to a cabinet meeting, the Duke of Mondale had begged Hyatt to speak to Susannah, Lady Belvedere, for him. How could Socrates deny his old friend, who was also going to be his father-in-law someday? As Mondale insisted, Hyatt had more time, and he did know the young matron better. Better than he wanted to.

So aside from all the other reasons he had to be aggravated with Miss Treadwell, Socrates added having to fend off a married trollop without offending her. Dash it if Susannah wasn't willing to trade invitations to her ball for invitations to his bed. He'd had to hint about a previous involvement, though he hadn't visited Lady Ashford in days, sending the widow an expensive gewgaw instead of listening to her complaints at his continued absence. Already enduring a relationship with a spoiled Society dasher, Socrates was in no hurry to take up with another, and a married one at that, even if her husband did spend all of his time at his clubs, as she claimed.

In addition to lying about the state of his affairs, Hyatt had to make up a Banbury tale about the Treadwell ladies being connections of his grandmother's, and his request for invitations a favor to her. He could not simply say the women were playing at constable and crook, and needed to interview the other guests. He could not, most definitely not, let Lady Belvedere think he wished the ladies invited for his own sake. For one thing, she'd be liable to withhold the invites out of spite or jealousy. For another, she'd spread the story all over Town, that Hyatt was smitten with the attics-to-let antidote.

What a waste of his time! The visit to Lady Belvedere's was everything he hated about so-called Polite Society: the subterfuges to protect one's privacy, the pretenses to protect one's reputation, the twenty minutes of prattle to get one scrap of paper that no one wanted in the first place.

And it was all Maylene Treadwell's fault, with her lies and lunacy. It just might be her fault, he was beginning to suspect, that Lady Ashford's voluptuous figure did not interest him, nor Lady Belvedere's bold manners. Damn her.

So aggravated was he that Lord Hyatt was not watching his steps as carefully as he might have been, if he suspected paper-skulled prelates might be praying in the street. Socrates almost tripped over the kneeling minister, then begged his pardon, offering a hand to help him up before the man's words penetrated his musings. By Zeus, the dusty deacon was damning her, too! The earl drew his arm back to shove the words down the dastard's throat, then caught himself. Good grief, he'd been about to clobber a man of the cloth.

And he agreed with him, by George, that the treacherous Miss Treadwell's chances of getting into heaven were slimmer than the lamppost to which the cleric was now clinging. Still, he could not let the man keep spewing his brimstone in front of her house. Now that he'd invoked his grandmother's name to get her the invitations, Socrates convinced himself that Maylene's reputation reflected upon him and his family.

First he politely suggested that the preacher go elsewhere, then he threatened to call the Watch. Finally, he tossed some coins onto the plate. And more coins. Reverend Fingerhut's convictions were too strong, or Lady Tremont's brandy wasn't strong enough. He went back to decrying the evil inside Treadwell House. Hyatt went in.

"Nice try, my lord," Campbell told him, leading him toward the library, where Miss Treadwell was already entertaining a caller.

A caller? Bloody hell, little Miss Treadwell, with her cherub's curls and angel's blue eyes, was entertaining a Covent Garden convenient! And he'd worried what people would think if they heard the sermonizing. If word of this visit got out, Miss

Treadwell might as well rip up the invitations in his pocket. Max would be the only gentleman who spoke to her.

And the demented female was all set to make introductions, to a woman she ought never have acknowledged, and a man with whom she oughtn't be alone. Worse yet, her guest was patting Miss Treadwell's hand as she stood to leave. "Oh, no need to do the pretty, ducks. Lord Hyatt and I are old friends. Aren't we, Soccy"

Chapter Nineteen

Soccy? Maylene had to remember to close her mouth as Fleur Lafontaine glided past her and stroked the earl's cheek. No need to wonder how close friends the two were. She was not jealous, she swore to herself. She was outraged. After all his pompous piety, Hyatt was purring like a kitten. "I'll see you to the door," she said to mademoiselle. And her turned back told his lordship that she'd see him when hell froze over.

Instead of following her hostess, though, Fleur latched her silk-clad arm onto Hyatt's elbow, choosing the male to escort her as naturally as water ran downhill. Good grief, Maylene thought as they went past her, chatting cozily, he wasn't the one, was he? The father of Miss Lafontaine's child? The thought was making her nauseated. No, that was Fleur's heavy perfume.

Campbell opened the door and stepped back, bowing. While Hyatt was busy checking on the churchman on the cobblestone, Maylene hissed in Fleur's ear, "Is he the father?"

"Who? Your darling butler?" She stopped teasing when she saw how serious Maylene was about the matter. "Soccy? No, more's the pity. But you shouldn't be getting your petticoats in a pother, lovey, even if he were. The Ideal's not for the likes of a poor gambler's gel."

Who was on the shelf, with a bosom, compared to Fleur's, as flat as that selfsame shelf. "Of course not," Maylene protested. "I would never suppose . . . That is, I only wished to ascertain the facts of the matter."

Fleur smiled her disbelief. "The fact is, it never meant tuppence who the papa was then, and it means less now. I want to find the boy's new father, not his old one."

"Yes, of course. I will be consulting my mother, then, as we discussed."

Miss Lafontaine turned, winked at Campbell, blew a kiss at Hyatt, and smiled once more at Maylene. Then she accomplished what no one else had been able to do that day. She got rid of Reverend Fingerhut.

"Bernie? Is that you? Lud, it's been an age since Mother Mcready's."

"No, no. You must be confusing me with someone else, madam. Mother who? No, I'm sure we never met." But he took off down the street so fast the skirts of his black frock coat billowed out behind him like a crow's tail.

Fleur tossed her head. "How many devouts can there be with dimples on their butts? Follow him, driver." She stepped into her waiting carriage, calling, "Ta ta, my cherries. Bony chance."

Hyatt did not wait for an invitation, and he did not wait for Campbell to close the doors before dragging Maylene back toward the book room.

"My God," he shouted as soon as they were down the hall. "How could you think of entertaining the likes of her? You might as well rip up Lady Belvedere's invitation, if she doesn't rescind it herself."

Maylene crossed her arms over her suddenly, by comparison, paltry chest. "I should not have to remind you, my lord, that whomever I choose to entertain is no business of yours. No more than your, ah, acquaintances, past or present, are any concern of mine. Now that you have brought it up, though, my lord, is there no woman in all of London that you have not kissed?"

Deuce take it, Socrates thought, did she have to keep reminding him of the liberties he'd taken? He was having enough trouble forgetting, himself. He ran his fingers through his hair, disordering the dark curls. "I knew you'd be throwing that back in my face the minute I saw the blasted female."

"Her name is Mademoiselle Fleur Lafontaine, in case you have forgotten." In case he'd known so many high-flyers, she implied.

Pacing the book room, Hyatt said, "Her name is Florrie

Fountain, and she's one of the most notorious wh—ah, women in London."

And the most successful, Maylene added to herself, watching his long strides wear out the threadbare carpet.

"You do know that she isn't respectable, don't you? Blast it, you're not that much the fool, I swear."

That might have been the closest Lord Hyatt had ever come to a compliment, so Maylene chose to consider it as one. Somewhat mollified, she answered, "I know that Miss Lafontaine has a problem."

"Tell her to take it to Gilly Pimstoke. He's her current protector. Or that attics-to-let apostle outside. Lud knows her soul needs praying for."

Maylene shook her head. "No, she came to my mother and me for help, and I have promised to try to get it for her."

"Zounds, you'd help Napoleon if he had a hangnail, and enough of the ready, wouldn't you?"

Maylene went toward the door, indicating that the interview was over. "You have made your opinions perfectly clear, my lord. Good day."

"No, Miss Treadwell, it has not been a good day." Socrates reached into his coat pocket and extracted the vellum cards. "I spent all morning wheedling these out of Susannah, Lady Belvedere, and now I see they will be wasted. You are intent on ruining your reputation, and mine with it, it appears. Next you'll be having Florrie in to take tea with Lady Crowley, I suppose."

"No one's reputation is going to be injured, Lord Hyatt. Miss Lafontaine has agreed it would be best not to call here again. I can send her a written communication if we discover any answers to her inquiry. She was actually relieved that she need not attend my mother's gatherings. I think she is somewhat afraid of the spiritual aspects."

"More likely she's afraid Gilly Pimstoke will slip her lead if she's gone. The bloke's as rich as Golden Ball." He nodded, then slammed the invitations down on her desk so hard the inkwell teetered and would have fallen if Maylene hadn't caught it. Some of the ink splashed on her fingers. He handed her a handkerchief of softest white linen—with his crest em-

broidered on it. "Then, here. Now you have everything you
want: Mondale's blank check and a passport to the Polite
World. Go and make the most of your opportunities, Miss
Treadwell. I shan't stand in your way if Florrie Fountain won't.
Land yourself an eligible *parti* or take a page from Florrie's
book and hook yourself a wealthy protector. Just let the duke
off your fishing line!"

A protector? He thought she could be a . . . a rich man's mistress? One tiny part of Maylene was gladdened that he thought
she could attract a gentleman; the rest of her was incensed at
Lord high-and-mighty Hyatt's lewd suggestion. She tossed his
handkerchief back in his face, which left a trail of ink down his
cheek and on his immaculate white neckcloth.

"I would have continued to help the duke because he needs
assistance, and that is what I do, my lord. But now I swear I will
move heaven and earth to find his daughter for him and then
I'll . . . I'll see she marries Lord Shimpton instead of you!"

Some days a mother was a girl's best friend. Other times, a
young woman might wish she'd been born under a cabbage
leaf. This was one of those times.

Lady Tremont arrived home in a wondrous mood, not in the
least exhausted by spending the duke's money. Aunt Regina
might need to rest after trying on corsets and such, but the
baroness was full of enthusiasm. And to find a handsome, well-
funded gentleman closeted with her daughter, why, her cup run-
neth over. Luckily, it did not spill on Lord Hyatt, since he was
already oddly mussed, with tousled hair and a black streak
along his cheek. If Campbell had not assured her that there had
been other company during his call, she might have been concerned. Now she was more concerned with keeping him at
Treadwell House, to Maylene's horror.

Lady Tremont invited the earl to stay to tea, meager though
it would be after the priest's depredations. Then she had to exclaim over the invitations to Lady Belvedere's ball, which he'd
been so kind as to bring in person. Everyone knew how busy
his lordship was, with his many interests, so his consideration
was even more gratifying. Had he seen the latest showing at
Somerset House, and did he support the Corn Laws? Had he a

horse entered at Newmarket, and what did he think of shell pink crepe for Maylene?

Maylene thought black would be better, for she was sure to die of embarrassment. Her mother was going on, though, explaining to Hyatt that they'd decided white was too insipid, especially since she wasn't any dreary young miss, and the brighter colors were too strong for Maylene's delicate complexion. Didn't he agree? Maylene's complexion took on the fiery hue of mortification.

"Mama, I am sure his lordship has better things to do than discuss fashions."

"Nonsense, Lord Hyatt is a man of style himself. He can give us excellent advice. Aunt Regina thought the Belgian lace would do for an overskirt, whilst I liked a softer pink netting. Which do you prefer, my lord?"

The fact that her daughter sat silently through the conversation did not bother Lady Tremont one whit. A mother knew what was best for her girl, even if the foolish chit refused to make a push to engage the Ideal's interest. One smile, Maylene's doting parent believed, and Hyatt would lose his heart to her darling. He was more likely to lose his temper, Maylene could swear, since he never seemed to have that emotion under control when she was around. If he shouted at her mother, Maylene vowed to herself, she'd toss the entire inkpot at him. Then the teapot. She frowned, and her mother kicked her ankle as they sat side by side on the sofa.

As if aware of Maylene's threats, Hyatt was being polite, for now. In fact, he seemed to be enjoying himself hugely, at Maylene's expense, of course, for he had to know how uncomfortable Lady Tremont's unsubtleties were making her. Goodness, her mother was being so obvious that Maylene wished she could crawl back under that cabbage leaf. Now Mama was practically begging Lord Hyatt to dance with Maylene at the ball, since she'd know so few gentlemen there.

Hyatt had to agree, since he was drinking their tea and eating their last biscuit. He undoubtedly wanted to keep an eye on her anyway, Maylene supposed, to make certain she didn't entrap any schoolboy into an honorable offer . . . or steal any of Lady Belvedere's knickknacks. Her mother was busy proving their avaricious intents. She was also busy encouraging Hyatt to attend that evening's spirit-calling session.

"But, Mama, you know his lordship does not believe in the beyond."

"Then we shall just have to show him, won't we? I have very good feelings about tonight, my dears. I'm positive Max and Alex will have some answers for us. In fact, my lord, why don't you stay and take pot luck supper with us beforehand?"

Maylene was growing desperate. "But, Mama, you know how you like to relax in solitude before a meeting."

Her ankle got kicked again, for her effort. Much more of this and she would be too lame to dance at the ball, with Hyatt or anyone else.

"And you can play the pianoforte for his lordship while I rest and prepare myself," her mother concluded. "Aunt Regina will be happy to act as chaperone. Isn't that lovely?"

Listening to another amateur performance was about as lovely as a visit to the tooth drawer, and Maylene knew it well. Hyatt's polite refusal was a relief, and an insult, since he claimed a prior engagement for dinner that Maylene did not believe for an instant. He'd be honored to attend the séance, though, dash it.

"Mama, how could you?" Maylene wailed after he left. "The earl despises us. He thinks we are climbers and charlatans. Whatever were you thinking of, to invite him to the sitting, much less to dinner?"

"Grandchildren," was her fond mother's answer.

Chapter Twenty

Expectations sat like another guest at the round table that evening. Tonight, everyone seemed to feel, they would have answers. Even Lord Hyatt was eager, for he'd convinced his friend Mondale to make this the last try at Max, the dearly departed detective—and his dog.

He and Maylene shared the sofa by the hearth again, though she sat so far into her corner that the welting on the cushions was making indentations in her arm. She huddled in her shawls, despite the meager heat from the fireplace, while he lounged at his end of the couch, one midnight blue superfine-clad arm spread across the furniture back, where it could almost touch her bare neck. Maylene made sure not to lean back. He was quiet while Lady Tremont went through her routine of making everyone present swear that what they heard or saw here, stayed here. His fingers only started drumming on the sofa cushions when the baroness began her preliminary chants and swaying motion. Maylene scowled at him, but since she was always scowling at him, he paid her no mind.

Finally, Lady Tremont got down to serious business, greeting her dear friend Max with smiles and coos, then introducing the guests at the table.

"What's that, dear? Alex is there, too? How nice. Good doggy, Alex."

Lord Hyatt groaned. Maylene glared.

"And see who has come to chat with us tonight, dears. You remember Lady Crowley, don't you? She has been most eager to speak to her beloved Aloysius, you know. Just a few words, meant for him alone. Isn't that charming? What did you say, dear?"

Lady Tremont screwed up her forehead in concentration. "'*Sum, es, est, sumus, estis, sunt*'? Whatever is that, Max?"

Everyone at the table except for the duke was mystified. "First term Latin," Hyatt whispered for Maylene's benefit.

"I am not totally ignorant," she snapped back, having provided her mother with the conjugations.

Lady Tremont's brow cleared. "Oh, Lord Crowley is practicing his classics so that he can speak to some of the saints? How enterprising of him, to be sure. Lady Crowley is bound to be disappointed that she did not get to give him her message, but perhaps next time? Yes, I'll tell her to try again."

"And again and again," Hyatt muttered.

But Lady Crowley seemed happy enough with knowing the dastard she'd married was still safely dead. Her unsaid farewells could wait.

"And here is our brave Lieutenant Canfield," Lady Tremont was going on, "who was so concerned about his lost leg. Yes, I think he is looking much stronger now, too."

Canfield did have better color and had put on some weight. He managed his crutches much more skillfully and was a great deal less self-conscious of his missing limb. Aunt Regina had sent him to a prosthetics manufactory, Lord Hyatt had sent him to be interviewed as secretary to a member of Parliament from his home borough, and Maylene had sent him a smile of welcome.

"Speak up, dear, please. We are all concentrating as hard as we might, I am certain, but there seems to be noise in the background again. What's that? We should wave? Oh, waves."

Hyatt cocked his head, listening for the sound of rushing water he expected from the adjoining room. When none was forthcoming, he leaned toward Maylene and whispered, "What, you didn't have time to reroute your indoor plumbing?"

"If we had indoor plumbing, my lord, you can be sure we would use it for baths, not bamming the poor lieutenant."

"Then why the waves?"

Maylene wasn't certain herself. Her mother's imagination, insight, talent, or whatever rarely followed any play script. "Be quiet and listen, for goodness' sake. We might find out."

Lady Tremont's countenance took on a delighted expression.

"He did? Admiral Nelson himself? What an honor for our brave soldier!" She fell back in her chair and her face went blank as she underwent one of her transformations. After a few contortions, which seemed to alarm the Duke of Mondale at her side more than anyone, the baroness sat up again, with her cheeks puffed out and one eye squinted shut.

"What's this I hear," Lady Tremont barked out in a deep, thunderous bellow, "about some sissified soldier whining over his lost leg?"

The lieutenant sat at attention, color brighter than his scarlet uniform creeping up his cheeks.

"You gave it for your country, didn't you, soldier? Then be proud, damn it! You ain't a coward, are you?"

"N-no, sir!"

"Then stop hiding like a craven, worrying over the next life. Get out and live this one, by Harry. Live it for your mates who cannot, I say. You owe it to them, else they died for naught. Understand, soldier?"

"Aye-aye. That is, yes, sir."

"And remember that England needs more brave boys, even if they turn out to be land-lubber infrantrymen. It's your duty, soldier. You can still father children, can't you?"

Now Maylene was blushing as vividly as the lieutenant, who stuttered out an affirmative. Hyatt swallowed his laughter, thinking, damn, but this was better than Drury Lane.

"Humph. Then get on with it, dash it. And that goes for the rest of you niminy-piminy lads at the table, too. Get on with it, I say. Put some wind in your sails, men, that's the ticket!"

Socrates wasn't finding the admiral quite as amusing now. Niminy-piminy? Him? And it was one thing for his own grandmother to urge him to start filling his new nursery. It was quite another for the Hero of Trafalgar and Lady Tremont, to say nothing of her passed-on paramour and his previous pet.

Speaking of dogs, Lord Shimpton was nearly twitching in his seat. "Do you think it is my turn yet?" he whispered to Lady Crowley, whose hand he was squeezing in his excitement. "Lady Tremont said I could ask Mumsy about getting a dog tonight."

The widow rubbed her bruised fingers. "As soon as Lady

Tremont recovers. It takes great energy to connect with the spirits."

The baroness was drained, sagging against her chair back. Campbell offered a glass of water, and the duke, on her other side, was calling for smelling salts and the end of the session.

"I shall be fine," Lady Tremont claimed in a reedy voice, sipping the water. "And we have much too much to accomplish, to waste dear Max's visit. You are still with us, my dearest, aren't you?" Her eyes drifted shut, and she started rocking in her seat. Slowly, a smile came over her face, softening its contours, removing the signs of strain and ten years. "Ah, yes, Max, there you are. I am well, don't worry. Do you see who else has come to visit this evening, my dear? It's our good friend Lord Shimpton, come to chat with his beloved mother. What's that, Max? Lady Shimpton cannot speak to us this evening?"

"Mumsy? Is she ill?"

"Someone should tell the cawker she's dead," Hyatt murmured for Maylene's hearing only. The curls ruffled by the closeness of his breath tickled her ear, but she was tucked as far into the corner of the couch as she could go.

"You must be quiet or you will destroy Mother's concentration," she said. Heaven knew he was destroying hers.

"What's that, dear, she is practicing her Latin also?"

"Mumsy?"

"Oh, she's performing a cotillion! How lovely. Oh? She wishes to make sure her precious Frederick dances it at Lady Belvedere's ball? I'll tell him. And Maylene will teach him."

Maylene groaned as loudly as Lord Shimpton. He was more concerned with his mother's opinion than Maylene's toes, however. "But what about m'dog? I wanted to ask Mumsy what kind I should get!"

"Did you hear that, Max? The dear young man needs advice. Yes, I suppose Alex would know best, if you don't mind asking him." Lady Tremont tilted her head to one side, listening. "No, dear, I cannot understand the barking. Oh, Alex says he smells water? That's all he says? You're sure? What has that got to do with the proper dog for Lord Shimpton?"

Lieutenant Canfield offered the information that there had been a breed of water spaniel in Portugal. And the duke had heard that fishermen in the Canadian provinces used black retrievers to bring in their nets.

"Perhaps he's still getting Admiral Nelson's scent," Lady Crowley suggested. "I recall the one time I was on a sailing ship and thought I would never get the smell of dampness out of my clothing."

Hyatt was more cynical, naturally. "What, are you sending your suitor off on a wild-goose chase—or should I say wild-pooch chase—now that you have Canfield in your sights? I suppose you own shares of a shipping line."

"You know we own nothing of the kind," Maylene said, taking notes of the possible interpretations. "I am as confused as everyone else about the meaning, but that is the way the spirit world operates, you know. Oracles give useful answers, but not necessarily obvious information."

"Fustian. It's raining out, is all. It doesn't take a fried flea hound to smell what passes for spring showers in London."

No, that was Lord Shimpton.

Lady Tremont was continuing. "Well, perhaps Lady Shimpton will come chat with us again another time and we can ask her then. I am positive she knows just the perfect breed of doggy for her darling son. Meanwhile, Max, dear, do you recall our search for that young man, Mr. Joshua Collins?" A moment went by. "Alex smells water? Yes, dear, you already told us that. Lord Nelson has come and gone. But were you able to reach Winslowe? The missing gentleman is his heir, after all, so Winslowe should know his whereabouts. Oh, he never cared for that branch of the family? So he doesn't mind if the estate goes to the Evangelical Association Church of Repentance?"

Maylene minded that the reward money would go to them, too. She tried to signal her mother to try harder. "Do you hear music, Mama?"

"No music. Only water."

Maylene muttered, "Bother."

Her mother frowned. "Let us go on to the next guest, Max, dear. His Grace of Mondale is here again, even more concerned for his missing daughter. Have you or Alex managed to gain a clue as to Lady Belinda's location?"

Everyone held their breath while Lady Tremont listened.

They all exhaled on a sigh when she said, "Yes, dear, I know Alex smells water. That's all?"

The duke let go of the baroness's hand to wipe at his eyes. "I'll never find her now. My girl is gone."

In a firmer tone than she'd used before, Lady Tremont addressed the afterworld. "You know, dear, perhaps you should not be relying so heavily on Alex's assistance. When all is said and done, he is still a mere dog. What? Yes, I know he ran into that burning building to save your life, but even you must admit that was not terribly clever. Loyal, yes, but intelligent? No. Alex was a small dog. How could he have rescued you? If he could have carried his precious water, then . . . No, dear, I am not criticizing your dear doggy. Please do think about Lady Belinda though. Were you able to make contact with her mother?"

The duke lifted his head again. "Minty?"

"I see. She was sleeping peacefully, and you hated to disturb her. I doubt she'd be resting so comfortably were her daughter in peril, so that is something, Max. Thank you, dear. His Grace will take solace from that, at least. But can we try again, do you suppose? His Grace brought a pair of Lady Belinda's gloves and a stocking, so Alex might pick up her trail, as you suggested last time." Lady Tremont spread them on the table in front of her, then waved one of the gloves in the air. Then she sighed. "Yes, I know. Alex smells water."

The duke gathered his daughter's belongings and clutched them to his chest. They could all see that years of keeping his emotions in check were all that was keeping him from collapsing entirely. Hyatt swore, next to Maylene.

"Her friends are bound to know something," she said loudly enough for the duke to hear, hoping to give His Grace some reassurance. Max might have given up, but Maylene had not.

Lady Tremont nodded. "And who knows? Perhaps Max will think of something next time."

"There will not be a next time if I have any say," Hyatt told Maylene. "Can't you see what this is doing to Mondale? How can you be so cruel?"

"As cruel as giving him no hope at all? As sitting back and waiting for Lady Belinda to waltz in the door herself? I told you, my lord, this is not an exact science, with guaranteed results. His Grace knew that and was willing to chance having his hopes dashed. But Mama still seems convinced that the girl is not in peril."

Her mother, he thought to himself, was also convinced that she'd been chatting with an immortal mutt.

She was smiling again in that softer way reserved for Max. "We have one last inquiry tonight, dear. This is a complicated situation that needs your assistance. Nine years ago an infant was put out for adoption. His name was Francis. Yes, I know the new family would have changed it; that's why we need your help. You could track the boy down for us. You see, his true mother wants to make sure he is well provided for." Lady Tremont opened her eyes to look at each of the guests at her round table. "Let us all imagine the anguish of a young woman, forced to part with her flesh and blood, thinking she was doing the best for her child. But a mother never stops loving her babies." She glanced toward Mondale. "Nor a father, either, I suppose. In any case, the dear mother is now in a position to help her boy if he needs it, to smooth his way in life as no one helped smooth hers. Think about her search, my friends, and focus your mental energies on Mademoiselle Lafontaine, so Max can guide us to her son."

Try as she might, the only mental picture Maylene had was of Fleur's jewel-draped décolletage. Heaven knew what Hyatt pictured, but he was smiling.

After a minute more of silent concentration, Lady Tremont wiped a tear from her cheek. "Such an affecting story, don't you think, Max? Can you help? What's that, dear? Alex smells water? Bah!"

Chapter Twenty-one

Never doubt a good dog's nose. Alex just might have had more bravery than brains, more grit than gray matter, when he tore into that fire after his master, but he could smell water.

Lady Belinda was not aboard a ship of white slavers, as her father feared, but she could hear the waves washing ashore from her room at the humble inn outside Brighton.

Joshua Collins, meanwhile, was being soaked by his wife's tears as he lay on his sickbed, barely conscious of the basin of water she was using to bathe his fevered brow. Her wedding ring was all she had left to sell now, to pay for his care. "You have to recover, Josh, you simply have to. I couldn't live without you. Why, I'll throw myself into the ocean if you die, see if I won't."

As for Lord Shimpton and his search for the perfect dog . . . he spent the entire next morning trying to find members of the new Kennel Association, to ask about water dogs. In the afternoon, he was promised to Lord Hyatt, to see about a carriage and horses. Hyatt was annoyed he'd agreed to bear-lead the bone-head, and Shimpton was terrified of the imposing earl. Thankfully, the transaction at Tattersall's took no time at all, for Sir Howard Whitten had overplayed his last hand the evening before, and was down to his last shilling. Hyatt got to spend less time in the chinless clodpole's company, and Shimpton got a yellow-wheeled landau, two highbred bays, and the unemployed driver, for a song. Frederick thought his mother would be proud.

Shimpton also thought he'd drive round to Treadwell House to invite the ladies for a spin. Now that he had the carriage, perhaps Lady Tremont and Miss Treadwell would put their minds to finding him a bride. Acquiring the carriage had been easy as pie, the viscount told himself. How hard could it be to acquire a wife?

Harrison, the new driver, though, advised him that the horses were too fresh for a sedate stroll through the park. After standing so long, they needed to run before facing city traffic. So Shimpton agreed to ride out along the Richmond road for a bit before calling on the ladies. He quite enjoyed having eyes follow his handsome equipage as they left London behind. Of course, he'd be more pleased to have a companion sitting beside him on the burgundy leather seats—a four-footed companion.

Once they left the metropolis, traffic grew thinner, and no one was around to admire the landau and its new owner. The scenery grew boring, one tree looking very much like another, and the back of Harrison's hat was even less entertaining. Shimpton thought he'd take the reins. Harrison scratched his head. He'd been hired on to drive the bays and see they were groomed proper-like. That swell Lord Hyatt had made sure he understood. But the toff hadn't said anything about handing the ribbons over to any flap-eared flat in a puce waistcoat. Then again, the coxcomb was paying Harrison's salary; the Corinthian wasn't. "Can you drive, m'lord?"

"Of course. All gentlemen can drive. It's in the blood, don't you know?"

Harrison knew the nobs' blue blood was so thin they had to keep their snoots elevated so they didn't have nosebleeds all the time. He pulled up at a small inn and waited for his employer to climb up to the bench. Then he got down. He might be crazy to hand over the bays, but he wasn't stupid enough to put his own neck on the same line. "I'll wait here, m'lord, and order yer nuncheon."

"Food? Excellent, idea, Harrison. Wouldn't have thought of it m'self. I can see we'll rub along fine. You do like dogs, don't you?"

For lunch? Harrison tugged his cap, slapped the nearest rump, and headed into the inn.

Now this was more like, Shimpton thought, as the bays stepped out smartly. The breeze ruffled his neckcloth and a

dairy maid waved to him. As he guided the horses around a corner, though, waving back gaily, he realized the girl hadn't been
waving her greetings; she'd been warning him that her cows
were coming behind her along the road. Shimpton tried to slow
his cattle. Unused to his hand on the reins, the bays did not re-
spond, so Shimpton tried to pull them over to the side of the
road. But the breeze caught the end of his poorly tied cravat and
flapped a square of linen in his face. Shimpton jerked on the
ribbons. The cows were getting closer. The horses whinnied.
Shimpton whimpered. The landau's wheels ran off the roadway.

The uneven terrain unnerved the frightened bays even more,
so they thought they'd run away from it. Then one wheel hit a
rock. The landau tilted, tottered, then tipped Shimpton right out
into the ditch at the side of the road. The horses kept going.

With all the rain they'd been having, the ditch was half filled
with water—murky, muddy water, not improved by the cows'
passing. Even Lord Shimpton realized this immersion did not
count as his monthly bath. He tried to pull himself up, but the
steep banks were slippery, and his boots were filled with muck,
so he kept sliding back down into the thigh-high water.

What would his mother do? Shimpton wondered, sitting in
the ditch. She'd yell at him to stop being a nodcock, that was
for sure. He tried to consider what Lord Hyatt would do, but
could not quite imagine that out-and-outer ditching his carriage, much less appearing in his dirt, and that of Richmond.
The incident in the park had to have been a freak accident, undoubtedly Miss Treadwell's fault. So he decided to take Lady
Crowley as his example. She never seemed to give up nor to
lose her composure. She wasn't impatient with him, either, unlike Miss Treadwell, who was so competent she'd likely build
herself a flying machine to get out of the ditch. Lady Crowley
would just keep on, the way she did when that husband of hers
never came to talk with her at Lady Tremont's. Inspired, he decided that he'd walk back to the inn, in the ditch, once he figured out which direction to take.

After he'd waded for a bit, though, the viscount heard a piti-
ful whimpering. It wasn't coming from him, he was sure, so he
looked around. And there, on a half-submerged rock, shivering
and sodden, clinging with its last ounce of strength, was his

dog! Alex had said he smelled water, and here was water, smelly at that. And here was the most pathetic little creature on earth, waiting for him, Frederick, Lord Shimpton. No other being had ever needed him, no other life had ever depended on him. Shimpton reached out and lifted the tiny infant animal, then tucked it under his own wet coat, babbling words of comfort. He used the rock to boost himself out of the ditch, the sooner to reach the inn and warmth for his new friend.

As he trudged the last few yards, he rejoiced. The spirits hadn't lied! Lady Tremont and Max had to be smarter than anyone he'd ever known, wiser even than Mumsy. "I'll call you Neptune," he told the wee beastie that trembled against his chest. "The god of water—at least I think he was. Miss Treadwell will know. But you won't care, will you, Neptune, now that you've got me to care for you?"

And Lord Shimpton's new dog, Neptune, agreed in the only way he knew how. He meowed.

Once he'd seen the simpleton Shimpton off in his new rig and checked on the repairs to his own curricle, Lord Hyatt met up with Mondale. It was all he could do to keep the duke from heading down to the docks to question everyone he could find about recent sailings of the brigand brotherhood.

"You cannot believe that claptrap about water, can you?" Hyatt asked. "Granted the lady did a masterful job with Nelson, but to suppose that a dog that's been dead for over ten years can sniff out a young woman on a merchant ship is preposterous."

"Preposterous, but I have nowhere else to turn. The Runners have no new reports, and the longer their search takes, the colder the trail."

Hyatt couldn't argue with the duke's reasoning, only his results. "Perhaps Miss Treadwell will be able to gather a few more hints from Belinda's friends."

"Ah, then you have come around to thinking the young woman might be helpful after all."

"One or two of her ideas seemed reasonable," the earl conceded. "I still think she is a conniver and an adventuress, but, yes, she might turn up some information the Runners have missed."

"And you'll help her get close to the gels at the Belvedere do?"

Hyatt nodded. That chore could not be much worse than towing Shimpton through Tattersall's.

"Good, good. And don't look so downpin about it. I'm sure you'll find the baroness and her daughter as delightful as I do if you stop looking for chicanery. They are kind, caring women, Soc, if you could but see it. And deuced attractive, too, both of them. You hadn't used to be so cynical."

He hadn't used to be conversing with dead dogs, either.

Leaving the duke to his cabinet work, Hyatt decided to visit the jewelers, to buy a parting gift for Aurora Ashford. He hadn't been to call on her, hadn't invited her to meet him at his Kensington hideaway, and hadn't missed her at all. Obviously her charms had palled on him, so it was time to let her find another lover, if she hadn't already. He'd stop in at Drury Lane's Green Room to find a replacement mistress, he supposed, as soon as he got around to it. There was no hurry. Perhaps his concern for Belinda had dulled his appetites for other women. Something had. Socrates refused to consider that that something might be a prickly spinster with a poodle's topknot and a card shark's conscience.

Diamonds for the dashing widow, of course. Hyatt nodded at the first tray of bracelets the shop owner showed him. The most expensive of them would be cheap, if it saved him a scene of tearful recriminations. He took the cowardly way out and signed the back of one of his cards, for the messenger to deliver along with the gift. As he turned to leave the shop, a strand of pearls on one of the counters caught his eye. They were small but perfectly matched pearls, with coral beads separating each, and a coral and diamond chip fastener. They'd look lovely, his treacherous mind whispered, with shell pink crepe.

He doubted the silly baggage had any jewels to wear to the Belvederes'. She'd have had them on the night they all came for dinner, he reasoned. A duke, an earl, and a viscount surely demanded a female's finest folderols, even if the duke was nearly old enough to be her father, the earl was nearly engaged, and the viscount was nearly as bright as a green bean. And the duke was correct: Miss Treadwell ought to have some finery for the ball so no one would question her right to be there. Socrates knew he couldn't purchase the pearls for her, of course. Oh, he could present her with a filigree flower holder, a fan, or some other trifle, but nothing more, not without setting the cat among the pigeons. But the duke could. Mondale was going to escort the Treadwell ladies as an old friend of the family, and as such he could give the daughter of the house a birthday present, belated or early. His Grace would be pleased to reward Maylene for her efforts on his behalf, and he seemed to like the chit, besides.

Did Mondale like her too much? Socrates wondered, letting the pearls sift through his fingers. Could His Grace be thinking of marrying again, a younger woman who might still give him the son and heir he never had? Socrates felt as if he'd been punched in the stomach—worrying about his friend, of course. Jupiter, what a dance the minx would lead him! But no, Mondale was no fool, even if he was half convinced Lady Tremont had some influence with the afterworld. He was merely concerned with getting his daughter back, Socrates told himself.

He had the clerk wrap the pearls and send the bill to Mondale, then he picked out a pretty fan with mother-of-pearl inlay on the sticks. Hyatt decided he'd sign Shimpton's name to the flowers he'd select for the ladies, for the whopstraw would never think to do it. Satisfied, Socrates left the shop, whistling. Now he wouldn't be embarrassed to be seen dancing with the chit.

With all of the investigations they were undertaking, and all the preparations for their attendance at the ball, Maylene had to make lists of her lists. Her mother and her great-aunt were out shopping again, taking Nora to help with the selections. Campbell's nephews were out checking with shipping offices, in case Mondale's Bow Street Runners had missed something. His Grace had provided a miniature for them to carry, in hopes someone would recall such a pretty young woman.

Lady Belinda was so pretty, Maylene thought, no one would ever forget her, especially no one destined to be her husband. She compared the heiress's features to her own wayward curls—the combs never stayed where Monsieur Vincente said they should go—and her not quite straight nose. And her all too straight chest.

Lady Belinda might be near water, but Maylene was drowning in self-pity. She decided to go for a walk.

Chapter Twenty-two

Deuce take it, did the wretched female never have a care for her own reputation? There she was, strolling down Oxford Street, merry as a grig, with neither maid nor footman in attendance. Hyatt recognized Miss Treadwell's outdated straw bonnet instantly, and the way she carried her head, as if eager for life's next surprise. Yes, his pearls would suit her—Mondale's pearls, of course.

Socrates would have kept going on his way to his sparring match, but Miss Treadwell turned down the next corner. It was one thing for her to wander alone through the busy streets where she might be subject to rude stares and lewd suggestions. Only her reputation would be damaged. But for her to venture down narrow, less populated avenues was foolish beyond permission. His hands clenched into fists at his side, just thinking of some varlet waylaying the silly chit in an alley. Dash it, if Miss Maylene was going to be insulted, accosted, and manhandled, he was the man who was going to do it, none else.

He crossed the street and followed her, calling out as she paused in front of a doorway to check the number against a piece of paper in her hand. Another of her infernal notes, Hyatt supposed. Why couldn't she be at home with her embroidery like every other wellborn woman? Then again, Belinda wasn't sitting with her tatting either.

"Miss Treadwell, good afternoon."

Maylene hadn't been walking fast; why, then, was she suddenly out of breath? Not because of his lordship, of course. She'd seen many more attractive men this morning, well, one or two, she supposed. Most were dressed in the same biscuit pantaloons and midnight superfine, though few of the Bond

Street strollers could match Hyatt's broad shoulders or raffish tilt to his beaver hat. Few of them had looked at her as if she'd crawled out from under a rock, either. She curtsied, offering a reluctant, "Good day to you, too, my lord."

Hyatt pretended to look back and forth along the narrow street."Odd, I did not see your maid duck into one of these closed doors, but she must have, mustn't she?"

Maylene sighed. Of course his lordship would have to be at hand when she was bending Society's strictures. He was right to find fault, however, only if her behavior was any concern of his. It was not.

"Oh, my maid twisted her ankle," she fabricated. "Since I had a mere few more blocks to go on my errand, I left her on a bench outside the lending library."

Hyatt could not picture Miss Treadwell leaving an injured servant to suffer while she traipsed about Town.

"Oh, she was not badly injured. Nora merely needed a rest."

"Nora? Isn't she your mother's dresser? The iron-haired woman with the rheumatics in her joints? I could swear I passed her in Bond Street not twenty minutes ago, along with your mother and Mrs. Howard."

"Yes, well, I have an appointment, my lord. If you'll excuse me?"

"No."

"Pardon? I thought you said no, you would not excuse me."

"For once you heard right, Miss Treadwell. With any luck you will even understand. I cannot in good conscience leave a gently bred female alone on the streets of London. Who knows if whatever befell Belinda is still at large, to say nothing of the average cutpurse or footpad."

His jaw was clenched; he was not going to be budged. Maylene inclined her head. "Very well, you may accompany me, although such a sacrifice on your part is entirely unnecessary, I am sure." She opened the door without knocking and stepped into a cluttered hallway filled with desks, filing cabinets, and clerks at long tables. "You can wait here in the outer office."

He followed her right past the senior clerk, who pointed toward one of the younger men to escort her to Mr. Ryan's office.

Maylene glared at him over her shoulder, but he came in with her anyway.

Maylene made the introductions, for there was nothing else to do without creating a commotion. Hyatt nodded briefly, then took up a stance behind Maylene's chair, his arms folded across his chest. Ryan's Adam's apple bobbed a few times, but he politely offered wine or tea. Maylene refused both, for both of them. If Hyatt was thirsty, let him go to a coffeehouse or one of his clubs.

"I've come, Mr. Ryan, to tell you about last evening's findings." She could hear Hyatt snort in the background.

"You found something?" Ryan's watery eyes took on a shine that rivaled the oiled gleam of his hair.

"We feel that Mr. Collins might be near a body of water."

"We . . . ? Your lordship?"

"*We* believe nothing of the kind. For all I know your man might be at sea in a canoe or on the back of a camel in the Sahara. Lady Tremont's ghostly friend's dog smelled water, that's all."

If he were a papist, Mr. Ryan would have crossed himself. If Maylene had a cross, she would have put it through the dastard earl's heart. "It's a clue, merely, Mr. Ryan. Have you checked with the shipping offices for the passenger lists as well as the crew rosters?"

"We checked all of the boardings. The man is a violinist, Miss Treadwell, a music instructor. He would not have signed on as a common seaman, no matter what difficulties arose, though we would have heard about any untoward incidents in Bath."

"Is it possible a press gang was working anywhere near his last position?" she asked, dreading the thought of a sensitive artist aboard one of His Majesty's warships.

"In Bath? That's highly doubtful."

"But you said he'd left Bath, given notice. He must have made plans to go elsewhere, then. He simply did not arrive at his destination."

Ryan jotted down a note. "I'll make inquiries with the Navy, although those gentlemen are not very forthcoming. Are you sure Lady Tremont could not identify the music she heard last time? That sounded promising."

"No, I am sorry. The water is all she mentioned."

"Will she be trying again tonight?" the solicitor wanted to know. "We are running out of time."

Maylene stood and could sense Hyatt stirring right behind her. "No, I'm sorry, but the sessions are too exhausting for my mother to conduct with such frequency." And they were too aggravating when Max did not cooperate. "She needs to rest in between."

"In the Bond Street shops," the earl added helpfully. Maylene stepped back, hoping to make contact with his toes, but he'd moved closer to the door. She took a few steps in that direction, saying, "I will be sure to let you know if we—" She clapped her hand to her forehead and swayed on her feet. "Oh, I think I am going to —"

She did. Maylene swooned, right into Hyatt's arms. He caught her up and carried her back to the chair, where she lolled, limp. He started chafing her hands. "Dash it, Maylene, wake up!"

Ryan was wringing his hands. "What shall I do? Send for your carriage? Fetch her maid?"

Since neither of those helpful items was in the vicinity, Hyatt kept rubbing her hands and cursing. "Look in her reticule, man. Maybe she carries smelling salts like any respectable female." He tossed the solicitor her netted purse.

"Oh, I couldn't search her personal possessions!"

"Devil take it, give it back, then." Hyatt made to grab for the strings, but Maylene's eyelids fluttered.

"Water," she croaked.

"If you are playing Lord Nelson again," Hyatt shouted at her, "I'll wring your blasted neck!"

Maylene licked her dry lips. "Water, please."

"I'll go. Right away. Back in a flash." Ryan dashed out of the office. As soon as he was gone, Maylene brushed off Hyatt's hands and jumped to her feet, hurrying to shut the door.

"What the deuce?"

Maylene was already at the standing files at the back of Ryan's office, opening drawers and checking contents.

"Braverman, Byron. I wonder if that's . . . ? Eggerton, East-wood, Ah, Ladelow, Lafayette, Lagenthorpe. Oh, rats!"

"What the devil is going on? You could be arrested for what-ever it is you're doing—and me along with you!"

"I didn't invite you here, my lord, recall, so you can leave now." She continued riffling through the folders, muttering words no lady ought to know, much less use.

Socrates grabbed her shoulders to pull her away from the file cabinets, but she broke away to look through Ryan's drawers. "Good God, woman, have you no scruples at all?"

"Yes, and they tell me to help Fleur Lafontaine assuage her guilt at abandoning her baby. I'm not going to steal the child back, for goodness sake, only make some inquiries that would let her improve his lot in life. All I need is a name, but the records must be so old they are kept in the outer office, drat it."

She was about to sag back into the seat, defeated, when the earl said, "Try Fountain—Florrie Fountain."

She gave him a grin like the sun peeking from behind a mountain at daybreak on a spring day—after a long winter. "Foggarty, Foote, Forman. Yes! Fountain!" She glanced quickly at the top page. "Here, write this down."

"What, carry evidence that we tampered with the files? Don't be more of a peagoose than you must be. Read it and memorize the damn thing before Ryan gets back."

"You are right, of course," she told him, flashing another dazzling smile. "It's Macaleer, in Hans Town." With that, she shut the drawer, turned, and threw herself back into Hyatt's arms.

"Bloody hell," he cursed, then heard Ryan at the door. "She thought she was recovered and stood too soon. Here, give me the water."

"Oh, my," Ryan said as Maylene coughed and sputtered. "I thought she wanted to drink it."

By the time Hyatt hired a hackney and returned Miss Tread-well to Curzon Street, Maylene had recovered from her pique. Her hat never would. Neither would Socrates.

He sat opposite her in the carriage, arms crossed over his chest as he watched her fluff her curls and dab at her damp

neckline. Damn, he thought, the little fool had no idea what notions such actions could provoke in a man. And he was a bigger fool for having the notions. "You are totally without
principles and utterly incorrigible, Miss Treadwell. You have
betrayed that man's trust and forced me into committing dishonorable acts in order to protect your reputation."

"And you were brilliant. Thank you."

She sent him another of those sunshine smiles, the kind that
had to warm the coldest heart, he decided. So what if he was
the biggest fool in kingdom come? He smiled back. "I was,
wasn't I?"

"Definitely. Now all I have to do is check parish records for
Hans Town and have Campbell's nephews ask some questions
of neighbors' servants. We'll know in a few days if young Francis Fountain, or whatever the Macaleers call him, is in need of
his mother's assistance."

"And if he is not, will you still let Florrie go disrupt their
lives? Perhaps they don't want him to know he's not their flesh
and blood. Or that his mother is a light-skirt."

"I think that if the little boy seems content with his life, then
I will speak to the Macaleers and ask their preferences before
giving Miss Lafontaine their direction. That seems fair, don't
you think?"

"You are actually asking me, Miss Treadwell? Now *I* might
swoon."

When they reached Treadwell House, more in charity with
each other than they'd been since their first introduction, Maylene invited the earl in for tea.

As he followed her to the parlor, Hyatt asked, "What, your
private preacher hasn't eaten everything up?"

"Oh, Florrie—Miss Lafontaine, that is—frightened him off.
He didn't mind damaging our reputations, but his own was a
different matter. I only wish I'd had a chance to ask him the
name of his church."

"Good grief, never tell me you are thinking of joining his
congregation?"

"No, just an odd thought I had."

Lady Tremont and her aunt were already sitting around the
tea service. Maylene rang for fresh hot water while she listened

to them itemize their purchases. "What a lovely afternoon you missed, dear," her mother said. "And you also missed Lord Shimpton with his new pet."

Maylene reached for the plate of lemon tarts, to offer them to Hyatt. "Ah, he found a dog, then?"

"Not exactly." Lady Tremont recounted Shimpton's tale while Aunt Regina sat chortling.

"Do you really think he couldn't tell the difference? Not even Shimpton could be so buffle-headed, could he?"

The earl was carefully considering her questions, but Lady Tremont answered, "Oh, no, he knew it was a cat. A pretty little tortoiseshell kitten, now that it's clean and dry. But he swears he was fated to rescue the little mite, that Max and Alex foretold it and led his footsteps right to the tiny creature."

"And you should see him carry on with it," Aunt Regina added. "He wears the cat around his neck like a boa, saying he's going to start a new fashion. Now that I think of it, I had an ermine tippet once, with little glass eyes. I haven't seen it this age."

"It was a horrid weasel, and the moths got to it." Lady Tremont shuddered in remembrance.

Aunt Regina shrugged her padded shoulders. "At least it hides his weak chin."

"Perhaps there is a divine plan after all." Hyatt was smiling.

Lady Tremont was not. "You also missed Lieutenant Canfield, Maylene. He came to bid us farewell. He is returning to his family's home in Hampshire."

"How nice for him, Mama."

"Nice?" Lady Tremont was looking at her daughter the same way she used to when a much younger Maylene tore her petticoats. "He is going home to make an offer for his childhood sweetheart. He was so impressed with the dear admiral's words that he has decided to put his luck to the test."

"And I am sure he'll succeed," Maylene said. "A girl would have to be attics-to-let to let him get away."

Her mother might have been eating sour lemons instead of lemon tarts. "That's precisely my thinking. Why, with a little encouragement you could have—"

"But let me tell you our news, Mama, Aunt Regina. Lord Hyatt and I have accomplished a great deal today."

The earl and Maylene were smiling at each other, Lady Tremont noted. Now *that* was a great accomplishment, indeed. Miss Lafontaine's son could cross his own bridges.

Little Frankie Macaleer was not crossing any bridges, however. He was crossing the Atlantic Ocean.

Chapter Twenty-three

Fleur shed a few tears. She blotted at her darkened eyes with a tiny scrap of lace-edged lawn.

Maylene shed more. Hyatt handed her his monogrammed handkerchief.

Fleur's perfect complexion stayed unblemished; Maylene's cheeks turned all splotchy, her eyes red and swollen. Hyatt felt his own throat grow raw at seeing her tears.

"I thought you'd be pleased that the boy is well cared for and doesn't need anything, Florrie," he said.

"But it's the end of the world he's going to. I'll never get to see him."

Socrates refrained from saying that she'd made that choice nine years ago. "It sounds like a great opportunity for his father, to manage a sugar plantation in Jamaica."

"And the neighbors said the whole family was excited to be going," Maylene added. "Especially little Frankie and his sister."

"To think my boy has a sister," Fleur sobbed. "Why, it's almost as if I lost two babies."

Lord Hyatt had insisted on accompanying Maylene to Miss Lafontaine's little row house on the outskirts of Town. A ladybird's love nest was no place for a lady, but for Miss Treadwell to be meeting Florrie in public would have been worse. Now he was sorry he'd come. The place was respectable enough, neat and uncluttered, with no signs of Florrie's latest protector. And the women were weeping over good news. "Dash it, Florrie, you should be happy the boy doesn't need your blunt. He's never wanted for anything, and won't, if the father is as ambitious and hardworking as the local curate reported."

His words did not seem to comfort the flame-haired woman, for she cried louder. "Now that I've got the brass, it's too late to do any good with it."

Maylene blew her nose. Hyatt should have been disgusted at her sniveling and her flushed face. He wasn't. He wanted to comfort her—in his arms. Lud, where had that thought come from? He should be admiring the high-flyer's still stunning looks, rather than Miss Treadwell's high color.

"It's never too late to do good," she was saying now. "Why don't you take the money that you would have given to Frankie and donate it to a worthy cause? I know of a deserving charity."

She knew of an ugly Chinese urn. Socrates suddenly decided Miss Treadwell's eyes were shifty and her face was spotty. And she had that same revolting drip at the end of her nose as that makebait cousin, Tremont. She must have manufactured those tears the same way her mother scripted her conversations with the deceased. Damn her for being the Devil's handmaiden.

"There is an orphans' home in Bloomsbury, " Maylene continued, explaining to Fleur, "where my mother and I read to the children once a week. The orphans never have enough food or warm clothes, and they get almost no education. We do what we can, but it is a pittance compared to what the boys and girls need."

Hyatt sighed. Miss Treadwell was an angel. And she was beautiful, inside and out. Swollen face, squinty eyes, shaky morals and all—she was the most beautiful woman he'd ever seen.

"Orphanages are dreadful," Fleur agreed. "That's why I made sure my boy was going to be adopted, going to the solicitors all legal-like. I never wanted him to land in a place like that."

"But not every child can be as fortunate as Frankie—Francis—in his mother or in his adoptive parents."

"You're right, Miss Treadwell, and I'll do just what you say. I'll make me a generous donation in my baby's name. Aye, and get Gilly to cough up some blunt, too. He's likely fathered a few of the poor bastards himself in the orphans' asylum, so he'd ought. If I contribute enough of the ready, maybe they'll let me visit with the nippers, despite my, ah, profession."

Maylene was sure they would. "I'll speak to Matron for you.

Or you could come with Mother and me at nine of the clock on Tuesday morning."

Hyatt coughed. "I doubt Miss Lafontaine rises so early."

Maylene blushed, adding even more color to her reddened face. "You will be welcome whenever you choose to visit, mademoiselle. And here," she said, pushing forward the leather wallet that Fleur had paid her in reward money. "Add this to your donation."

"No, lovey, I can't do that. You earned it, fair and square. I asked you to find the boy and find him you did."

"But the children at the orphanage need the money much more than I do."

Fleur eyed her guest's worn gloves and unadorned gown. She wasn't so sure. It was going to take more than a fashionable crop and angel blue eyes to win the likes of the Ideal. She pushed the wallet back across the low table between them. "But you can help teach the tykes their letters, and I'd never be able to do that."

"And I'll add my donation to Florrie's so they won't miss yours, Miss Treadwell," the earl said, which caused Maylene to cry some more.

"You're a good girl, miss, and a real lady," Fleur told her. "And you deserve something special for the favor you've done me, and all those others you've helped. No, I don't mean more blunt." She held up her hand when Maylene would have protested. "Something just for you." Fleur reached up and lifted a necklace over her head and held it out to Maylene.

Now Socrates felt like crying. The pearls were bigger and longer than the ones he'd handed Mondale to give her.

"Oh, I couldn't," Maylene said.

"Of course you can, lovey. Gilly hates me to wear them anyway because another gent gave them to me."

Maylene looked over to the earl, who nodded. Then she put the pearls on, and Fleur led her to the mantelplace mirror to admire them. Socrates thought they looked absurd on the dull-as-ditchwater dress, with her face all tear-stained and her nose shining, but what he said was, "Exquisite."

Maylene spun around and embraced Fleur in a hug. Fleur

kissed her cheek. "Go on now, ducks, afore you make me all weepy-eyed again."

Then, in her excitement, Maylene turned and hugged Hyatt, too. He meant to kiss her cheek, and she meant to thank him for his support. Instead, their lips met—and stayed that way until Miss Lafontaine cleared her throat.

Florrie wondered what would have happened if she'd given the chit diamonds.

"I am sorry," Socrates said as soon as they were back in his open carriage, Jem Groom driving his chestnuts. He was not sorry at all.

Maylene did not pretend to misunderstand. She could feel the blush starting at her toes, which had barely stopped tingling from the pressure of his kiss. It was all she could do not to reach up and touch her lips in wonder. "No, do not apologize, my lord. It is I who must beg your pardon. Why, I practically threw myself at you. You were only . . . only reacting."

"Dash it, I am a grown man in control of my emotions, not an unlicked cub overcome by lust."

And she was a grown woman who eschewed emotions in favor of logic and reason. Yet they had shared a kiss—in front of a courtesan—that could have lit a fire in Florrie's hearth. "I am equally to blame, so let us forget that anything happened." She might forget her own name, sooner.

"But you still persist in thinking that I go around kissing every woman in sight, innocents as well as those in the muslin trade. As a matter of record, Miss Treadwell, I do not as a rule take liberties with young ladies, and Florrie and I were never lovers."

She stared straight ahead at the driver's back, wondering if he could hear their conversation and what he thought of it. "Please do not go on, Lord Hyatt," she said, before their words were bandied about the Running Footman or some other pub frequented by the serving class. "You do not need to explain."

Socrates did not *need* to explain; he wanted to. "Florrie was, ah, keeping company with a close acquaintance of mine. We became friends, that's all."

"I'm sure it is none of my business, my lord." The news was certainly giving her pleasure, nevertheless, for some reason.

"And that's another thing, all the 'my lord this' and 'Lord Hyatt that.' Blast, I cannot keep calling you Miss Treadwell if I am going to keep kissing you, Maylene."

Devil take the driver. "Are you, my lord?"

"Socrates. Or Soc."

"Are you, Soc?"

He was staring at her mouth, savoring the sound of his name on her lips. "Am I what?"

"Going to keep kissing me?"

"Heaven help me, it seems I have no choice." He leaned across the carriage toward her. Maylene closed her eyes and licked her lips.

"Curzon Street, m'lord," the driver called out. Then he muttered, "And not a minute too soon, neither."

As soon as the earl handed Maylene down from the carriage, an urchin ran up and handed them a printed page. *Repent,* it read. *Sin lives in Curzon Street. Raising the dead is the Devil's work. Cast out the witches among you!* Other pedestrians, whether out for a stroll or delivering their goods, had similar pages.

"I see Reverend Fingerhut has not given up his efforts to have us burned at the stake," Maylene said, trying to call forth a smile.

"I should have throttled the vermin while I had the chance."

"And I should have asked Miss Lafontaine for the name of his church."

"Do not worry, no one in this day and age is going to heed a word of his bilious babbling."

Except for the butcher who would not let his son deliver meat, the coal hauler who would not bring another load, and the two neighbors who crossed the street when they saw Maylene coming.

At least the weather was warm and, serendipitously, the ladies were promised to dine at Crowley House that evening. Socrates promised to look for the chawbacon churchman.

He was not attracted to the mop-top blond, Socrates told himself. Well, perhaps he was slightly drawn to her elfin looks and bright smile. But he was not growing fond of her, despite her plucky courage and determination. The chit had bottom. And a nice, rounded one at that. Very well, he was attracted and admiring. He was not interested in Miss Maylene Treadwell. Not at all. She was neither mistress material nor spousal stuff. The Earl of Hyatt's wife had to be rational, reasonable, respectable. His wife had to be the Duke of Mondale's daughter, wherever the hell she was. Socrates decided he would simply escort Miss Treadwell to the coming ball, see if she unearthed any clues to Lady Belinda's disappearance, and then avoid the troublesome Miss Treadwell for the rest of his barren, boring life.

Socrates was trifling with her, Maylene knew. That was all. He had so little respect for her that he could make improper advances, knowing she had no father or brother to defend her reputation, if she had a reputation worth defending. Being an original, an eccentric, a oner, was not the same as being untouchable—not to men of his wide experience and worldly tastes. My, how wonderful his lips tasted!

No, Maylene would not think about the bounder's kiss. The bounder's intentions could not be honorable, not while he was promised to Lady Belinda. Therefore, the Earl of Hyatt was making a May game of Maylene's emotions—if she let him.

She vowed to avoid him after Lady Belvedere's ball. That was only a few days away. It might be bruised, but her heart would survive.

Mr. Collins was going to survive, too. The highwayman's bullet had not managed to kill him, nor had the fever that ensued. Unfortunately, Joshua was too weak to walk, much less work. It would be months before he'd be able to play his violin, and the quartet he was to join in Brighton would long since have hired another musician. His young wife had traded the last of the few belongings the highwaymen had left them in exchange for this shabby room. But they were alive, and she refused to leave him. Furthermore, his darling bride had a plan. Whoever said you couldn't live on love alone had never met Mr. and Mrs. Joshua Collins.

Chapter Twenty-four

A pearl might not do much for the oyster's chances, but the duke's necklace surely enhanced Maylene's odds of becoming a success at her first grand ball. The necklace was beautiful, of course, and valuable, but it also lent her a confidence, a radiance that others would recognize and admire. If part of the pearls' reflected glow was due to the duke's disclosure that Lord Hyatt had selected the necklace with its coral beads, no one but Maylene had to know it.

She wore those pearls at her throat, Fleur's pearls woven into a crown atop her short hair, and Lord Shimpton's flowers at the high waist of her pale pink crepe gown, with its pearl-studded lace overskirt. The flowers, white rosebuds, had also been the earl's idea, Shimpton admitted. He would not have remembered to bathe for the ball, much less the obligation to his dancing instructor, without Hyatt's hints. It was the Treadwell butler, Campbell, who hastily brushed cat hairs off the viscount's claret-colored superfine, his eyes avoiding the saffron-waist-coat underneath.

The earl's nacre-decorated fan dangled off Maylene's wrist, when she was not admiring it. This gift was his, without round-aboutation, and she liked it best. She swore to put all of her misgivings aside and enjoy herself this evening, whatever it brought, especially if it brought news of Lady Belinda. The approval she read in Hyatt's hazel eyes when he called to escort them to the ball convinced her that a one-night lapse of good sense was forgivable, especially when he was looking so devil-ishly handsome in his elegantly subdued dark evening clothes. He wore a single pearl in his neckcloth.

The duke had also presented Lady Tremont with a pearl

brooch, on his own, without Hyatt's prompting. The gift was a
thank-you for all her assistance, he said, no matter the outcome
of their investigation. And Mondale also gave a set of pearl-
tipped hatpins to Aunt Regina, who wore them in her turban,
after biting them to make sure they weren't paste like the
strands she wore at her bony neck. All the ladies had new
gowns, slippers, gloves, silk stockings, and high expectations
for the evening. Aunt Regina even had new eyelashes.

A single grain of sand could irritate an oyster into making a
thing of beauty. The way every man at the ball was ogling the
beautiful Miss Treadwell's pearls—and her small but shapely
bosom—was irritating the hell out of the earl. He took himself
off to the card room after escorting the ladies through the receiving line.

The duke stayed by the grouping of chairs Lady Tremont selected, waiting for the opportunity to introduce Maylene to his
daughter's friends. Soon Lady Crowley joined them with her
niece, Miss Tolliver-Jones, who had been permitted to attend
even though her own presentation was yet a fortnight away. The
girl could get her feet wet in the social waters, Lady Crowley
declared, but she would not dance.

Unfortunately, Maylene had to. The minuet with Lord
Shimpton went better than she'd expected; she could still walk
at the end of it. Her steps might have included some hops and
skips that the dance obviously didn't require, but she was not
permanently lamed. Afterward, when she'd limped to her
mother's side, she suggested Lord Shimpton sit by Miss Tolliver-Jones to keep the younger girl company. Lady Crowley's
niece might be the perfect match for Shimpton, if she stopped
giggling at him.

Shimpton sucked on his high shirt collar. "Got nothing to say
to a chit. Not in the petticoat line, don't you know."

Maylene had an inkling. Then he asked, "Does she like
cats?"

Mentally adding a new requirement in a bride for the viscount, Maylene had to confess that she had no idea. "Why don't
you ask her? That will give you something to speak about."

Cats, it seemed, gave Miss Tolliver-Jones spots. That was the
end of the conversation. Shimpton chewed on his collar; the girl

giggled. Perhaps the two were not so well suited, Maylene conceded.

She reluctantly took her cousin's arm for the country dance now forming. Maylene could not refuse Grover, but she could manage to step on his foot when he held her hand too hard and long whenever the figures of the dance brought them together. She'd learned something from Shimpton, after all. At the conclusion of the set, Glover invited her to the refreshments room, the picture gallery, the balcony.

The day Maylene went off alone with the sniffling squeeze-stealer was the day pigeons took up roosts in her cockloft. Disgruntled, Grover took up a position on the other side of Miss Tolliver-Jones, who might have an annoying twitter, but she also had two thousand pounds a year.

Maylene danced the quadrille with the duke next. They had agreed that His Grace should act as normally as possible, to protect what they could of Belinda's reputation. People were beginning to ask for her, but gossip would dwindle if her own father seemed unconcerned. The duke turned out to be an elegant dancer with courtly manners, despite his obvious lack of concentration, as his eyes kept returning to Maylene's mother at the sidelines. Lady Tremont had put off her usual lavender gauze in favor of a new deep plum satin gown with a lowered neckline, with the duke's pearl brooch affixed at the vee of the décolletage. She looked beautiful, Maylene thought proudly, quite the handsomest dowager in the room, and the duke, it appeared, thought so, too. If those pearls were eggs, they would have hatched under the heat of his stare.

"Isn't it a shame that my mother considers herself a mere chaperone tonight, Your Grace? Why, she is a better dancer than many of the young girls. Of course, she might consider taking the floor if you were to ask her, " she hinted none too subtly.

"Do you think so?" His Grace almost left Maylene on the dance floor in his eagerness to reach Lady Tremont's side for the next set, a waltz.

The baroness hesitated. "Oh, no, I'm much too old for cutting a caper. And the waltz, oh, dear. Chaperones mustn't, of course. People will talk." Then Aunt Regina removed one of her new pearl hatpins and jabbed it into her niece's backside. Lady Tremont was on her feet instantly, the duke bowing over her fingers. "I'd be honored."

Maylene looked around. She would dearly love to waltz, but Shimpton hadn't been taught—a donkey could learn sooner— and she'd never chance letting Grover hold her so closely. Lady Belvedere was too busy finding partners for the younger girls, and gentlemen who might have offered now had to wait for her mother's return for an introduction. Maylene was just deciding this might be a good time to go to the ladies' withdrawing room to see if any of Belinda's friends might be there, now that the duke had identified some of them. Lady Crowley was nodding off while Shimpton enumerated his kitten's fine points, so Maylene thought she'd better pry Miss Tolliver-Jones out of Grover's grasp to accompany her, rather than leave the silly chit in his wandering hands.

Then Hyatt was bowing in front of her. "My dance, I believe."

Her fondest dream, she believed.

Maylene went into the earl's arms, telling herself what a dunce cap she was, how she greatly feared part of her would stay there forever, never to be reclaimed. Their steps matched perfectly, but they did not speak. Socrates was likely as afraid as she, Maylene thought, that they might argue and ruin the moment. They both knew the moment would have to last a lifetime.

When the dance ended, Maylene would have gone home to cry a hundred tears for every pearl of her necklace, for finding what she'd always wanted and not being able to have it. But Maylene would not drag her mother away, not when she was gaily strolling about the room on the duke's arm. Cousin Grover and Miss Tolliver-Jones were gone.

Maylene bit her lip. "Oh, dear, I'd better go after them."

"I'll go with you. We'll try the refreshments room first, shall we? Perhaps your cousin merely took the chit for a lemonade."

More likely he took her for a lesson the girl's innocence would not survive. Maylene nodded and followed Lord Hyatt through the crowded room. Before they reached the area set aside for punch and cakes, however, he was accosted by Aurora, Lady Ashford, whom Aunt Regina had helpfully pointed out to Maylene as Hyatt's current mistress. She was dressed in scarlet-trimmed black satin, with a heavy diamond bracelet on her silk-gloved wrist. The widow instantly draped herself over the earl's arm.

"Soc, darling, you haven't forgotten our dance, have you?" she purred, fingering the bracelet. "I wanted to thank you for the gift. I'm sure your little friend will excuse you."

Maylene couldn't help herself. She touched the pearls at her neck, staring at the matching pearl at Hyatt's throat. "Yes, of course, Lady Ashford. The earl is quite generous, isn't he? Thank you for the dance, my lord. I'll go find our missing friends, shall I? *All* our missing friends." She left no doubt she meant to remind him of Lady Belinda.

How was it, she asked herself as she made her way down the hall, that the sight of Hyatt not only stole her breath, but her wits, also? He needed but to look at her, and she forgot that he was arrogant, beneath contempt, and bespoken.

"Miss Treadwell? It is Miss Treadwell, isn't it?" The voice that finally penetrated Maylene's musings belonged to Lady Belvedere herself, an attractive young woman with an older husband and ambitions of becoming a Society hostess of note. Judging from the crowded rooms and corridors, she was well on her way to becoming a success. She was also on her way to the supper area to check on the provisions, she said, drawing Maylene along with her. Grover and the Tolliver-Jones girl were not there, Maylene could see, and she would have gone on to look in the card rooms except that Lady Belvedere had her arm.

"I hope you do not mind my asking, Miss Treadwell," the woman was saying as she led Maylene away from the public rooms and down a long corridor, "but is it true that you can find things?"

Maylene couldn't find her cousin standing here, but neither could she offend her hostess. Besides, Lady Belvedere might turn out to be another client. Heaven knew they could use another wealthy patron at Treadwell House. "I have been lucky at locating things in the past," she admitted, not mentioning the hours of hard work and research, the squads of young boys she employed, nor her mother's spectral suggestions. "Have you lost something, then?"

Indeed she had. Lady Belvedere had mislaid a locket, it seemed, a small gold piece of no particular value, except sentimentality.

"I am sure it will turn up tomorrow, when the servants make a thorough cleaning. It must have gone missing while you were preparing for the ball," Maylene suggested, thinking that an entertainment of this magnitude would take days of effort. It did, but not on Lady Belvedere's part. She'd merely directed her housekeeper and butler to hire more staff. No, the locket, it turned out, was not so much misplaced as misfound. Lord Belvedere had come upon the necklace that afternoon and had locked it in his study, down the hall from where they now were.

Maylene was confused. "But if you know where your jewelry is, ma'am, it is not lost."

"It's as good as lost, and so is my marriage if my husband thinks to look inside the locket. There was no time for him to do so, earlier."

"Inside . . . ?" Maylene prompted.

"Do not be dense, Miss Treadwell. You are reputed to have a wise head on your shoulders. There is a lock of hair inside the locket, a lovely brown curl."

Lord Belvedere's hair was gray. "I don't suppose your husband's hair used to be that shade?"

"Black," the young matron said with regret. "He already suspects something. That's why he stuck it away somewhere, and he's been watching me all night. I dare not go after the thing."

"But you think I should, is that it? Break into his locked study and steal the necklace? Good grief, ma'am, that is not finding a lost item, it is robbery!"

"Not if the locket is mine in the first place! And you would not have to break in because I have the spare key. You are my only hope, Miss Treadwell. Please do not let me down, or he'll banish me to the country or some dreadful place." She pressed the key into Maylene's gloved hand and turned. "La, Belvedere, there you are, just in time to escort me back to the ballroom. I was just showing Miss Treadwell the way to the library. She is a great admirer of books, aren't you, miss?"

Maylene hoped there'd be some law books.

Chapter Twenty-five

Socrates managed to disentangle himself from the limpetlike arms of Aurora Ashford before the supper dance, thank goodness, else he'd be forced to partner her through the meal, too. Obviously the lavish bracelet had sent the wrong message. Instead of ending their liaison, it had whetted her appetite for more: more gifts, more time with him, more chance of becoming the next Lady Hyatt. Attila the Hun had a better chance of getting into heaven. Devil take all ambitious women, he thought.

And devil take Miss Treadwell for disappearing again. The duke and Lady Tremont were so absorbed in their conversation that they barely noticed that half their party was missing. The old auntie had found someone fool enough to play cards with her, and Lady Crowley was snoring slightly, her head half resting on Shimpton's padded shoulder. The viscount had taken to playing cat's cradle with some yarn he'd found, unless the nodcock usually carried a ball of string in his evening clothes. Dash it, did no one care that Miss Treadwell was wandering about by herself, looking for the debutante and the dirty dish? Hyatt cared. He knew Maylene had as much consideration for her reputation as a rabbit, and as much social experience, despite her age and intelligence, as a lamppost. She'd never think that tongues would wag if she was seen poking into empty rooms and dark corners; she wouldn't realize that some of the young bucks had overimbibed on champagne to the point where a delicious morsel like Miss Treadwell might prove too tempting to resist. Socrates started down the hallway, glancing into the card rooms, the supper room, the billiards room, and the drawing room, where a string quartet played softly so some of the older guests could carry on their conversations, most likely about the lax morals of the younger generation, the earl supposed.

He opened a few closed doors down a less crowded corridor, to find embracing couples, a green youth casting up his accounts, and two old gents asleep with newspapers over their faces. "Pardon. Pardon. Try the window instead of the ferns. Pardon."

Then he opened the door to what he knew was Lord Belvedere's private office. There was Miss Treadwell, looking as guilty as sin, opening drawers in his lordship's desk. "Bloody hell." He turned and shut the door behind him.

Maylene looked up, not really surprised to see Lord Hyatt glaring at her. "It's not what you think."

"What I think is that you are searching your host's private belongings. Tell me I am wrong, Miss Treadwell, if you can." He was furious, at her for endangering her reputation and her very life—robbery was a hanging offense—and at himself for foisting a sneak thief off on the polite world, despite all of his earlier misgivings. She was not even embarrassed enough at being discovered to cease her scrabbling about in Belvedere's drawers.

"Lady Belvedere asked me to retrieve a piece of jewelry for her, that's all." Maylene hadn't wished to do this, but the pretty young countess had looked at her so pleadingly as she pressed the key into her hand that Maylene could not refuse to try.

Socrates did not believe her. "Belvedere gives the baggage everything she wants, not that it ever seems to satisfy the jade. He wouldn't be hiding her jewelry away."

"But I doubt that this piece was a gift from his lordship." She kept looking as she spoke. "Drat, this drawer seems to be locked. That must be where he put the locket."

"Or where he keeps his cash. You wouldn't be thinking of seeking your reward money, would you?" Susannah Belvedere was always accepting gifts from her cicisbeos; perhaps Belvedere was finally tiring of his young wife's indiscretions. Maylene's story might have a kernel of truth.

"Don't be absurd." She picked up a penknife from the desk to try to pry the drawer open.

"Stop that—you'll scratch the wood."

"You're right." She opened her reticule to look for a hairpin to try. With her hair so short, though, she rarely had use for the pesky things. She found her small sewing case instead. "Perhaps the needle will be long enough."

"Dash it, there's likely a secret catch to trigger the lock." Hyatt strode closer, looking over her shoulder. "Try the back of the top drawer." When that didn't work, he pushed her aside and knelt under the desk, cursing the while that once again he was involved in her larcenous dealings.

Oddly out of breath as his shoulder brushed against her thigh, Maylene said, "You can leave any time, you know."

His voice came back muffled, from near her feet. "You forget that I am the one who secured your invitations for you, for which I am sure to go to purgatory. The least I can do to protect my own name is keep you out of prison. Yes, here is the lever."

The drawer opened easily now, and Maylene forgot to resent his high-handedness. "You seem to have a few useful talents yourself, my lord."

Maylene moved some papers, a leather wallet, a pouch of coins, a dueling pistol, and a lace glove. "It appears that his lordship is not above a bit of dalliance himself. Ah, here is the locket." She made to reopen her reticule to place the gold piece inside.

"He'll suspect she took it, you know. That will be just as incriminating as whatever Belvedere might find inside. What is it, a miniature of her current lover? A painting of his eye? I suppose Susannah hopes to avoid a duel if her husband cannot identify the chap." He eyed the dueling pistol with an expert's assessment.

Maylene removed her gloves to pry open the locket. "It's a lock of hair, light brown."

Socrates reviewed the current scandalbroth. "Brenton Gilchrist. The man's a milksop. Couldn't hit his target if his life depended on it. Which it just might. Belvedere is a crack shot."

"With once-black hair—like yours, my lord." Maylene removed the brown curl, carefully placing it in her reticule, then she removed her folding scissors from the sewing kit.

The earl backed up. "Oh, no, you don't, May. I will lie and rob for you, even sit through your mother's mystic meander-

ings, but this is asking too much! My valet will have my whole
head if I let you go snipping off a lock or two."

"Nonsense, he'll never notice. And charity begins at home,
you know. The Belvederes' home. You wouldn't want poor
Gilchrist to be shot, or Lord Belvedere to have to flee the country, would you?"

"It might teach that trollop a lesson," he muttered, but lowered his head so she could destroy his perfectly groomed hair.

Maylene tried to be unemotional about the task, but she
could not help noticing how silky his hair was, how the citrusy
scent of him seemed to fill her head, how his breathing was so
close she could share the very air with him. The scissors wa-
vered.

Socrates tried to be unemotional about the task, but he could
not help inhaling her sweet lilac perfume or noticing how
smooth her skin was at the top of her breasts, above the neckline of her gown, just inches away from his bent head, his eyes,
his mouth. His head jerked.

"Oh, my."

"Oh, my" was not what a man wished to hear from a female
with scissors in her hand. He clapped a hand to his ears to make
sure they were both still intact. Red-faced, Maylene turned her
back, pretending to fuss with twining the cut hair into a loop to
fit into the locket, while she scattered the rest of his hair on the
floor, then trampled it into the carpet with her slippered foot.

She had just replaced the locket in the drawer when they
heard voices in the hall.

"I'll have his liver and lights, this time, my girl. You've
pushed me too far, by Jove. We leave for Yorkshire as soon as
I've sent Gilchrist to his Maker."

Slamming the drawer shut with his knee, Hyatt grabbed
Maylene into his arms, swinging her around so that his broad
back shielded her from view. He kissed her, filling her open
mouth with his tongue when she would have protested. Any ar-
gument she might have made died instantly as Maylene surren-
dered to feelings she had only imagined before. Like the
champagne she could taste on his lips, the sensations went
straight to her head—and her toes, and her stomach. Every inch

of her tingled, so she pressed herself closer to his broad chest. Socrates groaned.

"Eh? What's that? I thought this door was locked, by George. Talk to the servants in the morning, Sukey. Can't have every room in the house taken up with cuddling couples, dash it. And as for you, wife, we'll talk tomorrow. You two, carry on, I suppose."

As the voices receded, sanity returned. Hyatt's arms fell, and Maylene nearly did, too, her legs were so weak. She caught herself on the edge of the desk, then she caught her breath. "Th-thank you, Socrates. You have saved my reputation and Lady Belvedere's marriage, for the time being. Th-that was quick thinking." It was also the most shattering experience of her lifetime. Yes, the earl was decidedly talented in his own fields of expertise. He, of course, was unaffected, so she tried to be as nonchalant as possible. "Shall we return to the ballroom?"

"You go ahead. We should not be seen leaving here together, alone." Hyatt was so unaffected that he should not be seen in polite company, not till the uncomfortable signs of his alleged disinterest disappeared.

Lady Belvedere was waiting outside the ballroom. She pounced on Maylene and dragged her up the stairs to the ladies' retiring room.

"And I suggest you hold your fan over your lips until then, Miss Treadwell."

Maylene could still feel the burning, so assumed she looked thoroughly kissed. Oh, dear. At least Lady Belvedere was in no position to censure her behavior.

The countess almost wept when Maylene pulled the knotted curl out of her reticule. She tucked it into the immodest bosom of her gown, which Maylene could not think was a good hiding place, being such a scant expanse of material. Maylene explained about replacing the brown hair with black, which Lady Belvedere thought was a stroke of genius.

"And you can be sure I'll be making a handsome contribution to your mother's fund. Meantime, is there anything I can do for you tonight, Miss Treadwell? Is there some particular gentleman you would like to meet? I could arrange any number of dance partners for you. Of course, after you've been kissed

by the Ideal, I don't suppose any other man will do, but perhaps
you have some less elusive bachelor in your sights. An introduction is the least I can do, seeing that you have saved me
from my husband's wrath."

Ignoring the mention of Hyatt's sobriquet while she dampened a cloth to apply to her swollen lips, Maylene allowed as
how she would, in fact, appreciate being made known to Lady
Belvedere's sister and her circle of debutantes.

"Goodness, why would you wish to waste the evening with
the infantry?"

"I was, ah, hoping to discover a bit about Lady Belinda, His
Grace of Mondale's daughter. I did not wish to ask the duke, or
the earl, naturally."

"Ah. So the wind truly does blow in that direction. I've heard
the rumors, of course, of an understanding between the families
as well as of the chit's disappearance. And you, being of an in-
quiring mind, wish to know the truth, of course."

"If the lady is not returning to London any time soon . . . "
Maylene let her voice trail off, letting the countess make the
precise assumption Maylene expected her to.

"Then you will feel free to pursue Hyatt in earnest. Although
I do not understand your sudden scruples after what I saw in the
study. You did not seem to mind that he was partway promised
then." Lady Belvedere shrugged her elegant shoulders. If a
wedding ring did not keep Susannah from her pursuit of pleasure, an unannounced understanding certainly would not. Miss
Treadwell, however, was known to be an original. Perhaps that
was why she was still a spinster. "Very well, have it your way.
I'll see you meet the gels, but not tonight. You cannot know
much about young females if you think they are willing to
waste a minute of their evening chatting with another woman.
Why don't you come to tea tomorrow? I'll make sure my sister
and some of her friends are there."

Maylene nodded, and Lady Belvedere started to leave, to return to her guests and her own flirtations. "But a word of advice
first, Miss Treadwell, in exchange for the service you have
done for me."

Maylene was staring in the mirror. "Yes, I know, hold my fan
a bit higher."

"No, my dear. Set your sights a bit lower. Do you know why they call Hyatt the Ideal? Not just because he is a perfect specimen of manhood, but because he is the goal every woman strives for—the unattainable goal."

Maylene waited in the ladies' parlor for a while, hoping to regain her composure. Lady Belvedere had told her nothing she did not already know. Hyatt was not for the likes of Maylene Treadwell, no matter how many excuses he found for kissing her.

By the time Maylene returned to her mother's side, her lips were their normal size and color, her pearl diadem was straightened on her head, and her heart was firmly where it belonged, not on her sleeve. She need not have bothered. No one noticed her, not after they saw the condition of Miss Tolliver-Jones when she and Cousin Grover stepped back into the ballroom from the door leading to the terraced gardens. Miss Tolliver-Jones might be green as grass, but so was the back of her gown. The Treadwell House party left immediately afterward, to help Lady Crowley plan a hurried wedding instead of a come-out.

And no one noticed that the paragon of London gentlemen had been barbered by a baboon until much later, when his man helped the earl undress. The valet tendered his resignation.

Chapter Twenty-six

She had fallen into a pond full of ducklings, Maylene decided. That's what the young girls in Lady Belvedere's parlor reminded her of, anyway. They were appealing and adorable from a distance. Up close, they never ceased their quacking and flapping and hissing, pecking at each other, vying for the choicest square of stagnant water. They did not acknowledge the scrawny old hen on the shore.

Maylene tried to ignore the rudeness, the cuts, the curious stares, some of them hostile. She could not ignore the fact, though, that she would never learn anything about Lady Belinda if no one spoke to her. She moved over to where Lady Belvedere was pouring the tea for some of the girls' mothers.

"They won't speak to me," Maylene said worriedly.

"Of course not. You were the only one other than Lady Ashford whom Hyatt danced with last night."

"Oh, so they resent me for Lady Belinda's sake?"

"Goodness, no. They'd steal him away from her in a minute if they thought they could. They were jealous of you, is all. Why, I've a good mind to snub you myself. I've been setting out lures for the Ideal for an age. Not that he dallies with married women, more's the pity." The countess gestured with her teacup around the room. "No more than he'd look at these unfledged chicks."

"But he's looking at Lady Belinda," Maylene reminded the older woman. "More than looking, I understand."

"Oh, that's different. That's business, don't you know, the weighty business of selecting the proper wife to match one's lineage, wealth, and social standing. These silly geese are hoping the earl will lose his heart, therefore, his head, and thence his hand, to one of them. I misdoubt the man has a heart to lose. What do you think?"

Maylene thought that she had to stop acting goosish herself. She was going to find the earl's fiancée, that was all. Lady Belvedere recommended she try Miss Georgina Westmacott, a pale-faced girl sitting by herself at the pianoforte. She was one of Belinda's closest friends, Lady Belvedere recalled.

Miss Westmacott knew all about the rumors of Belinda's disappearance—and of Maylene's interest in the earl. She plunked the instrument's keys angrily. "I intend to write to Belinda today, to tell her about your making sheep's eyes at her earl," Georgina said. "She'll be back in Town before the cat can lick its ear."

"Ah, then you'll write to her aunt in Wales?"

The girl went even paler, a scattering of freckles showing on her cheeks. She was obviously torn between worry over her friend and resentment of Maylene. "I already tried there."

"I would like to write to Lady Belinda myself," Maylene said, "to explain that she really has nothing to worry about, no matter what gossip she hears. Have you any idea of where else I might send a letter?"

The girl shook her head, careful not to disturb her coiffure. She'd had to spend all morning with her hair wrapped in papers, while Miss Treadwell looked as if she woke up with a perfect head of curls. Georgina thumped out a dirge on the pianoforte.

"Surely she mentioned somewhere else? Someone she might visit when her aunt recovered?"

"Well, she did ask me about the bathing machines at Brighton. I went with my family last summer, you see."

Brighton? That was certainly near the water! "Did she have friends there, then? Someone else from school, perhaps?"

"No, everyone from our group at Miss Meadow's Academy is here in London having their Seasons, except for Marjorie, who married the Italian count, and Rebecca, who is in mourning in Lancaster."

"Did Belinda have any particular male friends, then? Someone she might have been interested in if Lord Hyatt hadn't offered? Someone her father might not have found so acceptable, perhaps?"

"No, Bel spoke only of the earl and what a fine match it was."

"I see. And did you know her well enough to be sure of her feelings, Miss Westmacott? I'd like to be certain, you see."

"I'll wager you would, " the younger girl sniped, ending her piece with a discordant crescendo. "We've been friends since our second year at Miss Meadow's, more than five years ago."

"Then you must be good friends indeed. Ah, where did you say Miss Meadow's Academy was located?"

"In Bath, of course."

Which was also wet. And which, oddly enough, figured in another investigation. Maylene had one more question: "Miss Westmacott, you play charmingly. Is Lady Belinda also musically inclined?"

The girl laughed. "I should say not. Why, she could barely read music, no matter how many private lessons her father paid extra for."

"Mama, we have to contact Max. I have an important question to ask him concerning the duke's daughter." Maylene doubted the duke knew the name of his daughter's private teachers, and she did not want to create a bumblebroth if her guess was wrong. The name would be easy enough to find out from the school, and still would not tell her Lady Belinda's current location. Either way, a missing heiress and a missing musician, both once from Bath, was too much of a coincidence to be ignored.

Lady Tremont, however, was not eager to conduct a session of spectral communication that night. Shredding her handkerchief, the baroness claimed that she was too fatigued from the ball. Besides, Lady Crowley was blaming her for Grover's scandal, Aunt Regina was suffering from a surfeit of lobster patties at the ball, and Max had proved unhelpful the last time. They would learn nothing new. Therefore, Maylene's mother stated, the poor duke should not have to suffer further.

"Yes, but His Grace might reveal something he hadn't thought important if we invite him back tonight; perhaps he knows someone in Brighton with whom Belinda might be staying. It is worth a try."

"But, dear, you can ask the duke your questions without asking Max about it. Simply send him a note."

Of course she could write to Mondale, or call on him, for that matter, but her mother had always insisted on including her bygone beloved in all the previous investigations. Maylene did not understand this deviation from their general practice, and her mother's obvious agitation was confusing her more. "Don't you want to speak to Max tonight? You are usually so eager for his company."

"No, no. Not tonight, dear. I swear, I am exhausted."

"Then tomorrow? Shall I invite the duke for tomorrow?"

"Oh, goodness. Tomorrow we are promised for the theater, and the next evening we should have your cousin Grover and Miss Tolliver-Jones over for dinner to celebrate their betrothal."

Maylene was willing to celebrate getting Grover out of their hair, but poor Miss Tolliver-Jones ought to be receiving condolences! "I think they will be off on their honeymoon by then, if Lady Crowley has anything to say about it and if she can procure a special license in time. The sooner the two are wed, the sooner the gossip will cease. Besides, I am sure the duke will not wish to wait so long before hearing our theories."

"Oh, do we have theories, dear?" Lady Tremont rose and kissed her daughter's cheek. "I knew you would figure it out, darling. You have such a knack for that kind of thing. I am truly blessed to have such a talented daughter." She started out of the room, but Maylene blocked the door.

"Oh, no you don't, Mama. You are not leaving until you explain why you are suddenly loath to hold a gathering and what has you so upset. Has the duke made you improper advances?" Mondale's friend was a rogue; the duke might very well be one also. Maylene wasn't sure what she could do about it, for a young woman of one-and-twenty could not challenge a duke to a duel, and their only male relative was hardly fit for the field of honor. Besides, Maylene did not believe in violence, unless, of course, someone had insulted her mother.

"His Grace? Of course not. He has been everything kind

and . . . and delightful." With those words, Lady Tremont sank onto the sofa, her head in the cushions, weeping.

"Goodness, Mama, an eminently eligible gentleman is treating you well, and all you can do is cry? That makes no sense. Don't you like Mondale?"

"Yes, I do," her mother wailed, dampening the sofa pillows. "But . . . but I don't think Max does."

Now was not, perhaps, the best time to remind her mother that Max was deceased. "Um, why would you think that?"

"Because he was so uncooperative at the last session, giving us nothing but that silly dog's yammering."

Maylene knelt by the side of the sofa, stroking her mother's hair. "But, Mama, if the people we are looking for are not in the beyond, it might be beyond Max's powers to help us locate them."

"No, he is upset, I know it. He thinks I am being unfaithful."

"How can you be unfaithful now, when you were married all those years? Heavens, you said Max was married, too!"

"But Max was merely fond of his wife, and I never cared for your father, no, not the slightest. He was not a very nice man, you know."

"But the duke is, and you do care for him?"

"Yes!" Lady Tremont moaned into the pillows, her shoulders shaking.

"And does His Grace reciprocate your feelings?" Maylene thought she knew, but wanted to hear her mother's opinion.

The baroness sniffled. "I think so, but he is so upset over his daughter that it is too soon to say. And he did love his wife, you know."

"And you loved Max. That does not mean you both have to be alone for the rest of your lives."

"But my dearest Max will be! Alone, that is, for the rest of eternity. Except for that stupid dog that ran into the burning building instead of barking for help. I never told Max, of course, but Alex had the brains of a flea." She sobbed again. Her words were muffled by the pillows. "And he had fleas, besides."

Maylene felt they were digressing. "But just because you feel affection for the duke and he for you"—Maylene crossed her fingers in hope—"doesn't have to mean that you cannot still love Max."

"I shall love dear Max forever," the baroness declared, her voice quavering. "But he is only a man, no matter how immaterial or immortal. What if he does not understand and thinks I am being disloyal to his memory? He'll leave me, and then, when the duke gets his daughter back, he'll also leave me. You'll go off and get married, if God is merciful and answers a mother's prayers, and I'll have no one! I'll be all alone with Aunt Regina!"

"Mama, Max loved you —you said so yourself. And his love stayed so strong even after he went aloft"—ashes, Alex, and all—"that he can come back from the beyond to comfort and guide you. How could anyone who loved so deeply, so endlessly, not wish to see his dear one happy?"

Lady Tremont lifted her head from the cushions before she suffocated. "Do you think so, dear?"

"I think we had better ask Max tonight to make sure."

And they'd invite Lord Hyatt, of course.

Chapter Twenty-seven

Oh, how vexatious, Max. You say that Lord Crowley made time tonight to come hear his beloved wife's final farewell message? The dear woman will be so sorry she missed him!"

The dear woman had not forgiven her friend for being related to a ne'er-do-well knave who went around compromising young females into advantageous marriages—advantageous to the balding baron, of course. Lady Crowley had also been too embarrassed to show her face in public, and too distraught over having to write to her sister and brother-in-law that their daughter was to be wed in the morning to a lecherous lordling with pockets to let. Then again, the chit's titters were so annoying, they ought to be happy to be rid of her at any price. Having Grover in one's family, despite the title, was a heavy price indeed. Lady Crowley envisioned nothing coming from the match but thin-haired, runny-nosed little sneaksbys with incessant giggles. No, Lady Crowley could not face leaving her bedchamber and her restoratives.

Without the widow, Lieutenant Canfield, or Sir Cedric and his wife, who had reconciled themselves to the loss of their son, they were a small group at Lady Tremont's round, dimly lighted table that evening. Even Aunt Regina had begged off, still feeling dyspeptic after her raid on Lady Belvedere's buffet.

There were so few gathered to join their mental energies, in fact, that Lady Tremont insisted Lord Hyatt and Maylene take up places at the table, along with Frederick, Viscount Shimpton; James, the Duke of Mondale; and Campbell, the butler of Treadwell House.

Maylene thought her mother might want her nearby for comfort, and was touched. Then she touched the earl's bare hand

and suspected her mother's motives as more matchmaking maneuvers. Drat! How was she supposed to concentrate on the beyond when she kept wondering what his lordship's skin felt like, beyond his cool, firm grasp. She supposed his body under the blue superfine, under the thin linen shirt, would be all-over hard with muscles, lean and— She caught herself from leaning closer, drawn by his citrus and spice cologne.

Shimpton's sweaty palm on her other side did not aid her in communing with the afterworld, either, for it kept her thinking of washing afterward. At least he no longer smelled so bad, if one did not mind the aroma of kippered herring that lingered about him, since the addlepate would insist on stuffing his pockets with treats for his kitten. The feline did not seem to mind at all, sleeping in a contented ball on his lap. Since the viscount had hurriedly purchased a striped waistcoat and dark pantaloons to match the little creature, the cat hairs did not show so much.

The evening had begun as usual, with Lady Tremont's chanting, swaying, and whispers of encouragement for everyone to focus their thoughts on their loved ones who had passed on. Her eyes firmly closed, Lady Tremont had called out to Max. And again. Then she had smiled, a beatific, blissful smile. Maylene could breathe again.

"Max, dear, you came. I was so worried and afraid. I don't know what I would have done if you left me again." She paused to listen. "What's that, dear? You couldn't help the first time? Of course not. I never blamed you for dying. For staying at an inferior inn, perhaps, or for sleeping so soundly after a night of indulgence, but— What did you say, dear? I cannot hear you because of the noise."

Maylene looked at Campbell, who shook his head. They'd had nothing planned for the session. His nephews were out making inquiries about the investigations with the lists the duke had provided, so the adjoining room was empty. Aunt Regina's groans could not be heard at this distance.

"It sounds like . . . " Lady Tremont's smile faded. "Oh, you brought Alex again. Yes, I brought Mondale, but it's not the same. No, His Grace is not a lapdog, Max."

Hyatt's brows were lowered, giving him his habitual severe,

dark look, but the duke was chuckling. Lady Tremont went on. "Yes, dear, I know Alex is good company, but must he bark so much when we are trying to converse? What's that? He's very excited tonight? Max, dear, Alex is always excited. I hope they have no carpets where you are now. But shall we get on with the night's inquiries? Yes, dear, I suppose that if we think loving thoughts for a moment he will calm down."

"Nice doggy, good Alex, " Lady Tremont chanted, urging the others to join in while she muttered under her breath, "I don't see why the little ratter cannot go on to the Happy Hunting Ground on his own for once."

The noise must have died down, for the baroness smiled again and started to announce Lord Shimpton's presence, who had come to talk to his much-mourned mama. That's when Max reported Lord Crowley's availability.

"Perhaps he will be free another night, dear, to honor us with his presence. With him going off in that carriage accident that way, the river and all, why, I am sure he'll want to say good-bye to his beloved wife, too. Meantime, Lord Shimpton has come to introduce his new pet to his dear mother." The viscount lifted the kitten onto the table, where it stuck its little claws into the linen cloth and arched its back at the candelabrum in the center.

The baroness freed her hands from the duke's on one side and Hyatt's on the other to clamp them over her ears. "Yes, I know it's a cat! Please tell Alex that it is all right! He says what? Max, what language! You should wash his mouth out with soap! No, not with a kitten, with soap!"

Shimpton quickly scooped the cat back into his lap, under his waistcoat, scaring the creature worse than any barking could.

"Lady Shimpton?" the baroness reminded Max with more than a hint of impatience. "Is she nearby to speak a few words to her loving son?"

She was. Lady Tremont grew stiff and still, trembling for an instant. Then her eyes snapped open, and her nose twitched. "I smell cat piss!" she shrilled in Lady Shimpton's voice. "Devil take it, sonny, you've gone and got a cat instead of a dog! And you should have been looking for a bride in the first place! Didn't I tell you so?"

"Mumsy? You said to find someone to love me. At least I thought that's what you meant. Neptune loves me."

"Neptune? What kind of asinine name is that for a she-cat?"

"He's a girl?" Shimpton pulled the kitten out of his waistcoat and held it up, dangling. While the cat yowled its displeasure, Maylene peeked over the viscount's padded shoulders and past his ear-high shirt points. "Yes, she is."

"How can you—"

Lady Shimpton's voice quickly interrupted: "Neptune? Petunia is more like it."

"No, I'll just call her Tune, I suppose."

Maylene felt like clapping. The viscount was developing a backbone after all these years. She hoped he'd try for a chin next. She reached over to pat the cat, which immediately sank tiny needlelike fangs into her hand.

"I suppose that puts you out of the running for the next Lady Shimpton," Hyatt whispered to her as he handed over his handkerchief to bind the puncture wounds. "He'll never take a wife his cat doesn't like."

Maylene just scowled at Socrates, then caught herself. Any more association with His Arrogance and she'd have permanent frown lines on her face. She had no intention of wedding Viscount Shimpton, no matter how much he improved. Now she had to worry about pleasing the cat, though, before she found him a suitable bride. Maylene was beginning to believe that such a female did not exist.

Lady Tremont, meanwhile, was recovering from her enactment of Shimpton's mother with the aid of a glass of water and the duke's solicitude. She was ready to move on. "Miss Lafontaine could not be with us this evening, Max, dear, but she sends her appreciation for your assistance in locating her son. Very well, Max, thank you to Alex also. Yes, I admit that he was correct when he said he smelled water, but he could have been a bit more specific, you know. Of course I do not expect a dog to know his geography, Max."

Socrates leaned closer to whisper in Maylene's ear. "And here I always thought it was another lover who could come between a twosome. Deuce take it if it's not a four-legged creature that makes the most awkward triangle. Never get a pet, Miss Treadwell, if you want to get a husband."

Lady Tremont ceased her one-sided bickering to say, "We are still seeking Mr. Joshua Collins, dear. Have you any new ideas where we might search?"

Maylene sat forward, intent on her mother's words. She did not expect to hear curses come out of her mother's mouth, at least not in her mother's own voice. "Damn it, Max. I know your blasted dog smells water. Now can you make the plaguey beast be quiet before I get the headache? We want to ask if you think Mr. Collins might be in Brighton. There is plenty of water there, you know. What's that, dear? Bother, I can't hear you. Now there's loud music besides the dog's incessant barking. What, is Lord Crowley practicing for the choir again?"

"What kind of music, Mama?" Maylene softly called.

" 'Tune'? Alex says 'Tune'? Yes, that is what Lord Shimpton is calling his kitten. For Neptune, don't you know, because he found the dear puss in the water, just as you said he would. Pardon, as Alex said he would. Yes, I think he is a good dog. No, we are not interested to know that chasing cats is not permitted in the hereafter. We wish to know if Mr. Collins is pursuing his musical career in Brighton. Do you hear violins, dear? What, they hurt Alex's ears? I am sorry for that, to be sure, but what about Mr. Collins?"

Lady Tremont shook her head and looked around at the little group. " 'Tune' is all I can hear over the music and the barking. Let's try our last inquiry, shall we?" She shut her eyes and concentrated. "Max, dear, are you still there?"

"Where the deuce would he go?" Socrates whispered.

"Hush," Maylene whispered back, squeezing his hand. "She is about to ask after Lady Belinda."

"Right, and we might miss Belinda's street address if we don't listen carefully to some reincarnated dog's yipping. I'll wager we all get cat-scratch fever before we hear an intelligent remark."

Maylene feared he might be right, for her mother's face was turning an alarming shade of purple and her cheeks were puffed out. "Yes, Brighton is on the water, and Tune is the cat, by heavens! I know Alex is excited to have the kitten around, Max, but he could try to be more considerate. A young girl is missing, and barking 'Tune, Tune, Tune,' at the top of his shrill lungs is no help whatsoever! He's that excited? Oh, dear. Yes, now I understand why animals are usually not allowed past the Pearly Gates. You have to go? Of course. But you will come back another time, won't you? Max? Dear? Oh, my. He's gone, and I never got to say good-bye." A tear rolled down Lady Tremont's cheek. "Now I know how Lady Crowley must feel."

"He'll come back, Mama," Maylene hastened to reassure her mother. "Max just has other, ah, responsibilities. But Alex did seem to be affected more when you mentioned Brighton, didn't he?"

"I think so, May, but there was so much barking and noise that I could not be sure."

"And you did not recognize the music?"

"No, I am positive it was nothing I have ever heard before."

"Then Brighton seems to be our only clue to both mysteries. We'll have to go, don't you think, Mama?"

Hyatt's eyes narrowed. Hell and damnation, what was it about this female that caused him to suffer from amnesia? Not five minutes in Miss Treadwell's company, and he could forget his principles, forget his promised bride, and forget what an unparalleled adventuress the vixen was. Then she'd make a comment like the one about Brighton and restore his memory all too jarringly, damn her. The Treadwell ladies must have gotten wind of his plans to take the duke to his country estate outside of Brighton next week, before His Grace gave himself heart palpitations with worrying over Belinda. Of course they would manage to wriggle an invitation somehow.

Socrates had noticed the way Lady Tremont was looking at Mondale—the way a hungry cobra looked at a mouse. She'd set her sights on a bigger goal than merely lightening Mondale's purse; now the baroness wanted the whole thing. Coiled to spring, she was not about to let the poor bastard get out of her range. And the duke didn't even realize he was prey. Unconcerned that he was not the owner of the manor house, Mondale was even now convincing the ladies that there was plenty of room at Hyatt's country place. They'd never find good accommodations on their own in Brighton, not with the summer sea-

son and the Prince Regent's descent on the city so nearly upon
them, Mondale explained. And why should they go to the additional expense, and suffer the discomforts and dangers of jour-
neying without escort, besides? No, they were assisting him
and Hyatt, the duke insisted. The least the men could do was invite the women to stay at High Oaks.

"Isn't that correct, Socrates? Tell them we'll be delighted to
have some female companionship."

About as delighted as the mouse.

Chapter Twenty-eight

*R*epent, read the placard. *Leave the dead to rest, not to witches.*

"Bloody hell, it's that pious pimple on God's backside again." Lord Hyatt was so angry at Maylene, so angry at the duke, and so angry at himself for being angry, that he ripped the sign from Reverend Fingerhut's hands, tore it in two, and smashed the stave it had been nailed onto against the lamppost outside Treadwell House. The reverend fled down the street before he met a similar fate.

"Tsk, Soc, that was a man of the cloth, no matter how deluded."

Socrates did not repent. Not a bit.

"It's not like you to be so violently wrathful. And you were nearly rude to Lady Tremont and her daughter. Ruder than usual, I should say. What's got into you?" the duke wanted to know. "You're not bilious from the ball like Mrs. Howard, are you?"

What had gotten into Socrates was what was getting into his house in Brighton. Not content to invite the treacherous Treadwell trio, His Grace had told Shimpton to come along, with his cat, naturally. And he was prepared to send a note round to Crowley's widow also, so that wretch's relic could escape the London grabble-grinders. The earl would rather have the preachy parson come visit. High Oaks was big enough to house any number of unwanted guests, though, and Hyatt had told the duke to invite anyone he wished—but not frauds and felons!

"How can you trust those females, Duke?" he demanded as they rode toward White's. "They have no evidence leading them to believe Belinda is in Brighton, no informants other than a fricasseed furball. They just want a holiday out of the City, a visit to Prinny's seaside, where they'll find other gentry to gull. Or worse."

"Worse? What could be worse than helping people overcome their grief, reuniting families, giving comfort and guidance to the misfortunate, like Shimpton?"

"Shimpton is not misfortunate; he's missing a few links in his chain, is all. But, dash it, you're making those women sound like humanitarians! They are hanging on your coattails, Mondale, trying to better their situation. First they wrest a blank check from you, then an invitation, now a house party. What's next? Your head on a platter? The dukedom? They will not be content with anything less, I swear."

"I thought you were over your irrational misgivings of the ladies, Socrates. In fact, I believed you to be growing quite fond of Miss Treadwell. You were certainly whispering in her ear half the evening."

Fond? Shimpton's cat was fond of kippers; Hyatt was obsessed with Maylene Treadwell. He dreamed of her day and night, but more vividly at night. Why, just touching her hand made him hot and bothered. Her riotous curls made every other ladies' twisted, braided, and artfully arranged locks seem like straw. Her eyes sparkled like sunbeams on water when she challenged him, and her smile could warm the longest winter. She smelled of lilacs and soap and woman, and if he could have one night with her, Socrates thought, he'd die content, especially if he could visit occasionally, like Max, and if she wasn't a scheming, shrewish sorceress, up to her pretty neck in skull-duggery.

None of this, of course, was anything Socrates wanted to relate to the father of the wench he wished to wed. He wiped a cat hair off his sleeve and said, "Miss Treadwell is well enough, I suppose. She'll do, but not as a house guest."

"I'm sorry, my boy, for misunderstanding. I did not mean to overstep. I'll get my man of affairs to find us a house to rent. If Lady Tremont and her daughter believe that there is a chance my Belinda is in Brighton, I am going."

"I won't hear of it. You'll stay with me, as will whomever you choose to invite. I'll manage. Lud knows the pile is big enough that I can find places to hide. But tell me, Duke, do you really think it possible that Lady Belinda is with this Collins chap they're also looking for? Miss Treadwell seemed to think it likely."

The duke stared out the window of the coach. "In a way, I am hoping so. Otherwise, I shall have to conclude that something terrible has happened to her." He brushed a drop of moisture from his eye. "My only child, don't you know. I am sorry, son, but I would rather see her married to a mail coach driver than lying in a ditch somewhere."

"I understand, Your Grace, honestly, I do. But are you sure the dastard means to marry her? I am sorry to mention it, but any loose screw who would run off with a wealthy young heiress who is halfway promised to another cannot necessarily be trusted to do the honorable thing."

His hand clenched on the overhead strap, Mondale stated, "Oh, he'll marry her, all right. If the scoundrel has spent these past days and nights with my girl, he'll marry her. I can still culp a wafer with my Mantons, you know. And the magistrate for Brighton is a good friend. Hell, Prinny is a friend, too, and he'll understand, after the trouble he had with his own daughter."

"I daresay we can come up with some story to save her reputation, then. Find some relation to swear she was chaperoning them or some such. "

The duke nodded. "Aye, and it might not be such a misalliance at that, if the fellow really does turn out to be Winslowe's heir."

"He'll be a duke." Hyatt agreed, "and you couldn't arrange a higher match for Belinda without finding a foreign prince. Further, Winslowe was known to be sitting on a fortune, so you won't be supporting some down-at-heels dancing teacher forever."

"A music instructor," the duke corrected. "But don't forget we have to find Joshua Collins before the inheritance is forfeited to some worthy cause. I'll send men tonight, but when can we leave for Brighton, do you suppose?"

After discussing the logistics of transporting the Treadwell ladies et cetera, *et* cat, as they entered the men's club, Hyatt waited until they were seated with a bottle of cognac between them before saying, "You sound convinced that Collins is our man and that Belinda is with him. This mightn't be some mutton-headed notion of Miss Treadwell's, might it, founded on nothing more substantial than the ravings of a toasted terrier? I mean, we have no hard proof that Belinda is even in Brighton, much less with a suddenly eligible *parti*. For all we know, the blasted musician might be an ogre who's snatched Lady Belinda away against her will."

The duke swirled cognac in his glass. "No one kidnapped her."

Hyatt raised one dark eyebrow at his friend's confidence. "Oh?"

"I hadn't wanted to mention it before, but I checked the modistes' bills as Miss Treadwell suggested. Devilishly clever female, that. I don't know why you'd call her mutton-headed."

Ignoring the question of Miss Treadwell's thought processes, Hyatt asked, "What did you find among the dressmakers' accounts then? An elopement ensemble? I did not know they labeled them as such."

"Negligees." It was a simple word. It said a lot.

"Not nightgowns?"

The duke shook his silvered head. "I am sorry, lad."

Sorry? Was the canary sorry when the cage door was opened? Socrates was happier than he'd been for weeks.

So was Belinda. "I did it, Josh! I did it!"

Joshua tried to raise himself with his one good arm, but fell back onto the straw pallet. Belinda hurried to place a pillow behind his neck and hold a glass of barley water to his lips.

"What did you do, sweetheart?"

"I rode with Asa into Brighton while you were asleep."

Joshua wrinkled his nose. "I thought you smelled fishier than usual." The sale of her wedding ring had permitted Belinda to move Joshua and their meager belongings to a room in a fisherman's cottage. The conditions were not much improved over the hedge tavern, but now they did not have to fear being murdered in their beds for the price of the clothes on their backs. Nor did Belinda have to worry any longer about evil looks from the men in the taproom. In addition, Asa's food was plentiful and nourishing, even if fish stew grew monotonous after the third meal. Exhausted by the move in Asa's fish cart, Joshua had slept for hours.

Belinda brushed the hair back from his pale forehead. "Bother the smell! Just listen, my love. I sold one of your songs to the director of the musicales at the Castle Inn! He looked at it and immediately insisted I go to a publisher, who is going to print copies tomorrow! He paid me, too! And the maestro liked the piece so much, he has commissioned another to play for the Prince Regent's arrival next month." She emptied a pouch of coins onto the mattress beside him. "We can start buying our own groceries and looking for better quarters when you feel stronger. I can even reclaim my wedding ring!"

Joshua turned to face the wall. "No, Bel, don't."

"But I miss it, Josh, although I hardly had time to get used to wearing it."

"No, I want you to take the money—take all of it—and go home."

"Home, Josh? My home is wherever you are, silly. I wouldn't leave you before, when that castaway quack declared you past praying for. I certainly won't leave you now that you are so improved."

He took her hand in his good arm and brought it to his dry lips. "Sweetheart, listen. I won't be able to play the violin, you know that. Not now, not soon, maybe not forever. I'll never be able to support you on what I can earn teaching rich merchants' brats their scales and set pieces. And selling my compositions is as chancy as the weather. You deserve so much better."

"Dearest, if I deserve your love, that is all I can hope for."

He ignored her words of devotion. "Look at how we are living now, Bel." He made her see the crude mattress on the floor, the faded, threadbare blanket, and the bare, stained walls and curtainless windows of Asa's back room. Their one remaining satchel was the room's only other furnishing. "I can never forgive myself for bringing you so low. A duke's daughter, living in a reeking hovel. And that's how it might be, forever."

Belinda was angry. "None of this is your fault! If we hadn't been set upon by those highwaymen, we would have had

enough for a little cottage, just as we planned. You've scrimped
and saved for two years, driving a hackney by day and playing
at night, just so we could do this."

"No, I drove the coach so we could meet sometimes in London, and so we had a carriage to drive to Scotland, even though
I knew it was wrong."

"And I lied to my father for two years about needing more
and more pin money, even though I knew that was wrong, too.
I betrayed my father's trust so we would have a nest egg until
you became an established composer and a recognized musician. With all our savings and my jewels, we would have done
fine on what you can earn giving music lessons, you know we
would have! And we will—we just need time!"

"No, I cannot watch you trying to iron your own gown or
bake bread. That's not the life you were meant to live."

"I'll learn, dash it, Josh. I will. And Asa didn't mind about
the fire. He swore he never liked that old rug anyway."

Joshua shook his head. "You'll learn, and you'll learn to hate
me."

"Never, my love."

He stroked her hair. "Go home to your father, Bel. You know
he loves you enough to forgive you anything, even this."

"I could never leave you, silly. When are you going to realize that I'd have no life without you? What, do you think I
could just resume my Season, dance at all the balls, then marry
my father's choice at the end? Even if I would think of doing
such a thing, that would be the most dishonorable act of all, for
Hyatt has every right to expect his wife's innocence, even if he
cannot have her affection. But we are married, Josh, you and I,
forever! There is no going back, even if we wished. The cere-
mony was legal, you said so yourself, not just a handfast ritual
that could be overturned. We made sure we had a real minister,
not the blacksmith, so we are married in the eyes of God, too. I
have our wedding lines, here"—she touched her chest—"right
next to my heart. I could be carrying your child"—she touched
her stomach—"here."

"Deuce take it, Bel, you cannot be breeding! Not when we
cannot afford to feed ourselves."

"Of course we can. Asa says he'll teach me to find clams

along the shore. You'll write a brilliant piece for the Prince, and he'll offer you a position at the Pavilion—composer to the future king!"

"But I am so weak, dearest, I don't know if I can write something suitable in time. And without an instrument to play it on . . . "

"The Castle Inn's conductor says you can practice there when you are ready. And I'll help!"

He laughed, for the first time in weeks, it seemed. "Ah, sweetheart, you know you can hardly carry a tune. You'll learn to bake pastries sooner."

"But I can transcribe the music for you. All those expensive music lessons my father paid for must be worth something." He laughed again, and Belinda almost wept at the sound of it. "You are an excellent teacher, my love."

He kissed her hand again. "I am, indeed. And you are an eager pupil."

Neither one was speaking of music now. Blushing, Belinda lay down next to him, so he could enfold her in his good arm. "And I am not done learning, my love."

He wasn't quite strong enough for another lesson, not yet. Kissing the top of her head, Joshua asked, "Are you sure you won't go, then?"

"Never. But I have to let Papa know where I am so he won't worry. That's the only thing interfering with my happiness, now that you are recovering. He cannot have our marriage annulled, not after so long, and perhaps his influence can get that lazy sheriff to look for the villains who stole our money. If we were wealthy enough to offer a reward, he'd have found them by now, you can be sure."

Joshua frowned. "I never wanted to be beholden to your father, sweetheart. I would not have married you if I could not support you myself. Dash it, you'd have been better off with Hyatt."

"Better, but not happier. I'd never have heard the songs in my heart."

Chapter Twenty-nine

Marco Polo might have had a smaller caravan, Socrates thought, but not by much. At least they had no camels, only one cat that needed frequent rest stops on the journey to Brighton. Shimpton and his pet were riding in his own landau, thank goodness, and the viscount's driver had been threatened with dismissal or dismemberment if he let the lumpkin take the reins. Lady Crowley rode with Shimpton because the duke's carriage was crowded with Lady Tremont, her daughter, and her aunt, who insisted on carrying her jewel box, her wig box, and her cosmetics box along with her. Three baggage carts followed, and two more coaches with the ladies' dressers and the gentlemen's gentlemen. Hyatt drove his own curricle, repaired in record time at great additional expense, thankful not to be immured with the impossible females. Mondale rode with him for the first leg of the journey. When they stopped to change the horses and refresh themselves, however, Lady Tremont suggested that His Grace and Maylene switch places after luncheon.

"For dear Maylene is looking peaked. Don't you think so, my lord?"

Hyatt thought she looked as delectable as a ripe peach, in her burnt orange traveling gown with its jonquil spenser. Her cheeks were flushed, although he could not tell if that was due to discomfort or her mother's maneuvering.

"My lamb has always been subject to carriage sickness, you know."

"Mother!"

But Mondale said he wished to speak with Lady Tremont about her psychical experiments, so the shift in seats was made.

Hyatt concentrated on his horses; Maylene concentrated on the scenery. They both concentrated on keeping their bodies from touching on the narrow seat. Neither noticed the solitary rider on a scrawny horse who followed behind their last baggage carrier.

When they drove through Brighton, the earl politely pointed out the various attractions, like the Marine Parade and Royal Crescent. He did not need to identify the Prince's Chinese Pavilion, for no other building could be so fantastical, not in England. Maylene made due note of the fresh sea scent, the chalk cliffs, and the bathing machines on the strand.

Socrates made note of how the moisture in the air was making her short ringlets curl even tighter under her brown bonnet.

A string of small fishing villages came next, and Socrates explained about the nets and the drying racks they saw. Maylene explained her quickened pulse to herself by the chill in the salt air.

"High Oaks, " the earl announced at last, as they drove up a long oak-lined carriage path.

The house was immense, Maylene could see when they were still ten minutes away, of brick and stone, solid and imposing, just like its owner. She made the requisite compliments to its Palladian columns and manicured grounds, and she asked the appropriate questions about the ages of the various wings. Then the carriage drive swung around to the other side of the house, the side facing the sea. Maylene was speechless; Hyatt was smiling at her reaction.

"It catches everyone that way the first time," was all he said.

From the front, the house looked all windows, each reflecting the diamond-dusted sparkle of the blue waters. Nearly every window had a balcony or a terrace or a covered porch, all different, all filled with planters of trailing vines and flowers. In the front of the house, just past the roadway, wild, untamed growth fell away to an endless vista across the water, with nothing but sea birds overhead.

"It's . . . it's magnificent," Maylene breathed. Just like its owner.

"I was hoping you'd like it," Socrates said, although he had not dared name his vague anxiety. The one time she and her family had visited, Belinda had been more concerned that the bright sunshine would bring out her freckles than with the appearance of the house. The duke's daughter was young, he'd told himself. She would come to appreciate the place as much as he did in time. Maylene already did.

He wanted to show her the beach, the stream that ran down to the water, and the gazebo he'd built on the cliff face, out of sight of the house, for picnics and such. He wanted to take her for a ride on the sand, for a sail in his boat, for a swim in the little cove. So what if the water would be frigid still? He could not picture the intrepid Miss Treadwell insisting on using the closed bathing machines back in Brighton. There were favorites places within the house, too, that he wanted to show her, to share with her—as a conscientious host, of course, until they found Belinda.

Maylene wanted to stare and exclaim and explore. The Prince's Pavilion in Brighton might be the most unique edifice in England, but this was the most wondrous. High Oaks was no fairy-tale palace, no romantic Gothic castle. It was a house, a marvelous, glowing house where children could grow and play and laugh. Little black-haired children, she let herself dream for a minute, with curly hair. But she was a mere guest here, uninvited and unwanted, she knew. So she would not dream of tiny replicas of Socrates Hughes, Lord Hyatt—not until they found Belinda.

The other carriages were arriving, discharging passengers, luggage, and servants to clutter up the view and drown out the sound of the waves. Regretting that he could not devote himself to one guest in particular, Socrates got busy seeing the others all welcomed and settled. He made sure the butler counted the silverware when Aunt Regina was around, that the cook ordered extra fish for the viscount's cat, that the housekeeper assigned the duke and Lady Tremont rooms at opposite ends of the house. He sent for the magistrate, sent for the local newspapers to read the *on dits* and events columns, and he sent for subscriptions to the public assemblies. If Belinda was here, he was going to find her.

The magistrate was distressed to learn that his old friend's daughter had disappeared, possibly into his district. He would have recognized her, he said, if the chit had been going out and about in the local Society. There had been a rash of robberies though, and, now that he recalled, one of them had involved a young couple. The young man was injured, but alive, so there'd been no need for a murder investigation, according to the sheriff. The magistrate had no idea what had become of the thieves' victims, simply assumed they'd passed on to their destination. He doubted the incompetent sheriff would ever find the highwaymen, since the man was a drunkard, the magistrate admitted. They had little enough crime as a rule, so his shortcomings never mattered. He'd go ask about that young couple, if the sheriff was sober enough to remember anything.

No one wanted to wait. As soon as the bags were unpacked and the travel dust was washed off, most of the party left for Brighton. Lady Crowley begged off, claiming the headache, though everyone knew she did not wish to meet any acquaintances who might have heard about her niece's fall from grace into a bankrupt barony. Lord Shimpton decided to stay at the manor with her and his cat, since Lady Crowley let Tune play with her embroidery silks. She didn't lecture a fellow, either, nor expect him to make conversation.

The others strolled along the cobblestone streets, up West Street, down the Marine Parade, along the Steine. Brighton was less formal than London, with strangers nodding and striking up conversations. No one had heard of a young violinist. Aunt Regina joined a group of old women at an ongoing card game, declaring that the old biddies would know everything that happened in town. They didn't know about a recently married couple. For that matter, they didn't know about marked decks, but they were learning.

For the next few days, Maylene and her mother, escorted by the duke and the earl, were rarely at High Oaks at all. They went to every concert or assembly at the Old Ship Inn or the Castle Inn, every promenade and private party where a string quartet or dance band was to play. They showed Belinda's miniature to everyone, and gave Mr. Collins's sandy-haired, slim-built description, to no avail. If not for the lack of results, Maylene would be having a wonderful time, not worried about money or what others were thinking of her or how she was dwindling into an old maid. She was having fun, for once, and believed her mother was also. Lady Tremont was blossoming in the duke's regard, and he seemed to grow younger daily. Maylene's mother never mentioned Max, and she was too rapt in the duke's company to be much help in the investigation, which threw Maylene and Socrates together more. Neither one complained.

And then Maylene spotted a familiar figure in a crowded coffeehouse. He moved away before she could point him out to Socrates, but she was positive she'd seen Reverend Fingerhut. He must have followed them from London, for surely he could have found other sinners in the metropolis to condemn when they left. But why? she wondered, then answered herself: the money, Joshua Collins's money.

"Oh, why did I not find out the name of his church?" Maylene despaired, sure it would be the same as the default recipient of the Duke of Winslowe's estate. She decided to write to Fleur Lafontaine that very afternoon, and possibly add visiting the nearby houses of worship to her investigation.

Hyatt thought she was seeing too much in the muckworm minister's appearance. "There's no reason to be fearful," Socrates said, trying to comfort her. "My men will see to it that he doesn't put his signs up or start one of his vigils outside High Oaks. Besides, only the gulls would hear his harangue."

Maylene knew that Hyatt employed a veritable army of grooms and groundsmen, most of them retired veterans, some missing an eye or a limb. They were devoted to Socrates and would protect him with their lives, but who would protect Joshua Collins if Fingerhut found him first?

That night they were to attend a concert at the Castle Inn, where a new performer was going to play with the ensemble. They were all so eager and excited about the evening that Maylene had been able to convince Lady Crowley and Shimpton to attend, since no one would notice them in the crowded rooms. The new violinist was middle-aged, however, and had reddish hair. The master of ceremonies pointed out the man's wife and her three well-scrubbed children, looking on proudly. Maylene resigned herself to another evening of no answers. Pleasant music, delightful company, an opportunity to wear her shell pink gown and see the earl's eyes take on a golden sparkle—but no answers.

The orchestra was performing the new song that was being played everywhere. Maylene had danced to it the previous evening, and was humming now beneath her breath to the familiar strains. Hyatt smiled at her, also remembering the dance, and the tune.

And then her mother jumped to her feet, right in the middle of the piece. "Tune!" she shouted.

Lord Shimpton looked around for his cat. "Tune? I thought they wasn't permitted, so I didn't bring her."

Lady Crowley was crawling under her seat as all eyes turned to them.

Socrates was groaning. Lady Tremont was about to start talking to her long-lost lover and his fried friend, right in the middle of a concert. The woman had gone from dotty to queer as Dick's hatband at the drop of a baton. He feared for Maylene, if her mother had lost her mind entirely.

"Mama?" Maylene and the duke tugged Lady Tremont back into her seat.

The baroness could hardly sit still. "That's it, I tell you! It's the tune, the one I heard! That's what Alex was trying to tell us! The tune!"

"That tune?" Maylene asked, waving her pearl-handled fan at her mother's flushed face. Mondale took it from her, doing a better job.

"The very one."

They had to wait until intermission to rush toward the conductor. Everyone else was trying to leave for refreshments, so they got more cool stares as they pushed and shoved their way forward. The man confirmed that the composer of the popular new air was indeed a Joshua Collins. No, he'd never set eyes on the man.

"Well, the lad has talent, anyway." The duke pulled out the miniature of his daughter.

"Yes, that's the pretty little gal who sold me the piece. Said her husband was laid up but recovering. He'd better be, for I need a new composition for the Prince's welcome reception. The Collins fellow will go far if he keeps on writing."

"He'll go to hell if he's harmed one hair of my poppet's head," the duke muttered, while Maylene and Hyatt got directions to the fishing village where Collins's wife said they were staying. It was nearly on the doorstep of Hyatt's estate.

"We'll see you and the others back to High Oaks," the earl declared to Maylene, "then go on from there."

"I'll see you in hell first," Maylene said, echoing the duke's words. "I am coming, too."

"Nonsense. A fishing shack is no place for a lady."

"If Belinda is there, I can be also."

Jaw clenched, Hyatt grabbed her arm when she would have hurried after her mother and the duke out to the street. "You are not going, and that is final. The situation could get ugly if they are not, in fact, married. The duke intends to bring his guns. So do I."

"What, you'd kill my reward—my duke? I am definitely going! Besides, you arrogant jackass, may I remind you that this is my investigation, that you would not even have been here if not for me and my mother? That you belittled our efforts from the beginning and mistrusted our motives? That you . . ."

They bickered all the way home, where they left Lady Tremont and the others after Maylene scribbled a message to Mr. Ryan in London and the duke fetched his dueling pistols. They argued about Maylene's willfulness and Soc's high-handedness while the duke primed his weapons, and the driver, a local man who knew his way, followed the narrow roads to the fishing village by the light of the moon on the water. Once again, no one noticed the lone, dark-clad rider who followed their carriage on a bare-ribbed horse.

Chapter Thirty

Belinda fainted when she saw her father. Joshua fainted when he heard he was a duke. What joy!

The newlyweds—the duke almost fainted with relief when he heard they were, indeed, legally married—recovered with assistance from the smelling salts in Belinda's reticule and the brandy in the duke's flask. After that, there was much crying and hugging and begging for forgiveness. Joshua's straw pallet was pulled out into the front room so he could rest, while Belinda wept on her father's lap in the cottage's only comfortable chair. Hyatt and Maylene were seated at the scarred wooden kitchen table, and Asa sat on the floor, relishing his mugful of fine liquor almost as much as he was relishing the noble company.

"B'gad, not one but two dooks under m'roof! I'll drink to that! And an earl? I'll drink to that, too, b'gad."

"Hush, poppet, I forgive you." Tears were running down the duke's cheeks, too. "All I ever wanted was for you to be happy. Didn't you know that?"

"But you wanted me to marry Lord Hyatt." The mention of the man she had so insulted brought fresh tears. "I tried to love him for you."

"Damn, you should have told me, poppet. I would have understood. Soc would have withdrawn his offer if you were unwilling. You didn't have to run away!"

Belinda wiped her eyes on the duke's handkerchief and stood, moving to kneel by her husband's side, pulling the blankets more firmly around him. "Would you have let me marry a poor music instructor, Papa?"

The duke could not answer her. He did bend toward Joshua

to say, "It is not what I wanted, young man, but I will welcome my daughter's husband. I might never approve of you, but I am not one to disown my flesh and blood. Belinda is all I have, and if I have to share her with a man not of my choice, so be it. In a month or so, when you have regained your strength, I will take you to London, help straighten out the details of your inheritance and investiture, introduce you to my clubs, see you seated in Parliament. Then I intend to take you to Gentleman Jackson's Boxing Parlor and beat the hell out of you. After that, if Belinda still wants you, I might forgive you."

Joshua nodded, but spoke to Belinda: "I am not sure I wish to be duke. My music . . . "

The duke was not about to lose a titled son-in-law in exchange for a starving musician. "Nonsense, you can do both. We already have a passel of poets in the peerage. Nothing wrong with a fiddler."

"But I don't know how to be a nobleman." Joshua looked toward Maylene. "All those estates Miss, ah, Treadwell mentioned, all that property, the people who rely on the dukedom for their livelihoods—I wouldn't have the least idea what to do."

The duke was losing patience. "You don't have a choice about being duke, boy, no more than I did. It's yours by birth. You're young. You'll learn the rest."

Maylene disagreed. "I'm sorry, Your Grace, but if His new Grace is half as gifted as Lady Belinda and that conductor in Brighton say, he has no business worrying over what crop to plant or which breed of hog to raise. Such a talent should not be wasted."

"Spoken like your mother's daughter," Socrates said with a laugh. "But you are seeing the responsibilities, Collins, not the rewards. You can finance your own musical productions if you wish, or hire a concert hall. You simply find honest, competent men to manage your holdings while you do what you are good at. You have the funds to hire an army of them—and I know of one army man I can highly recommend as your general steward to start."

"Lieutenant Canfield!" Maylene exclaimed. "The very thing!"

The duke nodded. "And it's not as if you are alone, lad. You're family now, and I think I have enough experience to give you good advice. My daughter expects great things of you. We'll all help to see that you do not disappoint her."

"I'll drink to that!" said Asa, before he fell over.

The duke reluctantly agreed to leave the young couple where they were until morning. Joshua was in no condition to travel in a cramped carriage over bumpy roads in the dark, with a storm coming on besides, and Belinda would not think of leaving him. Hyatt hauled the snoring fisherman onto his cot in the sleeping alcove, leaving him a handful of bank notes and the flask before they left.

The rain hadn't started when Hyatt handed Maylene into the coach, but the moon and stars were obscured by clouds, the narrow path lit only by the carriage lamps. The driver had to keep the horses in check, and the steady, slow motion soon put Maylene half to sleep after the excitement of the evening.

Socrates spent the trip reassuring his friend.

"Belinda seems happy, don't you think, Soc?"

Happy, in the rundown shack, sleeping on the floor? She'd looked exhausted, overwrought, and at least five years older than the last time he'd seen her the previous month, but yes, she seemed exceedingly happy. "Very. I think she will be even happier knowing they have your blessing."

"And Collins seems a decent chap."

Socrates yawned. "All wealthy dukes are decent chaps."

"And it's not simply infatuation. They've been faithful to each other for three years, it seems, since Belinda started taking those private music instructions. That must mean the marriage will succeed."

It meant Belinda had lied to him and her father for the past two years. But yes, such constancy boded well for the match, unlike many in the *ton*, where affairs lasted three months, and affections less. "I think they seem well suited," he said noncommittally.

"And your heart is not broken?" Mondale asked. "No, I can see it is not." What he saw was Maylene's golden head resting on Hyatt's shoulder while the earl held her secure against the swaying of the carriage. When a clap of thunder awakened her

with a start, Socrates whispered soft words and brushed butter-
fly kisses on Maylene's forehead until she went back to sleep.
The duke chuckled. "No, I don't think you are too devastated at
all, my boy. Not at all."

A fierce storm raged through the night, so it was late morning when the duke and Hyatt returned to the fishing village with
two carriages and three footmen. The duke almost had
apoplexy when he heard there had been a fire at Asa's shack in
the middle of the night. His little girl was covered in soot and
his new son-in-law, the genius duke he'd described to Lady
Tremont, was coughing fiercely. Asa was on a ladder, trying to
stuff rags into the charred hole in the roof.

"My God, were you struck by lightning?" the duke demanded.

"Not bloody likely." Asa got down and handed them a
painted wooden sign that was charred at one end. "Some bastard lit this and tossed it onto the roof, I'd guess. Makes no
sense to me."

Only a few of the letters were legible. Asa was scratching his
head. "I don't know nobody named Pent."

"Thank God for Asa's dog," Belinda put in. "His barking
woke me in the middle of the night, so I managed to get Joshua
and Asa out of the cottage. If not for the noise, we would have
died in our sleep. Then the rain came right after a bolt of lightning and put out the fire."

Asa was still scratching his head. "Thing is, I don't have me
no dog. Nearest one's at Lidell's farm, nigh three miles away."

"But I could swear I heard someone say 'Good boy.' "

Who says you can't teach a dead dog new tricks?

The magistrate came to High Oaks the following morning.
He was happy the duke had his daughter back, and happier still
to report that two highwaymen had been arrested the day before, and they still had some of the little lady's jewelry on them.
Of course now the magistrate had a new mystery. Some
stranger had been killed by a bolt of lightning outside of
Brighton during the storm last night. No one knew who he
might have been, but the poor sod's half-starved horse was un-

hurt, over at the livery stable if any next of kin wanted to claim the sorry beast.

"I'm sorry, Soc," Maylene said.

Since they had just shared a very satisfying kiss in the orangery, away from all the others, Socrates was surprised. "You are? I thought that was rather nice myself. Perhaps we'll have to try again, though, if you are disappointed."

Maylene blushed. "No, not the kiss."

"Ah, then you are sorry Aunt Regina has cheated my household staff out of a month's wages. Or that Shimpton's hellcat is using my prize Aubusson carpet to sharpen its claws. No? Then perhaps you regret foisting that solicitor fellow Ryan on me. The housekeeper is complaining that his hair oil is ruining the pillow slips."

"Don't be foolish. I mean that I am sorry you lost your fiancée."

Socrates kept his arm about her shoulders as they strolled through the glassed room, supposedly admiring the plants. The orange trees could have been sprouting shillings for all they noticed, or cared. "But my fiancée was found, remember? You ought, since you were the one who found her. In fact, I do believe you have boasted of nothing else for the past two days."

"I do not boast. And that's not what I meant anyway. I meant that I am sorry your intended bride is already married. All your plans, the perfect match you'd arranged, are all destroyed."

"Ah, that. Do you know, I don't regret that loss one whit. In fact, I do not consider it a loss at all."

"Really?"

He stopped their meandering and kissed the tip of her nose. "Really. You see, Belinda found herself a gifted violinist. It doesn't matter that she is tone-deaf or that he was poor. They are happy together, and I am happy for them. Besides, I found a talented lady of my own. You found my heart, Maylene mine. It was tucked so far away, a marriage of convenience would have been good enough, until I met you. Now only you will do for me, my love."

He had to kiss her again, to punctuate his words. When they stopped, and Maylene had caught her breath, she said, "You know I will not put up with Lady Ashford and her ilk, don't you?"

"Lady who?"

"A mistress, Soc. No matter how fashionable it might be for husbands and wives to go their own way after the vows are spoken, I will not tolerate that, I am telling you now."

"Earls and countesses set their own fashions, my pet. You are already mistress of my heart and my soul. There is no room for any other woman."

"And I'll never be like Belinda, you know."

He had picked some blossoms and tucked one in her curls. "What, you won't run off with the piano tuner? I should hope not!"

Maylene placed a matching flower in his buttonhole. "No, I mean I won't be the pretty, pliant little wife you wanted."

"No, you won't. So I'll just have to make do with the wife I love. At least I won't be bored. Belinda would have bored me to tears in a sennight."

She was still unconvinced. "And we can spend most of the time here at High Oaks?"

"By Jupiter, Maylene, it sounds as if you are marrying me for my house."

"That's another thing. Everyone will think I married you for your money. Will you mind being wed to a fortune hunter?"

"Not if it is you, my love. Everything I have is yours, you know that. Besides, you do have a handsome dowry—Ryan's reward money."

Reaching up to touch his cheek, Maylene smiled and said, "That's less than you spend on a horse. But if you ever lose your fortune and need more, I am sure Mama and the duke will be happy to provide for us. They'd do anything to have their privacy."

"So is there anything else, my May? Any other reason you can possibly find for not making me the happiest of men? I'm warning you, the only one I will accept is that you do not love me."

"Then I suppose I shall have to say yes, my lord. Not even I could find a gentleman that I could love more."

Some time later, while they were still sealing their vows of love, the butler coughed from the doorway. Looking anywhere but at the flower-decked, tousle-haired pair, he announced, "Forgive me, my lord, but there is a gentleman here to see Miss Treadwell. He says he is desperate and needs her help to locate his missing—"

Maylene and Socrates both spoke at once. "Tell him to get lost."

Epilogue

Lady Tremont was going to hold one last, official séance in Curzon Street. The duke insisted.

"Ah, Max, dear, there you are. I am so glad you came to visit this evening. Of course I have missed you, too. What's that? Yes, I have missed Alex, also. But look who is here to speak with us, Max. His Grace wishes to thank you and Alex for finding Belinda and Mr. Collins. The Duke of Winslowe, I should say. And for rescuing them, too, dear, from the fire. Of course I knew it was you." Lady Tremont sighed. "And Alex. That bolt of lightning that struck Fingerhut was a bit dramatic, but no, they would not have been safe otherwise. And, yes, you always did have good aim. What, you've been practicing? They have a cricket team there? How lovely."

She smiled again, listening. "You have encouraged Lady Shimpton to come watch the matches? How nice. No, the dear viscount does not wish to speak with her this evening, Max. He has decided to remember his beloved mama in his prayers from now on, instead. He is going to marry Lady Crowley, you know. Of course you did. And raise cats." She hurriedly put her hands over her ears. "I am sorry, Alex."

After a moment of muttering about unmannerly mongrels, Lady Tremont went on. "And dear Maylene and her earl are off on their honeymoon. Yes, I am delighted with the match you found for her, too. Ideal? Definitely. I think they should name their firstborn son after you, but it's early days yet.

"It's not? A girl?" She clapped her hands. "Maxine? I'll tell them, dear. What's that? What is going to happen to this house? Why, Aunt Regina and Campbell are going to continue the psychical research, of course. Will you come visit with them? Ah, only true love can bridge the distance? Well, if that does not work, they might establish a gaming den here. No, they would not water the wine. I don't think so anyway."

Aunt Regina shook her head vehemently, sending her wig askew. Campbell reached over and straightened it on her head.

"And, Max dear," Lady Tremont continued, "His Grace of Mondale insists on asking your blessings on our marriage. I think that lightning bolt convinced him he'd ought. You don't mind? Yes, I'll always love you, too. How could I stop now after all these years? And we can visit now and again? Of course, when you are not overly busy. Farewell, my love— Oh, I nearly forgot. Lady Crowley never did get to send her dear husband her last good-byes. Do you think he might . . . ? He is? How wonderful! Lord Crowley is listening, dear ma'am. What was it that you wanted to tell him?"

Lady Crowley patted her curls, patted Lord Shimpton's padded shoulder, and patted the cat on his lap. Then she licked her lips and said, "Bugger off, you bastard."

The walls shook with thunder, but the stars were bright and no clouds hid the moon. It was laughter, a man's deep, rich laughter, and they all heard it.

And the barking.

A Man of Affairs by Anne Barbour

Well beyond the normal age of courtship and marriage, a young woman resigned herself to a quiet life on her parents' estate. Then the adopted son of the Duke of Derwent arrived. His kind manner and passionate glances brought new, unfamiliar joy to the lady's heart. But the dashing gentleman had too many duties to his father to properly court her. It would take a scandalous heartbreak to bring them together in a love that would go against their families and society....

0-451-19693-7/$4.99

The Bartered Heart by Nancy Butler

Abandoned by his mother and raised by a tyrannical father, a young rogue vowed long ago to harden his heart against emotion. So when his fortune is lost, he sets his sights on a marriage of convenience and riches. But as he makes his way to the estate of a very eligible young mistress, he finds his route riddled with treacherous bogs, bungling thieves, and a beautiful waif in petticoats who may mean much more to him than any amount of money.

0-451-19826-3/$4.99

To order call: 1-800-788-6262